Why Beulah Shot Her Pistol Inside the Baptist Church

Ingram
12-3-04

WHY BEULAH SHOT HER PISTOL INSIDE THE BAPTIST CHURCH

CLAYTON SULLIVAN

NewSouth Books
Montgomery

NewSouth Books
P.O. Box 1588
Montgomery, AL 36102

Library of Congress Cataloging-in-Publication Data

Sullivan, Clayton, 1930-
Why Beulah shot her pistol inside the Baptist Church / Clayton Sullivan.
p. cm.
ISBN 1-58838-167-6 (alk. paper)
1. Baptist women—Fiction. 2. Mississippi—Fiction. I. Title.
PS3569.U3465W49 2004
813'.54—dc22
2004021673

Design by Randall Williams

Printed in the United States of America
by the Maple-Vail Book Manufacturing Group

To My Students

I

THE FIRST THING I'm gonna' do is tell you my name, and after I've told you my name I'm gonna tell you about the tub of trouble I've lived in for the past six years. My name's Beulah Rainey. I live in New Jerusalem, Mississippi. There ain't too much to New Jerusalem. If you blinked your eyes goin' through it you'd miss it. It's in Jones County about seven miles southwest of Laurel where they have the Masonite factory and a bunch of poultry plants. New Jerusalem has three stores, a big, consolidated school, and two churches. There's the Methodist church. And then there's the New Jerusalem Primitive Baptist Church. That's the church I've belonged to all of my life.

Up until three days ago I was a married woman. I was Ralph Rainey's wife. My husband's full name was Ralph Jefferson Davis Rainey. He never talked about or used his two middle names. He always went by "Ralph." But I ain't his wife no more. I'm now a widow woman. That's because three days ago Ralph upped and died on me. I wasn't expecting him to die. But that's sure what he done.

This morning we had Ralph's funeral at the New Jerusalem Primitive Baptist Church and then buried him in the cemetery that's across the road. Or at least I'm guessing they buried him. I didn't hang around to see.

Most people think when you've just come back from your husband's funeral you're gonna be real sad and down in the dumps. You're expected to be all teary-eyed and you're supposed to have a lump as big as an apple in your throat. But I don't. I'm goin' to be honest with you. For the first time in years I'm at peace on the inside. I'm as calm as a summer's breeze now that Ralph's gone. I'm not sure where he's gone but by golly he's gone. I won't have to mess around with him anymore. And I'm glad about what I done this morning at the end of Ralph's funeral service. I'm sure what I done made a lot of people mad. I know I made his mama and daddy mad. I made his two brothers mad. And I made his sister who lives over in Baton Rouge mad. But I don't care. If they don't like what I done they can kiss my foot.

I've got sense enough to know a widow woman ain't supposed to be talking the way I'm talking. But all I'm doin' is tellin' you what I think. Before I got married I was a Buchanan. And here in Jones County and around Laurel they say "Buchanans believe in talking straight." Or as my daddy has always said, "Buchanans call a spade a spade." So I'm calling a spade a spade when I tell you I'm glad Ralph's six feet under in the cemetery. Why do I feel this way? I feel the way I do because my husband was no good. My mama told me he ain't no good before I married him. But I didn't believe her. Of course I believe her now. To be up front with you, my husband was a bastard. That's exactly what he was: a bastard. And I sure oughta know. Because I was married to the bastard for six years. And don't nobody know a man like the woman who's married to him.

I'll admit most of my neighbors here in New Jerusalem have the idea Ralph was a fine, upstanding man. Everybody knew he was a deacon in the Baptist church and never missed a Sunday goin' to church. I wanted to believe he was a fine man too when I married him. After all, I'd known him all my life. The Rainey farm and my daddy's farm ain't but a mile apart by the way the crow flies. And my folks and the Raineys have always belonged to the same church. But after all I've been through with Ralph it doesn't ring my bell that he was a big-shot deacon who led the singing and helped take up the collection every Sunday at the New Jerusalem Baptist Church. Which is where, I listened to Ralph and let him con me into marrying him.

At the time it happened I didn't have sense enough to know a con job was being done on me. But one was. I remember exactly when and where and how it got started with me and Ralph. It started on a hot Sunday in June. The Sunday-morning worship service had just got over with. Most everybody had walked out of the church and was standing out front visiting and talking with one another. But I'd stayed inside. I'd stayed inside so I could do a little practicing on the church piano. I was sittin' at the piano and I was playing "Onward Christian Soldiers." Or at least I was trying to play it. "Onward Christian Soldiers" has a lot of sharps and flats and it ain't an easy song to play. By the way, me playin' the piano was more my daddy's idea than mine. He always said he wanted me to be good enough at playing the piano to someday be the pianist at the New Jerusalem Baptist Church. That's the main thing my daddy has always wanted me to be: the church's piano player. That's why I was taking piano lessons once a week. Every Thursday afternoon Mama would drive me seven miles up to Laurel so I could take piano lessons with Miss Hopson. Well—like I was saying—I was playing "Onward Christian Soldiers" when out of the clear blue sky Ralph walked over to the piano. Most primitive Baptist churches don't have pianos. But our church does. It has an upright Baldwin piano. Ralph stood right next to the piano and listened to me play. He didn't say nothing until after I'd finished the last stanza. I'll never forget what he said when I was through. He smiled at me and said, "Beulah, you sure can play the piano good."

When he said that I said, "Thank you, Mr. Rainey. It's mighty nice of you to say that." Back then—before I really knew Ralph—I always called him "Mr. Rainey."

He then asked, "Do you by any chance know how to play 'Sweet Hour of Prayer'?"

"Sweet Hour of Prayer" ain't like "Onward Christian Soldiers." It's easy to play on the piano. It doesn't have a lot of sharps and flats. I said, "I sure do."

Ralph said, "I wish you'd play me a little bit of 'Sweet Hour of Prayer.' I love that song. They sang it at my Granddaddy's funeral."

So I played him a stanza of "Sweet Hour of Prayer." When I'd finished playing it Ralph said, "I don't think I've ever heard 'Sweet Hour of Prayer' played any prettier. You know how to make this piano sound like an angel playin' on a harp up in heaven."

Him saying that made me feel real proud. It made me feel like I was a lady Liberace or somebody like that. But then Ralph leaned over the piano and said something to me I wasn't expecting him to say. He said, "Beulah, something about you has been on my mind for a long time."

I didn't have no idea what he had on his mind. Particularly I didn't know what he had on his mind about me. The fact is, I didn't know he'd been thinking about me. But I could tell Ralph was throwing his fishing line, fish hook, and fish bait toward me. So I went for the bait and I said, "What's that Mr. Rainey?"

He said, "I wish you'd marry me."

That's exactly what he said. He said, "I wish you'd marry me." He spoke them five words to me while he was standing beside the upright piano at the front of the New Jerusalem Baptist Church in New Jerusalem, Mississippi. Believe you me, when he said them five words to me you could have knocked me over with a chicken feather. Or with a wet pine straw. I bet Ralph had never spoke twenty words to me before. Yet here he was tellin' me out of the clear blue sky that he wanted to marry me. Which I'd never even thought about doin'.

For cryin' out loud, at the time I wasn't but sixteen years old. I still had another year to go in high school. Getting married never had crossed my mind, and it sure had never crossed my mind to marry Ralph. Or as I called him back then, "Mr. Rainey." He was older than me. It turned out he was twenty years older than I was. I knew he'd been married before. His wife had died from a brain tumor. Her name was Ruth Ann. She'd passed away a year or two earlier in the hospital up in Laurel. And I knew he was a daddy. Ralph and Ruth Ann had a boy they named Oscar. Oscar was born without any hay in his barn. Or without all his marbles in his bag. Which explains why he lives at the Mississippi Rehabilitation Center in Ellisville. Daddy says the center used to be called the Mississippi School for the Feebleminded. But they don't call it that no more. Instead, they've sweetened the name up and now they call it the Mississippi Rehabilitation Center. And that's where Oscar stays most of the time. On Saturdays Ralph would go and get Oscar and keep him over the weekend and bring him to church on Sunday. But Oscar liked staying in Ellisville better then staying with his daddy at New Jerusalem. The only other thing I knew about Ralph was that he had a farm and owned "Ralph's Place." That's his meat market and barbecue cafe in Laurel. The reason I knew Ralph owned a butcher shop and barbecue cafe is because my daddy was one of his regular customers. He was always stopping by "Ralph's Place" and buying barbecue. I couldn't count the times I've heard Daddy say, "Ralph Rainey has the best barbecue ribs in Jones County. His ribs are just as good as Letha's in Columbia." Letha is a colored woman who lives over near Columbia in Marion County and for years has made her living selling barbecue. Some people say she cooks the best barbecue there is. Daddy says Ralph's barbecue is just as good if not better.

I could tell I blushed the moment Ralph leaned over the piano and said, "I wish you'd marry me." My face turned as red as an apple at Christmas. And I got a feeling of butterflies in my stomach. The only thing I could think to say was, "Mr. Rainey, I ain't but sixteen years old. I ain't even out of high school."

Maybe that was a dumb thing for me to say, but at the time, it was the only thing I could think to say. He then said, "I wish you wouldn't call me Mr. Rainey. I wish you'd call me Ralph." That made me feel funny too. Ralph was twice as old as me. That's why I'd always called him "Mr. Rainey."

Ralph kept on talking. As he was talking I was sittin' on the piano bench and he was leaning on the piano. He laid it on heavy. Kind of whispering, he told me he'd been watching me for a long time. He said he'd been thinking about me for months. He said, "I think you're the prettiest girl in New Jerusalem. The fact is, I think you're the prettiest girl I ever seen."

You'll admit that was pouring the honey on thick. And I mean thick. Ralph tellin' me I was the prettiest girl he'd ever seen was the nicest thing anybody had ever said to me. My mama and daddy didn't never say nothing sweet or kind like that to me. No they didn't. All they ever done was boss me around. They'd say, "Beulah, wash the supper dishes tonight!" "Beulah, go shell some corn and feed the chickens!" Or Daddy would order me to practice my piano lessons so I could someday play "The Old Rugged Cross" and "Onward Christian Soldiers" in church. Mama and Daddy was always strict on me. They was strict because they was primitive Baptists. Which is what the New Jerusalem Baptist Church is. Don't nobody in our church drink or dance. Dancing is a sin. And none of the women use make-up like powder or lipstick. The reason they don't is because the Bible says you ain't supposed to use 'em. I'm not sure where the Bible says you're not suppose to use 'em but that's sure what it says somewhere. That ain't the only thing the Bible says. It also says somewhere that it's disgraceful for a woman to cut her hair. So none of the women who belong to the New Jerusalem Baptist Church ever cut their hair. They wear it long—which is what

I done—or some of 'em tie it in a knot which I done every once in a while. Brother Ledbetter is always preaching against women using make-up and cuttin' their hair. He feels real strong about things like this. Brother Ledbetter, in case you don't know, is the preacher at the New Jerusalem Baptist Church. Which is why people call him "Brother Ledbetter."

Maybe it's because I'd never cut my hair and I'd never used no powder and lipstick that I got so excited when Ralph told me I was the prettiest girl he'd ever seen. Back then—being just sixteen years old and having lived all my life in New Jerusalem—I didn't have sense enough to know Ralph was settin' me up. He was pumping me up with sweet talk like I was a circus balloon. And back than I didn't know that what a man says with his mouth don't always square with the way he acts. So what did I do while sittin' on the piano bench listening to Ralph? I'll tell you what I done. I lapped up what he said like a kitten laps up warm milk. Or like a dog gnaws on a ham bone. I couldn't get enough. I gotta admit I was a little ticked off when Ralph—after tellin' me over and over how pretty I was—popped me the question, "Beulah, are you a virgin?"

Somehow I felt him asking me that right there in the church was a little touchy and nosy. But I was so taken in by all he was saying that I said, "Oh yes, Mr. Rainey."

He said, "You mean Ralph. Please remember I want you to call me Ralph."

So I said, "Oh yes, Ralph." That was the first time I ever called him Ralph. I think it's kinda weird that the first time I ever called my husband by his first name was when I answered his question about me being a virgin.

He said, "I'd never marry a woman who wasn't a virgin. I don't want a wife some other man has fooled around with."

I was feelin' real awkward about Ralph askin' me if I was a virgin. So I said, "Maybe you'd better talk to Mama and Daddy about this.

I couldn't get married unless Daddy said it was all right."

Ralph said, "Beulah, if you want me to talk to your Mama and Daddy about you and me gettin' married, I'll sure talk to 'em."

Which is exactly what he done. Ralph come by our house two days later. The night before he come he called Daddy up on the phone. He told Daddy he wanted to come over the next evening and talk to him about something real important. Daddy told him, "Sure, Ralph, come on over. I'll be glad to talk to you."

After Daddy had hung up the phone he turned to me and Mama and said, "That's funny. That was Ralph Rainey. He says he wants to come by tomorrow night and talk to me about something important. I wonder what he wants to talk to me about?"

Maybe I should have kept my mouth shut. Maybe I should have let Ralph handle the whole thing by himself. But I didn't do that. I let the cat out of the bag. I looked at Daddy and said, "He wants to talk to you about me being his wife. Last Sunday after church Mr. Rainey told me he wanted to marry me."

The moment I said that Mama let out this big groan. She sounded like a stuck pig. She made a face and said, "You've got to be kiddin'."

I said, "Nope, I ain't kiddin'. Last Sunday he told me he wanted me to be his wife, and I told him he'd have to talk it over with the two of you and get your okay."

Daddy asked, "When did he ask you?"

I said, "Yesterday right after church. I was practicin' the piano and he come over and stood by the piano and when I got through playin' 'Sweet Hour of Prayer' he told me he wanted to marry me. That's exactly what he said."

Daddy said, "I'll be damn." Daddy don't usually cuss. He don't cuss unless something really gets his attention.

Mama cut bait. She said, "You marryin' Ralph Rainey is the last thing in the world I want you to do. He ain't no good."

Daddy got downright huffy. He didn't like what Mama said. Which is why he looked at her and said, "Why do you say that? He's a deacon at the church. He leads the singin' every Sunday. He's the best songleader our church has ever had. What do you mean sayin' he ain't no good?"

Mama said, "I know he ain't no good because of what Ruth Ann used to tell me."

Ruth Ann, in case you've forgotten, was Ralph's first wife. She's the one who died from a brain tumor.

Mama kept on. "Ruth Ann used to get me aside and tell me Ralph wasn't nothing but a hypocrite. She said he was a lollipop at church and at his cafe. That's the very word she used. 'Lollipop.' But Ruth Ann said that around the house—when it was just him and her—he could be as mean as a rattlesnake."

Daddy said, "I don't believe it."

Mama snapped right back, "Why would I make it up? For some reason which I never figured out Ruth Ann felt I was the only person she could talk to about Ralph because nobody else would believe her. She told me Ralph got so mad at her a time or two that he gave her a whippin'. One Sunday at church we went into the lady's room and she showed me some bruises she had on her legs where 'lollipop' had whipped her. She told me he used his belt and that his belt felt like hot water mixed with iodine. Them bruises was big. I seen 'em with my own eyes."

I could tell Mama and Daddy didn't see eye to eye on what kind of man Ralph was. So I didn't know what would happen when he came by the house to talk to them about marryin' me. But come by he did. Like I said, he come by the house on Tuesday evening. He and Mama and Daddy sat on the front porch. Mama and Daddy sat side by side in the swing. Ralph sat in a rocking chair. Me and Earline sat down on the front steps and listened. Earline is my baby sister. That's what we done. We didn't talk. We just sat and listened. While

we was listenin' I give Ralph the once over. Ralph would never win
a contest for bein' the best lookin' fellow in town. The main thing I
didn't like about him was his teeth. Ralph had buck teeth. They
stuck out like a horse's teeth stick out. His daddy and brothers have
teeth that stick out too. Their teeth stickin' out is how you can tell
if somebody in Jones County is a Rainey. Everybody says they all
look like horses. Of course they don't say that to their face. They say
this behind their back. There's a lot of things people say behind your
back that they don't say to your face. My granddaddy used to say that
if everybody knew what everybody else had said about 'em behind
their back there wouldn't be two friends left on the face of the earth.
I expect he's right about that.

Ralph got right down to it. He didn't beat around the bush. He
said, "Arnold, I've come by to tell you and Josephine I want to marry
Beulah."

Arnold is my daddy's name and Josephine is my Mama's name.

Ralph rattled on. "Since Ruth Ann died I've been mighty lonely.
I don't have nobody to talk to in the morning when I get up and I
don't have nobody to talk to in the evening when I get home. The
only family I have is Oscar and you know what kind of kid he is. His
roof don't have all its shingles. Like it is now, all I do is work and
work and work. I work like a Turk at my cafe and I work like a Turk
on my farm with Sumrall."

Sumrall, in case you don't know, is an albino who works for
Ralph. He lives in a shack on Ralph's farm. I've heard Ralph say he'd
never let a darky live on his place. But he let Sumrall live on his farm.
That's because Ralph believed an albino brings you good luck. I've
heard him say, "An albino is a two-legged rabbit foot. Let one work
on your farm and you'll get enough rain in the summer to raise a
good watermelon crop and cotton crop and corn crop."

Ralph kept on telling Mama and Daddy about how hard he
worked. He said, "I work from can to can't. But there ought to be

more to life than work. That's why I want to get married again. I can take care of Beulah. I can take care of her real good. I ain't sayin' for one moment I'm a millionaire. But between the farm and the cafe and the butcher shop I make a good livin'. At least the tax commission thinks I make a good livin' cause they're always on my tail for more tax money."

Ralph rolled on like the Mississippi River. He kept on talking about how lonesome he was and how he made a good livin' and how he needed somebody to help him out. At the time I didn't know what he meant about him needin' somebody to help him out. I learned later what he meant by that.

Daddy took his cigar out of his mouth and said, "Ralph, this all sounds mighty good to me. If you want to marry Beulah, I'm all for it. She'll make you a good wife."

But Mama didn't agree. She didn't agree one bit. She spoke up and said, "I've got my doubts. Beulah's too young to get married. She ain't but sixteen."

Ralph said, "Josephine, for cryin' out loud, sixteen ain't too young for Beulah to get married. A lot of gals here in Jones County get married by the time they're sixteen. That's how old Ruth Ann was when I married her."

Mama come right back at him. She said, "Beulah ain't got sense enough to get married. She's smart but she's still wet behind the ears. I think she oughta finish high school before she gets married. She ain't got but one more year and then she'll be through."

Daddy didn't see it that way. He said, "I quit school after the fifth grade and I've made it just fine. I've made a good living bein' a welder at Masonite. If finishin' the fifth grade was good enough for me, then I think finishin' the eleventh grade oughta be good enough for Beulah. Just who does she think she is? The queen of England?"

Mama said, "I've always wanted Beulah to go to college. She makes good grades. Miss McDonald—her math teacher—stopped me one day at the meat counter in the Jitney Jungle Grocery and told me Beulah was the smartest girl she'd ever taught math to. She said that to me out of the clear blue sky. You can go from one end of Jones County to the other and you ain't gonna find a single Buchanan who has ever went to college. I've always wanted Beulah to be the first Buchanan from New Jerusalem and Jones County to have a college degree. She'd make a good school teacher."

Mama wantin' me to go to college was news to me.

Daddy said, "That's the silliest thing I've ever heard you say. There ain't no need in the world for Beulah goin' to college. She'd make a better wife than a school teacher."

Like I told you, while Mama and Daddy and Ralph was talking about me and Ralph gettin' married, I sat on the front steps. I didn't say nothing. I just listened.

Mama, Daddy, and Ralph kept talking. They went back and forth. Saying the same things over and over.

Out of the clear blue sky Daddy farted. He farted a big one. It makes Mama mad when Daddy farts when we have company. She don't say nothing about him farting when it's just Daddy, Mama, Earline, and me. Mama said, "Arnold, what you just done is embarrassing. I've told you a thousand times not to fart when we have company. And Ralph here is company."

Daddy said, "Ralph ain't company. I've known Ralph Rainey all my life. Company is somebody you don't really know."

Daddy went on to say, "Ralph, let's leave it like this. I'm all for you and Beulah gettin' married. But Josephine here ain't. I think me and Josephine need to do some more talking just between ourselves. And I think I want to pray about this. Whenever I come to a fork in the road I believe in praying about which way to go."

Ralph said, "Arnold, that sounds good to me. And I'll tell you what: I'll pray about it too."

My daddy said, "After Josephine and me has talked some more

and after I've taken it to the Lord in prayer, I'll get back in touch with you and let you know what I've decided."

Ralph said, "I'll be waitin' and listening. Between you prayin' about it and me prayin' about it we're bound to figure out if the Lord wants me to marry Beulah."

With that Ralph stood up and shook hands with Daddy. He told me and Earline and Mama goodnight. "Goodnight Josephine. I wish you didn't feel the way you do. I hope you change your mind." He looked at me and said, "Goodnight, Beulah." And he looked at my baby sister and said, "Goodnight, Earline."

Ralph walked out to his Ford pickup and drove away. Every man in Jones County who can afford one has a pickup truck. Maybe a Dodge or a Ford or a GMC. They use 'em to carry feed in and to haul dogs when they're goin' hunting during deer season.

Mama and Daddy and Earline and me watched Ralph's pickup drive away on the gravel road that runs in front of our house. We watched its red tail lights until it went out of sight around the bend that's down the road.

A few moments went by and nobody said nothing.

Finally Daddy spoke. I remember to this day what he said. "Ain't this something. Ralph Rainey has come here tonight and said to me and Mama that he wants to marry Beulah. It ain't everyday a man like Ralph Rainey asks a woman to marry him. No sir! This don't happen everyday. Ralph's got property. You take his farm on the Okatoma River. I know for a fact it has five hundred acres on it. Two hundred acres are on the west side of the river, and three-hundred acres are on the east side. It's all good river-bottom land. It's as fertile as a cat's ass. He bought it for a steal from Henry Lassiter's widow. She got rid of it after Henry died so she could go live with her two boys in Birmingham. You plant corn in Okatoma River bottom land one day and the next morning you've got corn stalks five feet tall. Ralph's got a real nice brick home on the place. And he has two good barns. And he's got a goin' meat market and barbecue cafe in Laurel. He's bound to be makin' money. If he wasn't makin' money how could he afford every year to have a new Ford pickup and a new Buick car? And besides all this, he's a deacon at the church. Every Sunday he's there—leading the singin' and taking up the collection."

After Daddy had said all of them good things about Ralph, he looked right at me and said, "Beulah, you're one lucky gal and I don't mean maybe."

Quick as a flash, Mama said, "No she ain't. Ralph Rainey ain't no good. I've told you this but you won't listen to me. Or hear me. The reason I know he ain't no good is because of all the stuff Ruth Ann told me about him. Ruth Ann wasn't tellin' me no fib about him beating her up when he got mad. Ralph is like a dime. He's got two sides. He's got a good side and a bad side. I don't want Beulah gettin' mixed up with a guy like him. And besides, there's too much difference between his age and Beulah's. He's twenty years older than her. And he's got that nitwit son from his marriage to Ruth Ann. When Ralph brings Oscar to church all he does is sit on the front pew and pick his nose. Him pickin' his nose makes me sick at my stomach."

Daddy said, "I don't think Oscar's a problem. He stays most of the time at the Rehabilitation School at Ellisville."

Mama and Daddy went around and around. Daddy was all for me marrying Ralph and Mama was dead set against it. While they was talking they didn't say nothing to me. I'd about decided they didn't care what I thought. Just like a farmer doesn't care what a cow thinks when it's being hauled to market to be butchered for meat.

But believe it or not they finally got around to asking me how I felt.

Daddy looked over at me and asked, "Beulah, what do you think about marrying Ralph?"

Daddy's question didn't catch me empty-handed. That's all I'd thought about since Ralph stood beside the church piano and asked me to marry him. Should I or should I not? I didn't care one way or the other about his farm and barbecue cafe. They didn't mean twaddle to me. What bothered me the most about Ralph was his buck teeth which made him look like a horse. Them buck teeth I didn't like. And I didn't like what Mama had said about him whippin' Ruth Ann. But a whipping is a whipping. My daddy didn't have no guilt or brakes about givin' me a whippin' from time to time. When I did something he really didn't like he'd take his belt off and go to it on my rear end. He'd say time and again, "The Bible says spare the rod and spoil the child." Where it says that I don't know. But Daddy says it's in there somewhere. Which is worser? A whipping by Daddy or a whipping by Ralph? You tell me. Maybe Ralph wouldn't never give me a whippin' like he gave Ruth Ann. Maybe he'd changed. Maybe he'd treat me nicer. He was sweet as honey in what he said to me after I'd played "Sweet Hour of Prayer" on the church piano. He'd said, "I think you're the prettiest girl in New Jerusalem. The fact is, I think you're the prettiest girl I ever seen." Them's the sweetest words anybody had ever spoke to me. And getting married to Ralph would mean I'd no longer have to live with Mama and Daddy. That I liked. I liked it because Mama and Daddy was always sayin' to me things like, "Beulah, clean off the table and take the dishes to the kitchen." They'd say this to me after we'd eaten supper. Or they'd say, "Beulah, go get a broom and sweep off the front porch. It's got leaves on it." They treated me like I was their maid or slave. But the thing I didn't like the most was the way Mama and Daddy held the reins so tight on me. They did this because they was Baptists and didn't want me to sin. Daddy went out of his way to make sure I didn't sin none. That's why he wouldn't let me have no dates. Charles Stogner once asked me for a date to go to the skating rink at Laurel. Daddy wouldn't let me have a date with

Charles because the skating rink has a jukebox and Daddy said where you have a jukebox you have dancing and dancing is a sin. Or you take the way he acted the time Miss Hopson, my piano teacher, wanted to take all of her piano students to a music conference at the university down in Hatttiesburg. The piano conference was gonna begin at nine o'clock in the morning and go all day long and into the night. At night they was gonna have a piano concert by a real famous piano player who was coming down to Hattiesburg all the way from Chicago. Miss Hopson wanted all of her piano students to go to the conference and she wanted all of us to have fun. So she come up with a big idea. We'd go to the conference and attend the piano concert. Then we'd all spend the night at the Holiday Inn and eat pancakes the next morning at the International House of Pancakes on Hardy Street right across from the university. When she told me about it I got so excited I didn't know what to do. I went home and told Mama and Daddy what Miss Hopson was planning. She was gonna pay for everything herself. Miss Hopson don't really have to work. She has lots of money. Everybody says her father made a ton of money in the lumber business and left her more money than she'll ever be able to spend. She teaches piano lessons because she loves the piano. The moment I told Daddy what Miss Hopson's plans were my daddy said I couldn't go. I asked him why I couldn't go. He said a motel ain't nothing but a whorehouse. Why Daddy thought that I don't know because as far as I know he ain't never spent a night in a motel. But I've heard him call a lot of places whorehouses. He says a drive-in theater is a teenage whorehouse. The back seat of a car is a whorehouse. I begged him to let me go but he wouldn't budge. He wouldn't budge an inch. The next week when I went up to Laurel for my piano lesson I told Miss Hopson what my daddy had said about not lettin' me go. She said, "Your daddy is being unreasonable. I'll call him right now and get him to change his mind." I told her Daddy's extension number at the Masonite plant. She called him right then and there. I couldn't hear what Daddy said but I could hear what Miss Hopson said. She said, "Hello, Mr. Buchanan, this is Patty Hopson, your daughter's piano teacher. How are you today?" Miss Hopson was being real nice asking Daddy how he was. Daddy must have said he was okay because Miss Hopson said, "That's fine. I'm glad to hear that." Then she went on to say, "Mr. Buchanan, I'm calling you about the music conference they're going to have down in Hattiesburg in a few days. I've looked over the program and I can tell it's going to be high quality all the way through. I particularly want Beulah to go so she can hear the piano concert that'll be at night. They're bringing down a Chicago pianist and he'll be accompanied by the University of Southern Mississippi Symphony. Beulah tells me she has never heard a symphony orchestra before. I thought I'd let my students have a little fun by spending the night at the Holiday Inn. And then they can have a pancake breakfast the next morning. I'm picking up the tab for all this myself and I surely do want Beulah to go. She'll be exposed to a lot she hasn't been exposed to before. It'll be educational as well as a barrel of fun." I could tell Daddy started saying something. He must have said something about my safety or my conduct because Miss Hopson said, "Mr. Buchanan, don't you be worried. I'll keep a close eye on her. I can assure you she'll be okay." Daddy started talking again and Miss Hopson rolled her eyes and made a face like she didn't like what he was sayin'. The upshot of it was Daddy wouldn't give in. When the telephone conversation was over Miss Hopson put her arm around me and gave me a hug and said, "Beulah, I tried my best to get your daddy to change his mind but he wouldn't. I guess this means the door is closed." I wanted to cry. But I didn't. Buchanans don't cry in public. I didn't get to go to the concert. I stayed home. Everybody who went said they had a big time. They had a pillow fight at the motel. They went swimming in the motel pool. The next morning they ate pancakes at the International House of Pancakes.

I think Daddy should have let me go. Me going down to Hattiesburg and spending the night in a motel ain't the worst thing in the world you can do. I can think of a lot of things that's worser. The thought goin' through my mind was that gettin' married would be a quick way to get out from under the thumb of my mama and daddy. Maybe I wouldn't be bossed around no more. Maybe if I was married I'd get to go places. So when Daddy asked me what I thought about marrying Ralph, I said, "I think I'd like to." Them's the exact five words I spoke.

Daddy blew a big puff of cigar smoke, passed another loud fart, and said, "Then that settles it. Ralph and Beulah are gonna get married."

Mama spoke out real loud and said, "I think she's making a mistake. And I mean a big mistake."

With that Mama got up and left the front porch in a huff. As she walked into the house she slammed the door. I bet you could have heard that slam all the way down to the Okatoma River. That's the way Mama acts when she's mad about something. She walks away in a huff and slams the door. That wasn't the first time I'd heard Mama and Daddy disagree. And I figured it wouldn't be the last time.

The next day Daddy went by Ralph's barbecue cafe in Laurel and told him he'd prayed about it and had decided it would be okay if we got married. Ralph said he'd prayed about it too. As far as Daddy was concerned me marrying Ralph was the Lord's will. That's what he told me he told Ralph.

The Lord's will or not, no sooner had Daddy give the green light for me to marry than I hit a snag. When I think about the snag it still hurts. Two or three days after Daddy gave the green light we was all eatin' breakfast. By "we" I mean Daddy, Mama, Earline, and me. Daddy was dunking his biscuits in his coffee. Mama don't like for Daddy to dunk his biscuits in his coffee. She says it's not nice. When you dunk a biscuit in coffee you crumble it up in your coffee and let it get real moist and then you eat it with a spoon. That's what Daddy was doin' when he said, "We got to start thinking about Beulah's wedding."

In a real snappy voice Mama said, "Who're you talking to?"

Daddy said, "I'm talking to you."

Mama said, "Why're you talkin' to me?"

Daddy said, 'Because you're Beulah's mama."

I could tell Mama was still real ticked off because she said, "I ain't havin' nothing to do with Beulah's wedding. And when I say *nothing* I mean *nothing*. I ain't even goin' to it."

It really hurt when Mama said that.

Daddy said, "Josephine, that's not a nice thing for you to say."

Mama said, "Maybe it's not. But nice or not nice, I'm not touching her wedding with a ten-foot pole. I've told you Ralph ain't no good. If I went to the wedding I'd be as phony as a Jew singin' about Jesus at a Baptist revival. You and Beulah can handle the wedding all by yourselves. So go to it and best of luck."

I thought at the time Mama was being mean. I still think she was being mean. The Bible says you're supposed to honor your father and your mother. That's one of the ten commandments Brother Ledbetter is always preaching about at the New Jerusalem Baptist Church. I'm guessin' the commandment means you're supposed to love your parents. But how can you love your mama when she's mean to you? I think it's weird that your mama and daddy say some of the meanest things that's ever said to you. Even if I was makin' a mistake by marrying Ralph, couldn't Mama at least have gone along and kept her feelings to herself and her mouth shut? If she'd done that I wouldn't have been embarrassed by the way she was acting. I'll put it this way: can't a mama be kind to her daughter even when she feels her daughter is making a mistake? If I ever have a son or a daughter I'm gonna be kind and tender to 'em even though I know they're pissin' in their pants.

When Mama said she wasn't gonna have nothing to do with my wedding, Daddy said, "Oh shit." I could tell he was ticked off.

But then he said, "By god, I'll get something worked out. What it'll be I don't know."

Daddy went and told Aunt Carrie about the way Mama was acting. Aunt Carrie is Daddy's sister. She's married to Sam Casey. Everybody calls her husband "Uncle Sam." His real name is Samuel, not Sam. He was named after Samuel in the Old Testament. Everybody says Uncle Sam is the best carpenter in Jones County. And maybe he is. He ain't never hurting for work because people are always wanting him to fix this and fix that. Aunt Carrie and Uncle Sam have one daughter. Her name is Velma. Velma is older than me. When I was a little girl I used to spend the night with Velma. She and I had a big time chasing lightning bugs at night. We'd catch 'em and put 'em in a glass jar with air holes punched in the lid. Velma has become the black sheep of the New Jerusalem Baptist Church. I don't think she's a black sheep but Ralph's relatives sure think she is. They don't like her because she divorced her husband who was a Rainey and was kin to Ralph. Velma later remarried. She married the man who owns the Confederate Truck Stop on Highway 49 just north of Hattiesburg. Two weeks after Velma remarried they had a business meeting at the New Jerusalem Baptist Church and voted her slam out of the church. I know they voted Velma slam out of the church because I was there when they done it and heard what Brother Ledbetter said. He said Velma remarrying after she'd got a divorce made her an adulterer and he wasn't in favor of having an adulterer in the church. He said the Bible says a divorced woman ain't suppose to marry again. My sister—Earline—says her divorce is not the reason some people don't like Velma. Earline says people don't like Velma because they're jealous of her. They know she's now got money and can afford to drive a Cadillac.

Aunt Carrie listened to Daddy telling about Mama acting like a pouting pig over me marrying Ralph. Daddy later told me she said, "Josephine ought to be ashamed acting that way. Beulah needs her support." Aunt Carrie told Daddy not to worry. She said she and Velma would take care of the wedding. Which is exactly what they done.

Velma had me come down to Hattiesburg and meet her at the Confederate Truck Stop. She took me across town to McRae's Department Store in the Cloverleaf Mall. She picked out for me the prettiest white dress I'd ever seen. It had gold embroidery all over it. When I tried it on it made me feel like a princess. Velma also bought me a pair of white shoes and a white hat with a fancy veil on it that came down over my face. The clerk said it was a pillbox hat. I'd never heard of a hat being called a pillbox hat before. Velma also bought me a frilly pink dress which she called my "going away" outfit. On top of all that she bought me a pretty blue blouse and a matching pair of blue slacks. She told me, "You wear this blouse and these slacks on your honeymoon." When I walked out of McRae's Department Store with all of them new clothes in them big boxes I felt like I was floating on a cloud. They even gave me a cute little box to carry my pillbox hat in. The box was round like a donut.

One week later Ralph and I married. Our wedding was on a Saturday morning at the New Jerusalem Baptist Church. Ralph said he could spare two days for a wedding and a honeymoon. He'd have to be back at his barbecue cafe and butcher shop by early Monday morning. A nice crowd was at the church to see me and Ralph get married. Like she said she wouldn't, Mama didn't come. She stayed home and pouted. When Mama is really mad she pouts and don't talk to nobody. For a week before the wedding she wouldn't say nothin' to Daddy or to Earline or to me. She wouldn't answer the phone either. Her not comin' to my wedding was embarrassing and really hurt my feelings. But Daddy and Earline was there. So was Velma and Aunt Carrie and Uncle Sam. Ralph's mama and daddy came. So did his two brothers. One is named Dewey and the other one is named Harold. Pauline and Luella was there. They're Dewey's and Harold's wives. Bessie was there. She's Ralph's sister who lives in Baton Rouge. She drove all the way from Baton Rouge to New Jerusalem just to be at our wedding. The one person who wasn't there I thought might be there was Oscar. Ralph didn't want him there because he said Oscar wouldn't know what a wedding was. So Oscar stayed in Ellisville.

I wore my new white dress with gold embroidery that Velma had bought for me at McRae's Department Store. I had on my new white shoes and my new pillbox hat with the veil that come down over my face. My sister Earline was my maid of honor. Ralph wore his dark blue suit and his maroon tie. His daddy was his best man.

Brother Ledbetter done the ceremony. I thought he'd never get through. That's the way Brother Ledbetter is. He can ramble on and on. He read from the Old Testament. And then he read from the New Testament. He had a book of poems about love and marriage and he read some of them. Then he got off on divorce. He talked more about divorce than anything else. He said he didn't want me and Ralph to ever get a divorce because gettin' a divorce is sin. Why he wanted to hit so hard on divorce the day we was gettin' married was beyond me. Aunt Carrie told me later he wasn't aiming what he said at me and Ralph but was aiming at Velma. Like I told you, Velma divorced her first husband and married the husband she has now and got voted out of the New Jerusalem Baptist Church. I tell you right now: Brother Ledbetter don't like Velma and Velma don't like Brother Ledbetter. She says he's full of baptized crap. She and Brother Ledbetter don't even speak to each other. They give each other the cold shoulder treatment.

When the wedding service was over we had some real nice refreshments. Aunt Carrie and Velma had set up a table at the back of the church and had covered it with a white linen table cloth. I could tell they'd really gone to a lot of trouble. On the table were two bowls of nuts. Them bowls had all kinds of nuts—pecans, peanuts, cashews, and almonds. There was another bowl of little round, green mints. There was a big bowl of cherry punch with a big piece of ice floating in it along with a fancy silver dipper and green paper cups for everybody to drink out of. Where that fancy silver dipper came from I've never found out. I keep forgettin' to ask Velma or Aunt Carrie where they got it.

What really stole the show was the wedding cake which was sittin' right in the middle of the table. Velma had it baked at the Jitney Jungle Grocery in Laurel. It was covered all over with white icing and was decorated with little red rosebuds. On top in the very middle was a little toy bride and groom. The groom had on a black suit and the bride had on a red dress that matched the rosebuds on the cake. In her hand she was holding a red umbrella. I couldn't believe my eyes when I seen that umbrella. Also on top of the cake in pink icing was writing which said, "Best Wishes to Beulah and Ralph." It was all so nice. I wished Mama had been there to see how nice it was. But like I said, she was home pouting because she didn't want me to marry Ralph.

Ralph and me left the church about the middle of the day. Just before leaving I went to the lady's room and took off my white bride's dress and put on the pink "going away" dress Velma had bought for me. Velma helped me change into it. Everybody waved at us and told us goodbye as we drove off. For our honeymoon we drove down to the Mississippi Gulf Coast. Our honeymoon lasted Saturday afternoon and most of Sunday. When we got down to the coast I seen something I'd never seen before. I'm talking about the Gulf of Mexico. The Gulf of Mexico took my breath away. It was so big and so pretty and so shiny. I didn't know there was that much water in all the world.

Ralph and me got on the highway that runs along beside the gulf.

Ralph said, "This is Highway 90. It goes all the way from the Louisiana line clean across Mississippi to the Alabama state line. When I was in the navy I was stationed for a year at Pascagoula where the shipyard is. So I know this coast pretty good."

After I was married to Ralph I learned all about the navy. Ralph was proud of having been in the navy. That's where he became a cook and learned the food business.

While we was driving toward Biloxi Ralph said, "We gotta find a motel where we can spend the night."

Ralph mentioning a motel made me feel funny on the inside. I'd never spent a night in a motel before. The only thing I knew about motels was Daddy saying they was whorehouses. That's the main reason he wouldn't let me go with Miss Hopson to Hattiesburg for the piano conference. Miss Hopson was goin' to let all of her piano students spend the night at the Holiday Inn and go swimming in the motel pool. Daddy told me, "I'm not gonna let you spend the night in a whorehouse."

Me and Ralph started looking for a motel. I spotted this motel called the Broadwater Beach.

I said, "Why don't we try this one? The sign out front says it's a motel."

Ralph said, "Okay. We'll give it a try."

We pulled up in front of the Broadwater Beach Motel. Ralph said, "You stay here. I'll go in and see if they have a room."

While Ralph was doin' that I got out of the car and looked around. I couldn't believe what I saw. The Broadwater Beach was fancier than the motels in Laurel. I mean it was a lot fancier. It had this big swimming pool with a waterfall. People in bathing suits were sitting around the pool and were soaking up the sun. Everwhere I looked was palm trees and flowers. And the motel had the greenest grass I'd ever seen. The grass was being watered by pretty, little sprinklers that stuck up out of the ground.

Ralph come out of the motel and said, "Let's get back in the car and keep looking."

Which we done.

When we got back in the car I asked, "Didn't they have no room?"

He said, "Yeah, they had a room. But they wanted to charge me seventy dollars for one night. Can you believe that? Seventy dollars! I ain't about to pay seventy dollars for a motel room. No way."

I thought to myself: Ralph, we're on our honeymoon. We ain't gonna be down here but one night. What'd be wrong spending seventy dollars for a nice motel room? But it was his money. So I kept what I was thinking to myself.

We got back on Highway 90 and away we went. We was still goin' toward Biloxi. A sign beside the highway read "Biloxi Straight Ahead."

Ralph said, "They've got a big airbase in Biloxi. It's one of the biggest bases the airforce has."

I said, "I didn't know that." Ralph was tellin' me a lot of things I didn't know.

The next thing I said was, "Look, Ralph, there's a Holiday Inn. Why don't we try it?" I kinda wanted to stay at a Holiday Inn to make up for not being able to stay at the Holiday Inn in Hattiesburg the time Miss Hopson took all her piano students to the music conference.

Ralph said, "I'll pull in and check out their prices."

So we pulled up in front of the Holiday Inn. Ralph hopped out and went inside and was back in thirty seconds.

He said, "They're worse than the Broadwater Beach. They want seventy-five dollars for a room. I'm not gonna let these robbers hold me up. That much money for a room ain't nothing but highway robbery."

So we got back on the highway and headed again toward Biloxi.

I was enjoyin' the ride. To my right was the Gulf of Mexico. Between the highway and the gulf was a pretty sandy beach. Some couples was out there walking on the sand and holding hands.

I said to Ralph, "I hope you and me can walk on that beach sometime this evening or night and hold hands like those folks out there are doin'."

He said, "We'll do that."

I was glad Ralph said that. We was on our honeymoon and so far he hadn't shown me no tenderness and honey talk. I thought that was what a honeymoon was all about. I was wanting a lot of tenderness and honey talk like he gave me the Sunday he stood beside the church piano and said all of them sweet things to me about how pretty I was.

We hadn't drove very far before Ralph said, "Let's check this motel out."

I said, "Which one?"

He said, "This one that's painted yellow."

Sure enough. There was this motel that was painted yellow. It was the brightest yellow I'd ever seen. The sign out front read "The Twinkling Star Motel." I'm gonna be honest with you. When I looked at that motel my heart sank. It sank into the ground. It wasn't near about as nice as the Holiday Inn or the Broadwater Beach. I could tell the rooms was real little and was crowded next to one another like pigs in a pig's sty. But I didn't say nothing. I was gonna let Ralph handle us gettin' a place to spend our honeymoon night.

Ralph drove in and stopped in front of the Twinkling Star Motel office. The motel office was real little too and had an open window you could see into. There was a man sittin' in the office and as soon as we stopped he yelled out the window, "Do you folks need a room for tonight?" I could tell the motel man had on a brown denim shirt and was wearing a straw hat. His straw hat was the kind you buy at a hardware store to wear when you're working out in the yard or in a garden. Since he was sittin' inside the motel office I couldn't help but wonder why he was wearing a straw hat. That didn't make sense to me.

Ralph yelled back, "Yeah, I need a room. How much do you charge?"

The man in the straw hat yelled back, "Thirty dollars a night. That's the best deal on the Mississippi Gulf Coast. You can't beat it."

Ralph answered, "How about comin' down to twenty-five dollars?"

The man in the straw hat came back at Ralph. He said, "You must be a Jew."

Ralph said, "I ain't no Jew. I'm a Baptist."

The man in the straw hat said, "I didn't think you looked like a Jew, but you're sure acting like one. I'll come down to twenty-five dollars. But I ain't goin' no lower than that. I gotta make a profit. You can have room eight up there on the right side. Here's the key."

With that he put a key on the shelf in front of the open window. Ralph got out of the car and picked up the key. He said, "You say room eight on the right side?"

The man behind the window said, "That's right. Room eight. Believe you me I'm losin' my pants on this deal. I still say you're a Jew."

Ralph laughed and said, "Nope, I'm a Baptist."

Ralph got back in the car and we drove a few feet and parked in front of room eight. Ralph and me got out of the car and got our two suitcases. Ralph unlocked the door to room eight and we walked inside. The room smelled musty. It smelled like it had been closed up for a year. It had a window air conditioner.

Ralph said, "Let me turn on the air conditioner. It's hot in here."

Which he done. I looked around at the furniture in the room. To be frank with you, it wasn't very nice. There was a bed, a table, a chair, and a twelve-inch television set. The bed and the table and the chair looked to me like they'd been on Noah's Ark. The floor was covered with linoleum. But what can you expect for twenty-five dollars? I wished we'd stayed at the Holiday Inn or at the Broadwater Beach. One thing I learned in a hurry about Ralph. He was tight with a dollar. I bet I heard him say a thousand times "a penny saved is a penny earned."

No sooner had each one of us used the bathroom than Ralph said, "I'm hungry. All I had for dinner was them wedding refreshments and they ain't holding me. Let's go get something to eat."

That was fine with me. So we got in the car and got back on Highway 90. We hadn't drove very far before Ralph spotted a Western Sizzlin Steak House.

He said, "There's a Western Sizzlin. They have got one of them in Laurel. Let's stop and eat there."

We parked and went inside the steak house. Ralph said, "Since this is our honeymoon let's order the T-bone special."

Which is what we done. We ordered two T-bone specials with a baked potato. Ralph let me know in no uncertain terms that he was a fan of Western Sizzlin Steak Houses. He said, "I couldn't count the number of times I've eaten at the Western Sizzlin in Laurel. They really know how to cook a steak."

He went on to explain he ate a lot of barbecued chicken and ribs at his cafe. But sometimes he got tired of barbecue and needed a grilled steak. Which is when he'd go to the Western Sizzlin. He added, "Course now that I'm married I hope I can have a lot of vegetable suppers at the house. There ain't nothing better for you than good cooked vegetables. By the way, Beulah, do you know how to cook vegetables?"

I said, "Oh yes I do. Mama had me working in the kitchen before I was ten."

He said, "That's good. I'm glad to know that."

After we'd finished them T-bone steaks we headed back west to the Twinkling Star Motel. On the way back we stopped at a Baskin-Robbins Ice Cream store and bought a cone of ice-cream. Mine was strawberry. As far as I'm concerned there ain't no better flavor of ice cream than strawberry.

As we pulled into the Twinkling Star Motel Ralph blew his horn and waved at the old fellow in the office who'd asked him if he was a Jew. It was getting late but he was still wearing his straw hat.

We parked in front of room eight. Ralph looked at me and said, "You said a little while ago you wanted to walk on the beach some. Why don't we do that before it gets too late."

I said, "I'd love to." Which is what we done. I'd never walked on a beach before. The fact is I'd never seen a beach before. You won't believe how much sand there is on the Biloxi beach. All of that sand and all of that wavy water with the tide comin' in just blew my mind.

As we walked down the beach me and Ralph held hands. I could tell he was gettin' lovey. Which is what you're supposed to do on your honeymoon. We hadn't walked too far before Ralph said, "I think I'll smoke a cigar."

Him saying that caught me by surprise. I know this sounds silly, but for some reason or other I hadn't caught on that Ralph smoked. Which is why I said, "I didn't know you smoked."

He said, "Yep, I do. At least once a day I smoke a cigar. I never smoke more than one. Smoking ain't good for you, but it helps me to relax."

He reached in his shirt pocket and pulled out a cigar. He then put it in his mouth and lit it and started puffing away. The way cigar smoke started comin' out of Ralph's mouth you'd of thought he was a steam engine puffing up a mountain.

Ralph said, "This cigar is a Swisher Sweet. Them's the only kind of cigars I smoke. I like the way they smell. And I like the way they taste."

I asked, "What kind of cigar did you say that was?"

He said, "It's a Swisher Sweet. It's a small cigar put out by the King Edward cigar folks."

That was the first Swisher Sweet I saw Ralph smoke. But it sure wasn't the last. Every day we was married he smoked a Swisher Sweet.

After a while we left the beach and walked back to our room at the Twinkling Star Motel. I began to feel real funny. And unsure of myself. I knew the time had come for me to go to bed with Ralph and I didn't know what to expect. I was a virgin. I'd never dated. I'd never been around men except men like Daddy and Uncle Sam. I knew Ralph would want sex. The thing I was wondering was: did I want it? What was I supposed to do? How was I supposed to act? I didn't know the answer to them questions.

Ralph asked me, "Have you got a nightgown?"

I said, "Nope, but I've got some pajamas."

He said, "Why don't you go to the bathroom and put 'em on."

Which is what I done. I took off my "going away" dress and put on my pajamas. I looked in the bathroom mirror and took my comb and combed my hair. I was doing my best to make myself look pretty. When you're a primitive Baptist and can't use makeup you don't have too much to work with when it comes to tryin' to look pretty. I excused myself on the john and then opened the door to our motel room. The moment I opened the door I seen that Ralph had put on his pajamas. They was fire-engine red. My pajamas was light green.

Ralph said, "I need to take a leak." Which he went into the bathroom and did.

When he came out of the bathroom I took one good look at him. And you know what grabbed my attention the most? His buck teeth. Like I've said, all the Raineys look like horses. But I was gambling that livin' with a horse would be better in the long run than livin' with Mama and Daddy who could be so mean to me and Earline.

As soon as Ralph stepped out of the bathroom he said, "Beulah, I want us to sanctify our marriage bed."

I didn't have no idea what he meant. And so I said, "What do you mean by that?"

"Before you and me go to bed for the first time I think we ought to pray." That's what Ralph said. I didn't know you was supposed to pray before you went to bed together for the first time. I didn't know what to pray about and so I said to Ralph, "That's fine with me but you do the prayin'."

He said, "Sure. I'll do the prayin'."

Ralph got down on his knees and I don't remember word for word what he prayed but it went something like this: "Oh dear God, me and Beulah is about to have sex together for the first time. I know St. Paul says in the Bible that it's a good thing for a man not to touch a woman. But St. Paul also says in the Good Book that it's better to marry than to burn. And oh dear God, ever since Ruth Ann died I've been burning for somebody to love. I want to thank you for little Beulah here who has come into my life to take Ruth Ann's place. Help me to be a good husband to sweet little Beulah and help her to be a good wife to me like Ruth Ann was. I pray this prayer in the name of Jesus who died on the cross so we could be saved through his blood. Oh thank you Jesus. Amen."

Them is almost the exact words Ralph prayed so he could sanctify our marriage bed in the Twinkling Star Motel. I didn't like it one bit that he called me "sweet little Beulah." Everybody said I looked grown for my age. I remember Aunt Carrie saying two days before the wedding, "Beulah, if I didn't know better I'd say you was at least twenty-five years old." You take my boobs. If you could have seen my boobs when I was sixteen you'd have understood what Aunt Carrie meant. I may have been a primitive Baptist from New Jerusalem who didn't use makeup, but my boobs wasn't second class to nobody. And I didn't like Ralph talking about Ruth Ann in his prayer. I particularly didn't like him saying I was gonna take her place. But since it was our first night together I kept my mouth shut. At times it's best to keep your feelings to yourself. Particularly if them feelings is raw.

So to bed we went. I thought we'd both get naked. But we didn't. Ralph kept his red pajamas on. I didn't take off my pajama top. But I did take off my pajama bottoms. I did that because Ralph said, "Take off your pajama bottoms. That way I won't have no trouble gettin' to it." That's the exact word he used. "It." I didn't appreciate him callin' my cherry an "it." But that's sure the word he used. An "it." After I took off my pajama bottoms we done some kissin' which I didn't like all that much. The reason I didn't like him kissing me all that much was because Ralph's kisses tasted like a Swisher Sweet cigar. I found myself wishin' he'd brushed his teeth and used some Listerine mouthwash before sanctifying our marriage bed. The next thing Ralph done was to rub my boobs a little. The next thing he done surprised me. He put some saliva on his fingers and wet my cherry. Since I knew the way his breath smelled it made me wonder if my cherry was smellin' like a Swisher Sweet cigar. After he'd wet my cherry he put a rubber on his dick and stuck it up my cherry. He then started pumping away. It must have felt good to Ralph because the moment he started pumping he started moaning. He didn't say nothing to me. He just pumped and moaned and pumped and moaned. As soon as he jacked off he pulled his dick out and turned over and went to sleep. He hadn't been asleep two minutes before he started snoring. I lay there on the bed and listened to Ralph snore. I done that after I'd put back on my pajama bottoms. I bet it took me at least an hour to go to sleep. So much was goin' through my mind. When a lot is goin' through your mind it ain't easy to go to sleep.

I bet us havin' sex for the first time in the Twinkling Star Motel in Biloxi didn't take more than two minutes. Three minutes at the most. It may have felt good to Ralph but it didn't feel good to me.

The reason I know it felt good to Ralph is because of the way he grunted and moaned. But for me it hurt while we was doin' it. The way Ralph had sex that first night we was together was the way he done it all six years I was married to him. On average he's wanted it three times a week. Usually on Monday night and on Wednesday night and on either Friday or Saturday night. And every time it was the same. Put on a rubber, stick it in, and pump away. Then turn over and go to sleep and start snoring like an Illinois Central freight train on the way to Chicago. The only time Ralph let up on having sex was when I had my periods. During my periods I didn't have to have no sex with Ralph. I'd pretend my periods was longer than they really was. I'd keep on wearing a Kotex or a Tampax several days after my period had stopped. Sometimes Ralph would say, "Beulah, your periods sure do last a long time." And I'd say, "I know they do but there's nothing I can do about it. It's just the way I'm made." Some women love to go to bed with a man. Maybe sex is good if you're havin' it with a man who is tender and kind and sweet talks you and knows how to work you up and get you in the mood. But Ralph never got me worked up. Every time after we'd done it I'd turn over and think about how it hurt. It got to the point where me havin' sex with Ralph wasn't nothing more than meat rubbing against meat. From time to time I'd wonder if it'd feel better if maybe I was doin' it with somebody else besides Ralph. But I knew that doin' it with somebody besides Ralph would be wrong. That would be committing adultery and goin' against Mount Sinai. The ten commandments came at Mount Sinai and one of those ten commandments says "you shall not commit adultery." At least once a month Brother Ledbetter preaches a sermon in which he shells down hard against committing adultery. He says over and over that committing adultery would be sinning against Moses and Mount Sinai. Brother Ledbetter shells down as hard on committing adultery as he does on women wearing lipstick and having their hair cut short. So in his sermons he'll say time and time again we've got to bow down before Mount Sinai and hold fast to Jesus. Sometimes while preaching a sermon Brother Ledbetter will start chanting. He says he starts chanting when the Spirit comes down upon him. You can always tell when the Spirit has come down on Brother Ledbetter. He gets a fixed stare in his eyes. He'll lift both of his arms real high over his head and he'll chant over and over "bow down before Mount Sinai and hold fast to Jesus. Bow down before Mount Sinai and hold fast to Jesus." While he's saying this he'll shuffle around the pulpit. And at times the Spirit will come down on everybody in the congregation at the New Jerusalem Baptist Church. Everybody will stand up and join in with Brother Ledbetter. Everybody will lift their arms real high and chant over and over "bow down before Mount Sinai and hold fast to Jesus." And sometimes when Brother Ledbetter is chanting and shuffling his feet the Spirit will come down upon Miss Priscilla King. Miss Priscilla is an old maid who is our church's piano player. She'll jump up and go to the piano and start playing music to go along with Brother Ledbetter's chanting and the congregation's chanting. On the church piano she'll play songs like "We're Marching to Zion" and "Since Jesus Came Into My Heart." You've missed a lot if you've never heard Brother Ledbetter and the congregation of the New Jerusalem Baptist Church chanting "bow down before Mount Sinai and hold fast to Jesus" while Miss Priscilla plays "We're Marching to Zion." It will make goosepimples come over you from head to toe. Or at least it used to make goosepimples come all over me.

2

R ALPH AND ME slept together Saturday night and on Sunday morning we woke up a little before seven. Ralph rolled out of bed and took a leak in the john. After he'd finished I went to the john too.

Ralph stuck his hand under his red pajamas and rubbed his stomach and said, "I'm hungry as a horse. I'm always hungry in the morning. Where do you want to eat breakfast?"

I thought it was real nice of Ralph to ask me where I wanted to eat breakfast. My daddy sure never would have done that. The evening before when we was driving to the Western Sizzler I'd seen an International House of Pancakes restaurant. I'd always wanted to eat breakfast at one of them restaurants with the tall blue roof. And so I said, "I think I'd like to eat breakfast at the International House of Pancakes. We passed one last night on the way to the steak house."

Ralph said, "That's fine with me. That's where we'll go and eat breakfast."

We got dressed. I put on the blue blouse and blue slacks Velma had bought for me at McRae's Department Store in Hattiesburg. I think I looked real snazzy in 'em. Of course if you're a primitive Baptist like I was you'd better not look too snazzy. Brother Ledbetter wouldn't like that and when he don't like something he'll let you know about it.

We left the Twinkling Star Motel and drove to the pancake house. When we walked inside the International House of Pancakes it took my breath away. It was too pretty for words. It had a real tall ceiling shaped like an A that went up and up and up. The booths was padded and was covered with what looked to me like blue leather. I thought to myself, "Ain't this nice. These pretty blue booths match my new blouse and slacks that Velma give me." The waitresses had on pink uniforms and little white aprons. I felt like I was in Switzerland or in some far away country like that.

Me and Ralph ordered buckwheat pancakes and Virginia ham and coffee which the waitress brought to the table in this cute little coffee pot. While we was eating them buckwheat pancakes Ralph asked me, "Have you ever seen a battleship?"

I said, "Goodness gracious heavens no."

Ralph went on, "We ain't too far from Mobile. Over there at Mobile they've got the *U.S.S. Alabama* docked on the Mobile bay. When I was in the navy I was stationed at one time on a battleship. Let's drive over to Mobile and go through the *U.S.S. Alabama.*"

I said, "That sounds great to me."

The waitress who waited on us was named Frances. She was just as nice and sweet as she could be. She come back to the table three or four times to ask if there was anything we needed. She filled up our coffee pot twice. I thought to myself, "You can't be nicer to a customer than Frances has been." I was kinda hacked on the inside when Ralph said right before we got up to leave, "I ought to tip that old gal. But I ain't gonna do it. This is the one and only time I'll ever be in this cafe and I don't tip a waitress if I know I'll never see her again." That was exactly what Ralph said and I didn't think it was very nice. But I didn't say anything because after all we was on our honeymoon and you don't want to say anything that might rub your husband the wrong way while you're on your honeymoon. So Ralph paid the cashier what we owed and then we left.

Ralph and me got back in his car and headed east for Mobile. Ralph's car was a Buick. Its color was maroon. Maroon was Ralph's favorite color. Every tie he owned was maroon. So was a sweater he wore in the wintertime.

We kept goin' on Highway 90 until we come to Pascagoula. When we got to Pascagoula Ralph said, "Here at Pascagoula is one of the biggest shipyards in the world. Asshole yankees don't think southerners from Mississippi and Alabama have sense enough to build ships. But I'm tellin' you right here in Pascagoula, Mississippi. they build some of the best and biggest ships you'll see anywhere."

We kept on goin' east. We came to the Alabama state line. Beside the highway was a pretty sign which read "Welcome to Alabama." The sign even told who the governor of Alabama was. I forget his name. When I read that sign I felt real funny on the inside. I really did. Now I was goin' into Alabama. I never dreamed I'd be so far away from New Jerusalem and Jones County and Laurel. But here I was! Leaving Mississippi and goin' into the state of Alabama. That was one of the reasons I decided to go ahead and marry Ralph. I figured I'd see more of the world married to him than I'd see if I kept on living with my daddy who said motels was whorehouses.

We finally got to Mobile. There was tall buidings and traffic everywhere. Out of the clear blue Ralph asked me, "Have you ever drove through a tunnel before?'

I said, "Never have."

He said, "Well, you're gonna drive through one now."

And sure enough straight ahead was a big sign reading "Bay of Mobile Tunnel." And there was yellow flashing lights tellin' us to slow down. Which Ralph done.

Around a curve and into the tunnel we went. Ralph said, "This here tunnel goes under a part of the Mobile bay."

If I told you how long that tunnel was you wouldn't believe me. That tunnel went on and on and on. It was lighted with I bet ten thousand lights. I couldn't believe that we was driving under water. But Ralph said that was exactly what we was doin'.

We come out of the tunnel and about as far as you can throw a rock was the Mobile bay. Oh my it was pretty. And floating right there on the bay was the *U.S.S. Alabama.*

I can't tell you how big the *U.S.S. Alabama* is. I didn't know a ship could be that big. Me and Ralph went all over it. We went from top to bottom. Ralph showed me the deck and the guns and the place where the sailors slept. We went down to the engine room and looked at the big engines. We spent the most time in the kitchen and the place where the sailors ate. Ralph explained to me that he worked in ship kitchens the entire time he was in the navy and that was where he learned the food business. Going all over the battleship was a lot of work. I had to climb ladders and walk up narrow steps and squeeze through small doors. I sure was glad I had on slacks and not a dress.

After we'd gotten done with goin' through the battleship Ralph and me drove back to Biloxi. The sun was in our eyes. Ralph said, "The bad thing about driving west late in the afternoon is fighting the sun all the way." On the way back we stopped at the McDonald's in Ocean Springs and ate a Big Mac along with some fries and a Coca-Cola.

We finally got back to Biloxi and the Twinkling Star Motel. The motel had thirty rooms. I know because I counted 'em. Fifteen was on one side and fifteen was on the other side. Like I've said, they was all painted sunflower yellow. Before each door was a yellow clay flower pot. An azalea bush was growing in each one of the pots. They looked sickly. I thought they needed watering and fertilizer. I was wishing again we'd spent our honeymoon night in a motel like the Broadwater Beach.

Ralph parked in front of room eight. There wasn't but two other cars parked at the motel. Ralph looked around and said, "Their business is slow today. It's slower than molasses on a cold day in

January. Counting our car and them two cars over there they don't have but three rooms rented. You can't make any money renting three rooms out of thirty."

We got our suitcases out of the room and put 'em in the trunk of the car. Ralph said, "I've got to stop at the office and pay my bill." We got in the car and drove to the office at the front of the motel. I could see the old-timer we'd rented the room from the day before. He still had on a brown denim shirt and he was still wearing his straw hat. I could tell he had this rotating fan blowing straight on him.

Ralph got out of the car, took twenty-five dollars out of his wallet, and put it on the shelf in front of the office window. When we'd checked in the day before the old fellow wearing the straw hat had been real friendly. He'd had a big smile on his face. But he wasn't friendly when we was checking out.

He barked at Ralph, "You owe me fifty dollars."

Ralph said, "You must be mixed up. Or maybe you've forgotten. I squeezed you down from thirty dollars to twenty-five. And that's what I've paid you."

The old timer barked again. "Look at the clock. What does it say? It says four o'clock. Our checkout time is three o'clock. You've stayed an hour past three so you owe me for two nights instead of one."

Him sayin' that really ticked Ralph off. He got red in the face. That was the first time I seen Ralph get mad. When he gets mad his face turns red. He said, "Listen, buddy, I can count. You don't have but three customers today. I'm not about to let you charge me for an extra night on a slow day like this. There's twenty-five dollars and that's all you're gonna get. Take it or leave it. And you can call the police and have me arrested if you want to."

That's what Ralph said and with that he got back in the car and we drove off. I've got to say I think Ralph was right. It didn't make sense for the man in the straw hat to stick us an extra night because we'd stayed an hour past checkout time.

As we was driving off Ralph said, "In this world you've gotta be careful. If you're not careful people will rip you off. Every person you meet wants to put his hand into your pocketbook as deep as he can."

After Ralph had calmed down he said, "You know something, Beulah, this is Sunday. And I ain't been to church. I can't believe it. I never miss goin' to church. But since this is my honeymoon I guess it's okay for me to miss goin' one time. I bet Brother Ledbetter preached a riproaring sermon this morning. That's what I like about his sermons. They're always rip-roaring. If he's not preaching on the book of Revelations he's preaching on the blood. If he's not preaching on the blood he's preaching against divorce. If he's not preaching against divorce he's preaching against women cuttin' their hair and using makeup. Brother Ledbetter really knows how to lay it on the line."

Ralph kept on talking about Brother Ledbetter and what a great preacher he was and how he believed Brother Ledbetter had the second blessing which explains why he was such a great preacher. I didn't understand what Ralph meant by saying that Brother Ledbetter had the second blessing. I started to ask him to explain what it meant but I decided not to. Maybe some day I'd understand what the second blessing was all about.

We turned off of U.S. 90 and got on U.S. 49 and headed north for Hattiesburg and Jones County and New Jerusalem. While we was headin' north on U.S. 49 Ralph said, "I'm anxious to get on back home. When I ain't there 'Ralph's Place' falls apart." "Ralph's Place" is the name of Ralph's barbecue cafe and meat market. He went on to say, "And besides that I'm always afraid the help will steal me blind when I'm not there to keep my eye on the cash register."

We got back to Ralph's farm about nine o'clock at night. After we'd gone inside the house Ralph said, "I'm hungry. That Big Mac ain't gonna hold me. I know there's some wieners in the refrigerator and some buns in the breadbox. Let's you and me fix us some hotdogs before we go to bed."

Which is what we did. We boiled the wieners and toasted the buns and fixed hotdogs which we ate along with potato chips and two glasses of milk. We then went to bed. Ralph wore his bright red pajamas again. I could tell he was horny. So we had pussy again. He done it the same way he'd done it at the Twinkling Star Motel. He done it quick and to the point.

Early Monday morning Ralph rolled out of bed. He shaved and took a bath. I could tell he was in a hurry. He said, "I usually eat breakfast before I leave but not this morning. I'll grab me a bite somewhere. I want to get to the store and see what kind of business we done on Saturday." He went on to say, "Beulah, make yourself at home. Look around the house and see where everything is. I'll be home this evening around seven. I want you to be sure and have me a good hot supper when I get here. The hotter the better."

With that Ralph hustled down the back steps. He got in his pickup truck and headed out for Laurel. He took off like a house on fire.

The first thing I done after Ralph left was to fix me a little breakfast. I ate some Cheerios and wheat toast. I then did what Ralph told me to do. I looked his house over. The first room I looked at was the living room. It had a sofa, a coffee table, and three stuffed chairs along with a rug on the floor that had a lot of blue flowers on it. Drapes were over the windows. There was pictures on the wall that I thought was real nice. One picture had a bubbling stream of water with lots of trees and mountains in the background. A pretty little deer was sipping water out of the stream.

The next room I looked over was the dining room. In the dining room was a big table with eight chairs around it. Next to the wall was a china cabinet with glass doors. There was enough dishes in the china cabinet to feed the Russian army.

I went through all the bedrooms. There was three of them. All of them had double beds along with a dresser in each one. On one dresser was three pictures of a young boy. I could tell they was pictures of Oscar. I recognized Oscar because Ralph was all time bringing him to the New Jerusalem Baptist Church. On another dresser was four pictures of a woman. They were pictures of Ruth Ann. I wished they were not there. I wished Ralph had put them up somewhere before he brought me home to be his wife.

I looked over the two bathrooms. Each one of them had a tub, a lavatory, and a commode. I could tell they was old. They reminded me of the bathroom at the Twinkling Star Motel.

And then there was a kitchen which had a stove and a refrigerator and a table with a lot of pots and pans hanging over it. The kitchen had a pantry with still more pots and pans and with all kinds of groceries on the shelves. I could see everything from black pepper to sugar to cans of sardines. Out on the backporch was two deepfreezers which Ralph kept locked all the time.

I could tell a lot of Ralph's furniture was old. I found out later it'd belonged to his daddy's mother. But some of it wasn't old. Ralph told me he'd bought some of his furniture from Hudson's Bankrupt Store in Hattiesburg.

Out in the back of the house was a garage and a barn. Both of 'em was painted white.

Before Ralph left to go to his cafe I'd told him I was gonna take his car and drive over to Mama and Daddy's house and load the car up with my stuff. By "stuff" I mean shoes and clothes and underwear. Ralph had said, "That'll be fine with me." Which is what I done. I drove over to Mama and Daddy's house. Daddy wasn't there. He'd gone to his job at the Masonite plant. But Mama was there. And so was my baby sister Earline. I pulled up in front of the house and got out of the car. Earline came out of the house. I could tell she was upset. She came to where I was and whispered, "Mama is still mad about you marrying Ralph. She hadn't stopped poutin'. She won't say nothing to me and she won't say nothing to Daddy. It's been like a briar patch around here." Earline went on and said, "Mama is acting like a donkey." I said, "I've come by to pick up my clothes and shoes so I can take 'em to Ralph's." Earline said, "I'll help you bring 'em out. But don't say anything to Mama. Just pretend she ain't here." Earline and me went inside to my room. Earline and me took my clothes out to the car and put 'em on the back seat. I'd brought two cardboard boxes that was on Ralph's back porch. Earline and me put my odds and ends in these two boxes. All the time I was moving my stuff out Mama stayed in the kitchen. She wasn't sayin' nothing. Like Earline said, she was pouting. The last thing me and Earline needed to get out of my room was my shoes. As I was gettin' ready to go back in the house and get my shoes you won't believe what happened. Mama come out on the front porch. She had my shoes in her hands. She took my shoes and threw all of them out in the yard. She threw 'em at me like they was trash. Without sayin' a word she turned around and walked back in the house. As she walked back in she slammed the door. Her doin' that made me feel awful. Just awful. If I live to be as old as Methuselah I'll never forget the hurt I felt on the inside of me when Mama threw my shoes out in the front yard. I had tears in my eyes. Earline said, "I can't believe Mama did that." But that's sure what she did. Some mamas and daddies think that simply because they're your Mama or your daddy that gives them the right to be just as mean to you as they want to be. They don't know that you've got feelings too.

I took my clothes and shoes back to Ralph's and put 'em in the bedroom. Ralph had told me that morning he wanted a hot supper ready for him when he got home. So about six o'clock I started fixin' Ralph's supper. I wanted it to be a good one. Particularly since it was the first one I'd cooked for him. If there was anything I knew how to do, it was cook. I'd helped Mama out in the kitchen since I was knee-high to a turtle. Before he left Ralph had told me where the key to the deepfreezers was. He'd said, "I keep the deepfreezer keys in the brass teapot over the sink." Sure enough, that's where they were. I unlocked one of the deepfreezers and took out some corn and lima beans. I cooked them along with two sweet potatoes. I cooked a pan of Mexican cornbread and fried some porkchops. I made a big pitcher of iced tea. When Ralph got home that evening I had him the best vegetable dinner you've ever seen. I was real proud of it. It was the works: corn on the cob, lima beans, sweet potatoes, pork chops, and Mexican cornbread with iced tea. He and I sat down and ate at the kitchen table. Ralph ate like he was Noah the day he come off the ark. When he was through he looked at me and said, "Beulah, I'm here to tell you that you're one terrific cook." Him saying that made me feel good. It really did.

When he'd finished eating his supper Ralph looked at me and said, "What are we gonna have for dessert?"

His question caught me flatfooted. I hadn't fixed no dessert. Fixing a dessert hadn't crossed my mind. And so I said, "Gosh, Ralph, I forgot to fix one."

Ralph said, "I'll let it slide by tonight. But from here on I want you to have me a dessert. Maybe a piece of pie or a piece of cake."

I said, "What kind do you like?"

He said, "My favorite pie is pecan pie and my favorite cake is angel food cake with ice cream."

I said, "I'll have you an angel food cake tomorrow night."

He said, "That'll be just fine."

Ralph then pushed his chair back from the table and ripped off this big belch. From the way it sounded you'd of thought somebody had fired off a shotgun. Ralph never belched when he was eating out in public. He only belched when he was eating at the house. I listened to Ralph belch for six years. Him belching got on my nerves. But I never said anything to him about his belching. I spent the first sixteen years of my life listening to my daddy fart and the next six years of my life listening to Ralph belch.

After belching the next thing Ralph did was to light up one of his little Swisher Sweet cigars. Ralph's cigars smelled different from my daddy's cigars. Daddy always smoked King Edward cigars. Ralph always smoked a Swisher Sweet. After he'd blown two or three smoke rings in the air he looked at me and said, "Beulah, I've been doin' a lot of thinking today about you and me. I think it would be a good thing if you understood right up front what I'll be expecting you to do now that you're my wife."

Smoking his Swisher Sweet wasn't the only thing Ralph was doing. He had a toothpick in his right hand and he started cleaning between his teeth. I learned that's another thing Ralph did all the time. He picked his teeth as much as he belched.

He went on, "I need to let you know what I'll be expectin' out of you. You know what the Bible says. It says, 'Wives, obey your husbands.'"

Ralph was all the time quoting the Bible to me. Particularly when he had some point he was tryin' to put over. He could pick out a verse here and he could pick out a verse there. Earline said Ralph fired Bible bullets. Maybe she was right. Whenever he wanted to put a point over he would fire a Bible bullet at you. The way he started quoting the Bible to me about wives obeyin' their husbands made me feel uptight. All my life I'd been bossed around by my mama and my daddy. Now Ralph—in so many words—was tellin' me he had a right to boss me around since he was my husband. Which is why the very first week I was married to Ralph I began to wonder if maybe I'd jumped out of the fryin' pan into the fire. Jumpin' from the fryin' pan into the fire don't make things easier. Or better.

Ralph started spellin' out to me what he wanted me to do now that I was his wife. He explained, "I need to leave the house every morning around a quarter to seven. I can do a better job runnin' my cafe and meat market if I've eaten a good breakfast before I leave the house. So I want you to get up every morning when I get up and I want you to fix me a man's breakfast. When I say a man's breakfast I mean a big breakfast. I want scrambled eggs, bacon, home-made biscuits, molasses, and hot coffee. When I say hot coffee I mean *hot* coffee. As far as I'm concerned there ain't nothing worse than a cup of luke-warm coffee. And from time to time I'd like for you to change it up and have hot cakes for breakfast. When I come home every evening I want you to have me a good home-cooked supper like the one you fixed tonight. Only don't forget the dessert. Supper ain't supper if you don't wind it up with a dessert like pecan pie or angel food cake. I get home every night around seven o'clock give or take a quarter hour. So when I get here I want you to have my supper ready to eat. And—like my coffee—I want it to be pipin' hot."

All the time Ralph was tellin' me what he wanted for breakfast and what he wanted for supper he was smokin' his Swisher Sweet and picking his teeth with a toothpick. Every evening he spent a lot of time picking around his gold tooth. I've told you Ralph had buck teeth. One of his front teeth that stuck out was covered with gold. I don't know what you'd call it. Maybe you call it a filling or maybe you call it a crown. I'm not sure what the right word is. All I know is that one of his front teeth was covered with gold. One time he told me he was fixed up with that gold tooth by a navy dentist in Charleston, South Carolina. Ralph was really proud of his gold tooth. He'd take a toothpick and clean around it time and time again.

I sat across the table from Ralph and listened to what he was saying. I listened with both ears. I'll be honest with you. I didn't like the way he was giving me these marching orders about breakfast and supper. And I sure enough didn't like it when he started talking about his first wife Ruth Ann.

Ralph said, "Beulah, I hope you can be a good wife to me and for me like Ruth Ann was. Bless her heart, she got up every morning and fixed me a big breakfast and every night she had a hot supper waiting for me when I come in. I'll never forget the way she could fry green tomatoes. She knew how to bread 'em and fry 'em just right. But that ain't all Ruth Ann did. Every morning after she'd cleaned up the house she'd get in the car and drive up to my cafe and help us get through the noon rush. The main thing she did during the noon rush was take orders and handle the cash register. I could always trust Ruth Ann to make the right change and to be nice to my customers. She'd make 'em all feel at home. That's one of the secrets of running a cafe like 'Ralph's Place.' You've got to be nice to your customers so they'll keep comin' back time and again. It's that repeat business that keeps you in the black. Without repeat business you'd go broke before sundown. Ruth Ann would always stay at the cafe until around four or five o'clock and then she'd come home and fix me my supper."

He added, "So to make a long story short, Beulah, I'm hoping you'll be a good wife for me like Ruth Ann was. She was a jewel. I want you to do like she done: fix my breakfast, help out in the cafe, and then fix me a hot supper."

All this Ruth Ann bullshit was news to me. Before we got married Ralph hadn't said nothing to me about working every day in his barbecue cafe. And before we got married he hadn't sung the praises of Ruth Ann all the way to the blue sky above. I began to feel like a Ruth Ann double. Or like I was supposed to be her shadow.

What Ralph didn't know was: I was wishin' he'd be tender and lovey to me. I was hopin'—since we'd gotten married—that he'd come home in the evening and hug me tight. And give me kisses. Lots of kisses. And tell me how pretty I was like he done the time he leaned against the church piano and told me how pretty I was and how he'd been thinkin' about me and how he wanted to marry me. But some husbands don't act that way. After they get married they ain't sweet and tender to you no more. They don't feel like they have to be. After all, they've married you. They've got you like them lightning bugs me and Velma used to catch and put in a fruit jar. And when it comes to sex they might as well still be masturbating. Instead of using their fist they use your crack and masturbate in it. They jack off in your cherry.

If I'd had any sense I'd of sized up the situation up front for what it was and I'd of said, "Ralph, I can tell this here marriage between you and me ain't gonna work out. You don't want a wife. What you want is a Ruth Ann substitute. And what you want is a wife who'll be an unpaid employee. But that ain't what I want to do with my life. So I'm packin' my suitcase and I'm goin' home to Mama and Daddy. I won't have to give you back no wedding ring because you didn't give me one."

By the way, that's one of the things that disappointed me about my wedding. I kept thinking Ralph would mention getting me a wedding ring. You can get real nice wedding rings that don't cost too much at Wal-Mart or Service Merchandise. But Ralph never mentioned buying *me* a ring. So I didn't buy *him* one. Velma had told me she'd give me the money to buy Ralph a ring if we had a double-ring ceremony. But that never come up. So I let it slide by.

But me thinkin' about sayin' I was goin' home to Mama and Daddy wasn't nothing but hot air. And I knew it. Mama was mad at me. She'd thrown my shoes out in the front yard. If I'd gone home she'd of really rubbed it in about me marryin' Ralph. She'd say, "I told you and your daddy that he ain't no good." And she'd say, "I told both of you that out on the front porch the night Ralph come by here to talk about him marryin' Beulah. But you two had your minds made up."

So what was I gonna do? Nobody wants you when you're sixteen years old and don't have no money and no education. Some parents have enough money so they can fix their daughters up as far as money is concerned. I've heard Velma talk about this. She said Dr. Roland Hodges and his wife fixed their daughter up in such a way that every month she gets a check for four thousand dollars. Dr. Hodges is a urologist in Laurel. Daddy calls him a peter plumber. Can you believe that? Gettin' a check every month for four thousand dollars! And not even having to work for it. That's what every girl needs—a check rollin' in every month for four thousand dollars. If you had that you wouldn't have to kiss any man's butt. You could tell 'em all to go to hell. Of course I don't go around tellin' folks to go to hell. I'm just thinkin' about what you *could do* if you for sure had four thousand dollars a month comin' in.

So there I was. No education. No money. And a husband who wanted me to be Ruth Ann's shadow. The way I saw it I had two choices. One choice was to throw in the towel and give up. But giving up doesn't solve anything. The other choice was to make the best of it and keep on goin'. I wasn't about to give up. No way was I gonna do that. I'm a Buchanan and Buchanans don't give up. I remember Granddaddy sayin' "Don't ever give up because you don't ever know what might turn up." I think that's a pretty good rule to live by. So instead of givin' up, I made the best of it. I gave it all I had. I want you to know that for the last six years I've busted my fanny bein' Ralph Rainey's wife. I've got up every morning and I've fixed him a big breakfast. I've come home every evening and I've fixed him a pipin' hot supper with everything from meat loaf to pecan pie. Six days a week I've drove up to Laurel to work in his barbecue cafe. I've took orders from customers and I've cleaned dirty dishes off of dirty tables. I've washed dishes and scrubbed greasy pots and pans. I've handled the cash register. I've been nice to the customers. I've smiled at them even when I didn't feel like smiling. I've said to 'em, "We sure do appreciate your business. I hope everything was okay. Please come back to see us." From time to time I've even helped out in the butcher shop. Ralph's cafe and butcher shop are under the same roof. All that separates them is a swinging louvered door. And besides doin' all of this I've helped out in the summer with Ralph's garden. I haven't told you about Ralph's garden. Every year I was married to Ralph he planted a garden that was the mother of all gardens. I can hear him saying, "Granddaddy Rainey had a garden. My daddy has a garden. So I'm gonna have a garden too. Only mine is gonna be bigger and better." So every spring and summer Ralph had him a garden. During the summer the days in Jones County are long. And they're hot. There ain't nothing hotter than the sun in Mississippi during the summer. Particularly in the middle of the day when there ain't no breeze or shade. When the days was the hottest and the longest is when I'd stay home and work in the garden. Ralph believing so strong about having a big garden is why he kept a mule on the place. Ralph's mule was named "JR." He said "JR" was short for the Jordan River. I don't know how many times I heard Ralph say, "Since I live at New Jerusalem I think I oughta have a mule named for the Jordan River." Every time he said this he'd laugh. I didn't think the name was funny and I didn't get the connection between New Jerusalem and the mule being named after the Jordan River. JR was as old as the hills. Ralph and Sumrall used JR mainly to plow the garden. I think I told you about Sumrall. Sumrall is the albino who lives on Ralph's place. Sumrall don't have no family. The reason everybody calls him "Sumrall" is because he was born and raised in Sumrall, Mississippi. That's a town not too far from Hattiesburg.

I hope you can see what I'm getting at. Being Ralph Rainey's wife has been work piled on top of work. I worked hard at Ralph's barbecue cafe and on Friday everybody who worked there got a paycheck but me. I didn't get paid nothing. And by *nothing* I mean *nothing*. The only thing we done other than work was to go to church on Sunday to the New Jerusalem Primitive Baptist Church. Believe you me, Ralph believed in goin' to church. He never missed a

Sunday. Not one. The way he put it, "I want to go to church so I can let my light shine for Jesus." The reason he said this is because of the Jesus board at the church. Five years ago Brother Ledbetter had a Jesus board built and put at the front of the church right between the pulpit and the piano. It's wired with electricity. This electric Jesus board is something. You oughta see it. I'm guessing it's about eight feet tall and four feet wide. Across the top in big red letters it says "Let Your Light Shine for Jesus." The way the Jesus board works is like this. The name of every person who belongs to the church is painted on it. Beside each name is a lightbulb and a switch. When you get to church on Sunday morning the first thing you're supposed to do is go to the Jesus board and turn on the lightbulb beside your name. Brother Ledbetter says that by turning on your lightbulb you're lettin' your light shine for Jesus. Every Sunday when he got to church the first thing Ralph done was to go and turn on the bulb beside his name. He always got a kick out of doin' it. I thought Brother Ledbetter's Jesus board was silly. But him and Ralph thought it was the greatest thing since somebody invented the wheel or figured out how to write and spell.

3

I HOPE YOU understand by now who I once was and I hope you understand who I now am. For the first sixteen years of my life I was Beulah Buchanan. I was the daughter of Arnold and Josephine. For the last six years I have been Beulah Rainey. I've been the wife of Ralph Rainey. Like I've just told you, these last six years have been like a wagon wheel goin' around and around and around. It's been the same thing over and over. Monday through Saturday I've worked at Ralph's cafe and on Sunday I've gone to church to let my light shine for Jesus.

During all this time I felt trapped like a mouse in a cat's paw. But then last February—about six months ago—things started changing. Things started changing because of what Brother Ledbetter done.

One day at Ralph's cafe the subject of preachers come up. How and why the subject of preachers come up I don't remember. But it did. I popped off and said, "We've got a mighty fine preacher at our church. His name is Brother Ledbetter. His full name is Brother Henry Ledbetter."

Quick as a frog chasing a tadpole Robert Hawthorn spoke up and said, "Henry Ledbetter! I've known that son-of-a-gun all of my life." Robert works at the Masonite plant with my daddy. The two of them is buddies. And he's a regular at Ralph's cafe. He eats with us at least three times a week. He says he can't get enough of our barbecue chicken and barbecue beans.

Robert went on to say, "Henry and I went to school together." I didn't know Robert knew Brother Ledbetter and I didn't know they'd gone to school together. And so I asked, "Where did you and the preacher go to school with each other?"

"At Salem." That was Robert's answer. Salem is a little community like New Jerusalem. It's across the county line in Naboshuba County.

Robert kept on talking. "Yeah, I've known old Henry Ledbetter all my life. It's hard for me to think of him being a preacher. His daddy worked for the county. His old man drove a road scraper in Naboshuba County for thirty years. I'll say one thing for him: he knew how to keep gravel roads in shape. Henry was the only son the Ledbetters had. Henry always had a hard time in school with spelling. The reason I know is because me and him was in the same grade. For three years we set side by side. He didn't have a hard time with arithmetic. Or reading. He just had a hard time with spellin'. In the sixth grade we had this teacher named Miss Motley. She really knew her stuff. She was a graduate of the teachers' college in Hattiesburg. Miss Motley believed the Good Lord in heaven above had put her here on this earth to teach pupils in Naboshuba County how to spell. She made progress with most of us, but not with old Henry. If you asked him to spell *cat* he'd say *k-a-t*. Or maybe *k-a-t-t*. If you asked him to spell *bird* he'd say *b-u-r-d*. If you tried to correct him he'd say, 'If b-u-r-d doesn't spell bird you tell me what it spells.' Old Henry gave Miss Motley fits. I remember her one day sayin' in class, 'Henry, you're, driving me crazy.'"

Robert went on to say, "Henry's full name is Henry Franklin Ledbetter. His folks named him 'Franklin' after Franklin Delano Roosevelt. That is why his nickname in school was 'Mr. President.' But he never used his middle name. As best I can remember he

dropped out of school after the tenth grade. Or maybe it was after the
ninth grade. He fooled around for a while working as a vegetable
man at the Top Dollar Grocery store. Then for two or three years he
drove a delivery truck for Acme Cleaners. He then became a used car
salesman in Hattiesburg."

That surprised me. Which is why I said, "You've got to be
kiddin'."

Robert said, "No I ain't. He became a used car salesman at the
Red Auto Barn on Pine Street. But one day, so he told me, he felt the
call to be a preacher. Which is what he is today."

Robert sayin' Brother Ledbetter had a hard time in school with
spelling and spelled cat the wrong way kinda hurt my feelings. I felt
I needed to put in a good word for Brother Ledbetter. And so I said,
"It may be that Brother Ledbetter dropped out of school after the
ninth or tenth grade and it may be he ain't never been to college but
I'm here to tell you I ain't never met nobody who knows as much
about the Bible as Brother Ledbetter does. He knows it from A to Z.
Particularly does he know a lot about the book of Revelations. He
can tell you what everything in there means. He's even figured out
when the second coming of Jesus is gonna take place."

I could tell Robert Hawthorn wasn't too impressed with what I
was saying. All I was tryin' to do was put in a good word for the
preacher. But I'm gonna be honest with you: ever since I've known
Brother Ledbetter I've been kind of afraid of him. Maybe "afraid"
ain't the right word to use. But I think you know what I'm getting
at. Maybe I should use the word "nervous." Or "shaky." I've always
been nervous or shaky around him. Ralph says he's a man of God.
And that he has the second blessing. And that he preaches powerful
sermons. I'll tell you one thing: you ain't never heard a preacher who
can shout the way Brother Ledbetter does when he gets all worked up
behind the pulpit. And you ain't never seen a preacher who can
shake his fist and stomp his foot the way Brother Ledbetter can when

he wants to put a point over. And you ain't never heard a preacher who can chant the way Brother Ledbetter does when he goes into a trance and says over and over, "Bow down before Mount Sinai and hold fast to Jesus!" "Bow down before Mount Sinai and hold fast to Jesus!"

Last February Brother Ledbetter done something I wasn't expectin' him to do. He done it the first time one Tuesday morning. What happened was this: I'd gotten up early and fixed Ralph's breakfast. Since it was cold I'd gone to the trouble of fixin' him pancakes. As soon as he was through eating breakfast he did what he always did. He got in his pickup truck and took out for Laurel to open up his cafe. I washed the breakfast dishes and done a little cleaning around the house like makin' up the bed. I washed a big load of clothes. I then dressed and got ready to leave the house to go to Laurel to help Ralph out at his cafe.

Just when I picked up my car keys and was gettin' ready to lock the front door, guess what happened? I looked out the front window and a car was drivin' up to the front of the house. I thought to myself, "Who in the world is comin' by the house this early in the morning?" I thought at first it might be a Fuller brush salesman. Or maybe it was Mormon missionaries. But I took another look and guess who it was? It was Brother Ledbetter. I recognized him and I recognized his car. Brother Ledbetter drives a black Pontiac. Velma says it shouldn't be called a Pontiac but should be called a peanut. The reason she says this is because she believes Brother Ledbetter keeps back for himself some of the church's peanut brittle money. Once a month all the ladies who belong to the New Jerusalem Baptist Church get together and make peanut brittle. They break it up into pieces and wrap 'em in clear polyethylene and take 'em to Laurel and Hattiesburg to sell on the streets. If you're a female member of the church you're expected to help out with the makin' and sellin' of the church's peanut brittle. I've helped out makin' it and I've helped out sellin' it.

Me and Earline have stood on the parking lot of the Wal-Mart store in Hattiesburg and sold peanut brittle to folks goin' in and out of the store. Most people smile and pass you by. I overheard one man say, "I wouldn't feed that candy to my dog." That really hurt my feelings. But from time to time somebody does buy a piece. And at the end of the day us ladies go back to the church and turn the money over to Brother Ledbetter. He says he uses it for missions and to feed the poor. Velma says he uses it to pay for his black Pontiac.

Brother Ledbetter got out of his car and looked around. I thought to myself, "Why in the world is Brother Ledbetter comin' by the house this time of the morning? What could he want?" I didn't have the slightest idea why he was comin' by. But he sure was. Brother Ledbetter closed his car door and headed for the front door. He walked up the steps and knocked on the front door.

I knew it was him and so I opened the front door and I said, "Good morning, Brother Ledbetter, how are you today?"

He said, "I'm just fine, Beulah. I thought I'd drop by for a moment and pay you a little visit."

That's one of the things country preachers in Jones County are expected to do. They visit you which is a very nice thing for them to do. But it struck me as being a little funny that Brother Ledbetter was comin' by to visit me so early in the morning. He'd never done that before. The thought that was goin' through my mind was that I didn't have no time for a visit. Not at that time in the morning. I needed to be on my way to Laurel to help Ralph get ready for the noon rush. There was a lot of stuff that needed to be done. There was everything from organizin' the cash register to makin' potato salad to slicing tomatoes. But I didn't think it would be very nice of me to say, "Brother Ledbetter, I don't have time right now for a visit from you. I need to get to work in Laurel." That wouldn't be respectful. So I said instead, "It's so nice of you to pay me a visit. Please come in."

Brother Ledbetter stepped inside and I closed the front door. Since I was tryin' to be nice I asked him if he would like something to drink. I suppose I should have asked him to have a seat. But instead I said, "Brother Ledbetter, could I fix you something to drink? Maybe a cup of coffee or a Coca-Cola?"

I was hopin' he'd say a Coca-Cola. I could fix that faster than a pot of coffee. I was tryin' to figure out some way to make his visit as short as possible. I knew Ralph would be lookin' for me and askin' "Where's Beulah? I wonder what's held her up?"

He said, "I'll take a Coca-Cola."

The next thing I asked was, "Would you like your Coke poured over ice?"

He said, "I sure would."

I then said, "Had you rather have your Coke here in the living room or back at the kitchen table?" I knew Brother Ledbetter knew where the kitchen table was with four chairs around it. He'd been in our house a lots of times. I said *our* house. I should have said Ralph's house. Ralph explained to me one day he kept everything he owned in his name and his name only. He said doin' that kept things simple. Brother Ledbetter said, "Let's go back and sit at the kitchen table."

I said, "That'll be fine." So back to the kitchen him and me went. Brother Ledbetter sat down at the table. Before he set down he took off his coat. Brother Ledbetter always wears a suit. I ain't never seen him without a suit on. Most of the time he wears a black suit with a white shirt and a red tie. Sometimes in the summer he'll wear a white suit. Or he'll wear one of them Haspel suits that has them light gray stripes. But most of the time he wears black suits. And that is what he had on the morning I'm tellin' you about. Them black suits make him look stern and serious. He looked like he was John the Baptist or somebody like that. Him wearing them black suits goes a long way toward explaining why I'd always been afraid of Brother Ledbetter.

I went to the refrigerator and took out two canned Cokes. I filled two glasses with ice. I poured up one Coke for Brother Ledbetter and I poured up the other one for me.

I put his Coke down before him and he said, "Thank you, Beulah."

I said, "You're quite welcome."

I sat down in the chair next to Brother Ledbetter. All the time I was thinking: why has he come by to see little old me so early in the morning? I figured he'd come by to talk to me about singin' in the choir. Or maybe he wanted me to teach a class in Sunday school. Or maybe he wanted me to help out more with the peanut brittle sales. I'd been told they was going slow.

Instead, he started talking about the weather. A week earlier it had snowed. It don't usually snow in south Mississippi. But believe it or not the week before we'd gotten a six-inch snow. That don't happen in south Mississippi but about once every twenty years. It almost closed everything down. The snow was all folks was talkin' about at Ralph's cafe.

Brother Ledbetter said, "I still can't believe we got the heavy snow we got. When it snows it makes everything look clean and pretty." On and on he went about the snow and about how the roads had gotten slippery and about how you couldn't tell for a while where the roads were and that was the reason why Mr. Elliot had drove off the road into a creek. Mr. Elliot is one of New Jerusalem's mail carriers. He's been a carrier for over twenty years. The second day the snow come down he had the bad luck of driving off the road into Magee's Creek.

And then it happened. It was the last thing in the world I expected to happen. But it sure happened. Brother Ledbetter put down his Coca-Cola. He reached across the table and put his right hand on one of my boobs. He didn't say nothing at first. He just started rubbing his hand back and forth across my boobs. He was rubbing them softly. I've already told you I have big boobs. Velma don't call 'em boobs. She calls 'em binoculars. She has big binoculars too. Call 'em boobs. Call 'em binoculars. I couldn't care less what you call 'em. All I know is Brother Ledbetter was running his hand back and forth across my boobs and the way he was doin' it made my cherry tingle. Ralph never did to me what Brother Ledbetter was doin' to me. He never went in for loving my boobs and working me up. All he was interested in was my crack. Or my cherry. All he ever wanted to do was jack off in my cherry and then turn over and go to sleep.

I'm gonna be honest with you. I didn't know what to do or what to say when the preacher started doin' what he was doin'. You might say I froze. I froze like a lizard or a roach does when it gets real still because it doesn't understand exactly what is goin' on. Or it doesn't understand exactly what it should do. Should it stay put? Or should it run like crazy? It don't know.

All I know is that Brother Ledbetter started talking to me in a low, quiet voice. His voice was kind of velvety. I'd never heard him talk like this before. I was used to him standing behind the pulpit at the church and bellowing away at the top of his voice like a whistling kettle. I was used to him bellowing things like "bow down before Mount Sinai and hold fast to Jesus." Another saying he uses over and over is "by the authority of the blood." Sometimes in a sermon he'll say something like "what I'm preaching today I'm preaching to you by the authority of the blood." It ain't no telling how many things he's said from the pulpit by the authority of the blood. Yet here he was sitting at the kitchen table with his hands all over my boobs and he was purring like a papa cat that's lapping up a bowl of warm milk. His voice was smooth as silk. It was sweet like honey. He said things like "Beulah, I want you to know I've always thought you was a mighty pretty woman." And "you've got a sweet pretty face." And "you're as cute as an angel." While he was sayin' these things to me he had a moony look on his face. He looked to me like he was in some kind of trance. It was spooky.

While he was tellin' me how pretty I was and that I was as cute as an angel I had a flashback. You know what that flashback was? I flashbacked six years ago to the Sunday Ralph had spoke to me when I'd gotten through playin' "Sweet Hour of Prayer" on the church piano. Ralph had leaned against the piano and had looked at me moony like and told me how pretty I was and how he wanted to marry me. Brother Ledbetter was talking to me the very same way Ralph had done.

Brother Ledbetter kept on pouring honey out of his honey jar. That's what some preachers' mouths are. They're honey jars. They're always saying sweet and nice things to people. But Brother Ledbetter was doin' more than being sweet with his honey jar. He was being lovey. He whispered to me, "Do you know why they named you Beulah?"

I didn't have no idea what the preacher was gettin' at. And so I said, "I don't know."

He said, "They named you Beulah because your name begins with the letter B. And B is the first letter in the word beautiful. Beulah and beautiful both begin with a B. That's why they named you Beulah. Because it begins with a B just like beautiful does."

That's what the preacher said. But I knew darn good and well that wasn't why I was named Beulah. I was named after one of my aunts. I could tell what was goin' on. Brother Ledbetter was goin' to town flirtin' with me. All the time he was sweettalking me he was rubbing his hands back and forth across my boobs which was making my cherry tingle more and more. Looking back on that Tuesday morning in February, I suppose I should have said, "Brother Ledbetter, you'd better stop this. What you're doin' ain't very nice." Or maybe I should have said, "Brother Ledbetter, I don't have time for this. I've got to hustle to Laurel and help Ralph get ready for the noon rush."

Or I could have said, "Brother Ledbetter, I'm a married woman. I'm married to Ralph Rainey and you know that just as well as I do. Ralph wouldn't like you doin' what you're doin'. No he wouldn't."

But I didn't say none of these things. Not a one. I sat there froze like a deer does at night when it stares at car lights. I sat there and let the preacher keep on doin' what he was doin'. You've got to understand that in New Jerusalem Brother Ledbetter is a very important man. He wears a suit and tie all the time. You'll never see Brother Ledbetter wearing overalls. Everybody in the church says he's a man of God. I've heard Ralph say at least a thousand times that he has the second blessing. Maybe it's because I believed Brother Ledbetter has the second blessing that I was stumped by what he was doin'. And didn't know what to say. Or what to do.

The next thing I remember is Brother Ledbetter standing up. He pushed his chair back from the table and stood up and took me by the hand. He whispered to me, "Beulah, honey, I want you to stand up."

I done what he told me to do. I pushed my chair back from the table and stood up like he had done. He pulled me real close to him and started huggin' me tight. While he was doin' this he kept on sweettalking me. He whispered, "You're so sweet. I've always wanted to hold you close to me like this."

Since we was real close to each other I could feel his dick. I swear to god it was as hard as an iron pipe. The morning I'm tellin' you about I happened to have on a real full skirt. It was a pretty green skirt I'd bought at the JCPenney Store in Laurel. I felt Brother Ledbetter's hand reaching down and pulling up my skirt. The next thing he done was to pull down my panties and put his finger on my clit. He started rubbing it real gently. Ralph never rubbed my clit. The fact is I don't think he knew I had a clit. That's the way it is with a lot of men in Jones County. They don't know a woman has a clit and that you can rub it and make a woman feel sexy.

I know exactly what you're thinking. You're thinking I should have said, "Brother Ledbetter, this is gonna lead to trouble. And I mean real trouble. So we'd better stop."

But I didn't. I think I was hypnotized. So I went along—like an oak leaf in the fall of the year floating down the Okatoma River. I was going whereever the current of the river took me.

Brother Ledbetter was in command of the situation. I was like putty. He whispered to me, "Beulah, let's go to the bedroom."

So we went to the bedroom. He told me to take off my skirt. Which I did. Since he'd already taken off my panties he could see my cherry. I stretched out on the bed while Brother Ledbetter took off his pants and underwear. He reached in his pants' pocket and took out a package of rubbers. He put a rubber on his dick and got on top of me and put his dick in my cherry. While he was doin' this he kept on sweet-talking me. He said, "You don't know how long I've wanted to do this."

He started pumping away. That's what a man always does when he has sex with a woman. He pumps away. Brother Ledbetter started sayin' "Oh this feels so good." He said that over and over. "Oh this feels so good." At least he was sayin' something. Ralph never said anything when we was havin' sex. He just moaned and grunted.

Brother Ledbetter finally jacked off. As he was jacking off he said, "Oh my god! Oh my god!" That's exactly what he said. He said "Oh my god" real loud.

After he'd jacked off he took his dick out of my cherry. He slipped the rubber off of his dick and wrapped it in his handkerchief. He put the handkerchief in his pocket. Brother Ledbetter put back on his underwear and pants. He also put back on his shoes which he had taken off before we had sex together. He looked at me and said, "Well, Beulah, I guess I'd better be goin'." And with that he left me stretched out on the bed. He walked to the front of the house and walked out the front door and got in his car. I could hear him starting his motor. And I could hear him drivin' away.

The very moment the preacher's car started down the driveway the phone started ringing. I figured it was Ralph calling from the cafe and wondering where I was and why I was late getting to the cafe. I wasn't about to answer the phone. There ain't no law that says you have to answer a phone simply because it is ringing. So I just let the phone ring away. It rang and rang and rang some more. While the phone was ringing I went to the bathroom and took a bath cloth and some Palmolive soap and washed my cherry. I looked in the mirror and combed my hair as best I could. I put back on my skirt and took another look in the mirror to make sure I looked okay. As soon as I was satisfied with the way I looked, I locked the front door, shot down the steps, and floorboarded it up to Laurel. I bet I drove Ralph's car a hundred miles an hour.

I parked behind the cafe where I always park and walked in the back door. The back door opens into the kitchen. The moment I walked in I could tell Ralph was mad. How did I know? I knew he was mad because his face was red. When Ralph gets mad his face always turns red like it did at the Twinkling Star Motel when the fellow wearing the straw hat tried to charge an extra day's rent because we'd stayed an hour past checking out time. Jesse Magee is one of the colored cooks who works for Ralph at the cafe. I've heard Jesse say, "I can sho' tell when Mr. Ralph is mad. His face looks like a tomato on fire." That's the way Ralph's face looked when I walked into the kitchen.

When I walked in Ralph looked at me and yelled, "Beulah, you're late! Did you hear me? You're late!"

I can still hear the way he yelled at me. "Beulah, you're late!" As though I didn't know I was late. Of course I knew I was late. That is why I'd floorboarded it all the way from New Jerusalem to Laurel.

In this real cutting voice Ralph said, "Why—may I ask—are you late?"

What—pray tell—was I gonna say? Suppose I'd yelled back at Ralph, "You want to know why I'm late? Okay, I'll tell you. Brother Ledbetter come by the house this morning to pay me a little visit. In case you don't know who he is I'll tell you. He's the preacher at our church. I fixed him a Coke to drink and while he was drinking his Coke he started flirting with me. He rubbed my boobs which is something you never do. We ended up back in the bedroom having sex together. In a nutshell that's why I'm late gettin' here to the cafe. I've been fuckin' with Brother Ledbetter." I hate to think what Ralph would have done if I'd said that. He would have hit the ceiling. He probably would have gone through the ceiling.

Or maybe I should have come back at him and said, "Ralph, let me tell you something. I've been workin' like a dog in this cafe for goin' on six years. I never get a paycheck. Never! Not one. You tell me I'm supposed to work here because I'm your wife. It's my duty. Doin' my duty I come here Monday through Saturday. The only reason I don't come in on Sunday is because we ain't open on the Lord's day. This is the first time I've ever been late. Right? So why don't you cool it?"

I could have said something like that. But I didn't. There ain't no need of arguing with Ralph when he's hot under the collar. So you know what I did? I lied. I lied through my teeth. I said, "It took me longer this morning to clean up the house than it usually does. And I had a big load of clothes to wash." Looking back on it and thinkin' it over, that wasn't a complete lie. Before Brother Ledbetter come by I'd washed a big load of clothes and I'd had to run them through the dryer. I'd had two dryer loads and that takes time.

When I got through talking about washing clothes Ralph snapped, "I don't appreciate you being late. The noon rush is gonna start and we ain't gonna be ready."

I bit my tongue and got busy organizing the cash register. You've got to make sure you have the right kind of change and the right number of one dollar bills and five dollar bills and ten dollar bills. You've got to make sure you have a good roll of tape in the register in case somebody wants a receipt. Like I said, I bit my tongue. My tongue is as full of holes as a piece of Swiss cheese where I bit it instead of snapping back at Ralph.

The noon rush that Tuesday was like it always is. About eleven o'clock workers from the Masonite plant start pouring in. And so did workers from the poultry plants. Laurel has some of the biggest chicken processing plants you'll find anywhere. Chickens and Masonite—them's the two things that keeps Laurel humming. Some of our customers are white. Some of 'em are colored. Some of 'em are Mexicans. They all know each other. Because they know each other they slap each other on the back. And they tell corny jokes. Like the one I heard last week. "Charley, do you know how you can tell the difference between a city slicker and a manual laborer like you and me?" "Nope, I don't believe I do." "Would you like to know?" "Sure would." "You can tell the difference between a city slicker and a manual laborer by the way they take a leak. A city slicker first takes a leak and then washes his hands. But a manual laborer washes his hands first and after that takes a leak. That's how you can tell the difference."

All our customers want their food in a hurry. That's so they can eat and have time for a smoke before goin' back to work. They storm through the front door knowin' ahead of time what they want to order.

They look at me and say, "Beulah, let me have a barbecue sandwich and potato salad. Along with a big, kosher pickle." And I'll say, "Right, comin' right up."

"Beulah, give me a fourth of a chicken with iced tea." And I'll say, "Your wish is our command."

"Beulah, I want a half of a chicken with baked beans and a Coke." And I'll say, "No sooner said than done."

It takes six of us to handle a noon rush. There's Ralph and me and four colored helpers. One of 'em is a man. I'm talkin' about Jesse Magee. Three of 'em are women. I'm talking about Rosie, Melinda, and Pearl. Jesse works the smoker. There ain't nobody who can smoke meat better than Jesse does. Ralph's specialty was always the grill and the Frymaster fryers. Rosie's specialty is baked beans and cakes. She makes the best chocolate cakes you'll ever put in your mouth. She knows how to take pork-n-beans and brown sugar and Worcestershire sauce and mix 'em together makin' the best baked beans you ever ate. Melinda and Pearl work behind the counter and help keep the tables clean. Me—I'm a jack of all trades. I work the cash register and take orders and clean off tables. If a wheel is squeaking, I grease it.

Most people don't have no idea what a hard business the cafe business is. You have to get there hours before you open and prep the food. Then you have to serve it to your customers. Most of our customers are nice and easy to get along with. A few of them are real pains. They want a five dollar meal for two bucks and then they feel they're paying too much. Worst of all you have to clean up at the end of the day after all your customers have left and you've put a "closed" sign on the front door. You have to keep the place clean. You gotta scrub the pots and pans and dump out the garbage and sweep and mop the floor. You have to do this to keep the health department inspectors happy. The health department inspectors can drop by your place any time they want to. They always carry clipboards. They carry them clipboards like they was golden tablets. They walk around your kitchen with sour looks on their faces. I ain't never seen one of 'em smile yet. But you have to be nice to 'em cause they can close you down if they don't like what they find. We ain't never been closed down. And we ain't never got any kind of health department warning.

And on top of all of this you have to keep your books. You have to make the payroll and send in your Social Security money to the government and pay your bills. If you don't pay your suppliers on time they'll put you on C.O.D. That stands for "collect on delivery." If you can't pay in cash when they bring your supplies to your place C.O.D. they won't unload 'em. You've got to have your supplies to stay in business. Praise the Lord I always paid our bills on time. The fact is I paid 'em ahead of time. But one time the Merry Merchants Company got our account messed up and sent out a load of supplies to us C.O.D. Them sending our stuff out C.O.D. made Ralph mad as a rattlesnake. He told the driver to take our supplies and stick 'em up his ass. He called up the Merry Merchants Company and told 'em what he thought. I heard what he said. He said, "I've been doin' business with you folks for years. I've always paid my bills on time. And now this morning you've sent my order C.O.D. and I want you to know that was an insult. I'll never buy anything else from you as long as I live." With that Ralph slammed the phone down. He was really hot. Mr. Whitehead the president of the Merry Merchants Company come out to the cafe and apologized to Ralph for the mixup and asked him to keep on doin' business with them. He said, "Ralph, it was an honest mistake. We had a new bookkeeper and she didn't know what she was doing." But Ralph had his mind made up. He told Mr. Whitehead, "From now on I'm buying all my supplies from Sysco."

Besides payin' your suppliers you have to make certain you send in your sales tax money to the state tax commission. The tax folks can close you down just like the health department folks can. What's my point? Runnin' a cafe is hard work. Runnin' a cafe ain't a job for softies.

4

BROTHER LEDBETTER's visit happened on a Tuesday morning. It took place right when I was gettin' ready to leave the house to go to Laurel. Five days later Ralph and me went to church. On the way to church that Sunday I felt as funny as a fiddle. I didn't know what would happen when I saw Brother Ledbetter. Which I knew was bound to happen as small as the New Jerusalem Baptist Church is. Sometimes there won't be more than twenty-five people there. When I saw the preacher what would I say? Or do? What would he say or do? I didn't know.

When I got to church guess who was the first person I met? You've guessed right. The first person I met was Brother Ledbetter. He was standing at the front door saying hello to everybody as they came in. You know what? I couldn't believe it. He acted like nothing had happened between him and me when he come by the house and fucked my pussy. When he saw Ralph he said, "Good morning, Ralph. Welcome to the house of the Lord. How are you doing?" Ralph said, "Preacher, I'm doin' just fine." He then looked at me and said, "Good morning, Miss Beulah. Welcome to the house of the Lord." When he spoke to us he had this ear-to-ear smile on his face. Brother Ledbetter was acting so sweet and nice you'd of thought he was a chocolate-covered cherry. That's one of the reasons I don't like preachers. Or it's the reason I don't like some of them. They try to be so sweet and nice all the time. It ain't natural to be sweet and nice all the time. Nobody else is.

I went along with what was goin' on. I said, "Good morning, Brother Ledbetter."

He said, "Blessings on you, Miss Beulah." And then he added,"Miss Beulah, just keep on lovin' Jesus." Brother Ledbetter is always tellin' people to just keep on loving Jesus.

Him talking to me like that after what he and I had done on Tuesday made me feel like a fool. It made me feel like a damn fool. And I felt like a fool when Ralph said to me, "Beulah, let's you and me go and turn on our lights on the 'Let Your Light Shine for Jesus' board." I did what Ralph told me to do. I walked down to the front of the church and I flipped the switch beside my name. When I did that the lightbulb beside my name lit up. There I was—Beulah Rainey—lettin' my light shine for Jesus. For some reason which I didn't understand I didn't like turning on my lightbulb, but I kept my feelings to myself.

During the morning worship service I had a hard time keepin' my mind on what was goin' on. Ralph led the singing. Miss Priscilla played the piano. I don't remember but one song we sang. We sang "Stand Up, Stand Up for Jesus." And Brother Ledbetter done the preaching. He was wearing his black suit. It looked to me like the suit he had on when he come by the house Tuesday morning. He had on a red tie with a diamond stick pin. Brother Ledbetter's diamond stick pin is shaped like a horse shoe. Most of the time he don't wear his diamond stick pin. He wears it only on Sunday. When the light hits it just right it sparkles like a little star.

Brother Ledbetter prayed this real long prayer which I thought he'd never get through with. He read out of the Bible. And then he preached a sermon from the book of Revelations. He really cut loose. The only thing I remember him sayin' was that there wasn't goin' to be but one hundred and forty-four thousand people in heaven. He backed this up with the book of Revelations and by the authority of the blood. But here's the rub. All the time Brother Ledbetter was saying there wouldn't be but one hundred and forty-four thousand people in heaven—which he said was about the number of people you have livin' in and around Jackson, Mississippi—I was thinking: five days ago you came by the house and rubbed my boobs and my clit and you took your pants off and got on top of me in the bedroom and fucked my cherry. That's exactly what I was thinking.

Try as hard as I could I couldn't think about anything else. And I found myself asking myself: what caused Brother Ledbetter to do what he did? During church that morning I came up with what I think is the answer. I got to looking real close at Brother Ledbetter's wife. I could see her because she's always in the choir where she sings alto. Every Sunday she sits in the same place. She sits on the end seat of the front row in the choir. From where I was sitting I could see her real good. Everybody calls her "Miss Sadie." She goes by the name of Miss Sadie even though she's a married woman. If you knew Miss Sadie you'd agree with me when I say she's odd. She's hard to talk to. When you say something to her she always turns her face to the right. And when she says something to you she always turns her face to the right. She never turns her face to the left. It's always to the right. You never talk to Miss Sadie head-on.

It's hard to talk to somebody if they ain't lookin' at you. But Miss Sadie don't ever look at nobody head-on. She always looks sideways. Yet the oddest thing about Miss Sadie are her hats. That's what I said: *hats*. Most of the ladies who belong to the New Jerusalem Baptist Church never wear hats to church. They may wear one on Easter Sunday but that's about the only time. But Miss Sadie wears a hat every Sunday.

And when I say every Sunday I mean *every* Sunday. You can count on Miss Sadie wearing a hat to church as certain as you can count on the sun shining in the day and the moon shining at night. Everybody knows she buys her hats at three places: at Bill's Dollar Store, at Fred's Discount Store, and at Hudson's Bankrupt Store. Miss Sadie believes in decorating her hats. That's her hobby. She'll buy a hat at Bill's Dollar Store and then decorate it with artificial flowers and leaves. Or maybe with ribbons. Or with just about anything you can think of.

Miss Sadie don't know it but all the ladies in the church make fun of her hats behind her back. They don't make fun of 'em to her face. When they're talking to her they pretend to like her hats. But then they go off and snicker about 'em. The lady in our church who snickers the most about Miss Sadie's hats is Barbara Lovett. Her husband is Roland Lovett who has the Texaco station in Ellisville.

You take the George Washington hat Miss Sadie wore to church four or five weeks ago. She'd bought it at Fred's in Hattiesburg. When she bought it it wasn't nothing but a round straw hat. But Miss Sadie took it and went to town on it. She decorated it with artificial red cherries. I never could figure out what those cherries were made out of. Maybe they was made out of rubber. Then again maybe they was made out of plastic or wood. All I know is they was artificial red cherries. On the very top of the hat she tied a little wood hatchet. She tied it with red, white, and blue ribbons. Miss Sadie turned up at church wearing this straw hat covered with red cherries with a hatchet on the top. When Mrs. Lovett saw Miss Sadie wearing this hat she said to her, "Oh Miss Sadie let me take a real close look at that hat you've got on. Oh my goodness! It's got sweet, pretty cherries on it. And it has a cute little hatchet with red, white, and blue ribbons. Who'd of ever thought of decorating a hat this way?"

Miss Sadie said, "Do you know why I decorated it like I did?"

Mrs. Lovett said, "I don't have the faintest idea."

Miss Sadie said, "What did George Washington do one day with a hatchet?"

Mrs. Lovett said, "He took his hatchet and chopped down a cherry tree."

Miss Sadie said "That's right. He cut down a cherry tree and when he was asked about it he owned up to it. He said, 'I cannot tell a lie.' So that is what my hat is all about and that's why I call it my George Washington hat. When people look at it it'll remind 'em you shouldn't tell a lie."

Mrs. Lovett said, "Why Miss Sadie, that's just wonderful. I love your George Washington hat. I really do. And who but you would have ever thought of decorating a hat with cherries and a hatchet?"

That's what Mrs. Lovett said before church when she was talkin' to Miss Sadie. But after church I heard her talking with Aunt Carrie and she said, "Have you seen that silly hat the preacher's wife has on today? She's decorated it with dozens of red cherries and a hatchet. It's the gaudiest thing I've ever seen. When I saw it I came within an inch of laughing in her face."

That's what Mrs. Lovett said to my Aunt Carrie. I don't have no better friend on this earth than Aunt Carrie. After all, she and Velma took care of my wedding. But even Aunt Carrie makes fun of Miss Sadie's hats. She told me one time, "The main reason I go to church is to see what kind of kinky hat Miss Sadie will have on."

I sat there in the church and kept on looking at Miss Sadie. As usual she had a crazy hat on. She had a blank expression on her face. She was as skinny as a bean pole. I bet she didn't weigh over a hundred pounds. She didn't have no boobs. She had gray hair which Mama said turned gray overnight. The story they tell about Miss Sadie's hair is that years ago she and Brother Ledbetter had a son. When he was four years old he got killed in a car wreck. They say that Miss Sadie's hair turned gray within a month after the wreck that killed her son.

I kept on looking at Miss Sadie and thinking. And then all of a sudden it hit me: if I was a man would I want to have pussy with a women shaped like a bean pole who has gray hair and wears stupid hats and doesn't have no boobs? Maybe the reason Brother Ledbetter come by the house all so horny was because he couldn't get the kind of pussy he needed from the woman he was married to. Maybe he'd gotten bored with her. Maybe Velma is right. Velma says people in Jones County have their heads in the sand when it comes to marriage. She says marriages are like shoes on your feet and tires on your car. With time they all wear out. So I guessed Brother Ledbetter's marriage had worn out on him. Maybe that's why there're so many divorces here in Jones County and up in Laurel and over in Ellisville. The marriages wore out and there wasn't no way to repair them. Where do you go to retread a worn-out marriage? I don't know. And I don't think you know either.

But I'm gonna move along. What I've got to tell you is that Brother Ledbetter started coming by the house to visit me time and time again. He'd come by most of the time on Tuesday morning. A time or two he come by on Thursday morning. Altogether since last February he's come by to see me between twenty and thirty times. Every time he's waited until Ralph left the house for Laurel to open up his cafe. Then he'd drive up to the house in his Pontiac and get out and come in. We always drank a Coke together. Then he'd start sweettalking me. "Beulah, you're so pretty." "Every time I see you I can't help but think how beautiful your face is." And he'd rub my boobs. And we'd go back to the bedroom and we'd kiss and hug some more and he'd put a rubber on his dick and fuck my cherry. And while he was fucking my cherry he'd say sweet things like "oh this feels so good." And before he did it he'd always rub my clit and put his finger up my cherry and make it tingle.

I know what you're thinking by now. You're thinking: why did you let Brother Ledbetter keep on doin' it? That's a good question. And I could give you all kinds of answers. I could put all of the blame on Brother Ledbetter. I could say something like this: Brother

Ledbetter cowed me. He was too much for me to handle. He's a mighty preacher who has the second blessing and knows all there is to know about the book of Revelations and has even figured out when the second coming is gonna take place. How could I—poor little Beulah—refuse a man like Brother Ledbetter?

Or I could blame Ralph for what I done. I could talk all day about how icy and unloving Ralph could be when he wanted to be. So me foolin' around with Brother Ledbetter was a way I had of striking back at Ralph. It was a way of gettin' even with him for being the kind of husband he was.

But somehow blaming the preacher or blaming Ralph don't get the job done of explainin' what was goin' on between me and the preacher. Looking back on all that happened I think I ought to be blamed too. It's a triangle with three sides. Brother Ledbetter ought to be blamed some. Ralph ought to be blamed some. But I ought to be blamed too. In all that happened I wasn't a little angel whiter than snow. I know what I could have done. The second time Brother Ledbetter come by the house to see me I could have said, "Brother Ledbetter, it'd be best if you and me didn't have nothing to do with each other. You're a man of God. I'm a married woman. What you and I did the last time you come by here was sinning against Mount Sinai. You know it was and I know it was. So it'll be best if you go your way and I'll go my way and we can still be friends but we'll be friends at arm's length."

That's what I could have said. But I didn't say that and I'm gonna tell you why. I didn't because Brother Ledbetter stirred up inside me feelings I didn't know I had. To put it another way, he woke up a part of me that had been sleeping. I'll be up front with you and tell you what it was. I found out I liked being kissed. I found out I liked a man holding me tight and sweet talking me and rubbing my boobs. I found out I enjoyed havin' sex. You know as well as I do that nice Baptist girls in Mississippi ain't supposed to like sex. Or if they do they're supposed to be ashamed of it. Think about the serpent and how Eve acted way back yonder in the garden of Eden. The serpent got Eve to sin by getting her to eat an apple. Then what happened? As soon as she ate the apple she became ashamed of her cherry. And she became ashamed of liking pussy. So what did she do? She covered her cherry with fig leaves. Velma says she's never understood why Eve used fig leaves to cover her cherry. Fig leaves scratch like crazy. Velma says Eve should have used oak leaves or banana leaves instead. Some people say the only women not ashamed of their cherries are whores. And they say whores are the only women who enjoy havin' sex. Well, I'm not a whore. I ain't never been a whore and I ain't never gonna be one. But I'm here to tell you: I enjoyed havin' pussy with the preacher.

That's what I mean when I say he stirred up inside me feelings I didn't know I had. He treated me so different from the way Ralph treated me. He'd take his time and kiss me and hug me and say sweet nothings to me. Ralph never done them things. He was always hot to trot. And he always smelled like onions and barbecue sauce. He smelled like onions and barbecue sauce even after he'd taken a bath and dabbed himself all over with Old Spice shaving lotion. Worst of all his breath smelled all the time like a Swisher Sweet cigar. That's why I didn't like for him to kiss me. He'd take a short cut when he was havin' sex and he'd wet my cherry with Swisher Sweet saliva and away he'd go. After he'd had sex he'd turn over and go to sleep. Notice I said after *he'd* had sex. I didn't say after *we'd* had sex. I said *he'd* instead of *we'd* because with Ralph I never had no climax. I knew how to climax by rubbing my clit. Every girl knows how to climax that way. But after you're married you don't want that to be the way you climax. You want your husband to cause you to come. But Ralph never caused me to come. I don't think he cared whether I come or not. Maybe he didn't know I could come. All he was interested in was jerking off for himself.

Brother Ledbetter wasn't like that. He wasn't like that at all. By the way, the second time he came by the house he told me he wanted me to start calling him Henry. He didn't went me to call him 'Brother Ledbetter' which is what I'd always done. I remember him saying, "Beulah, I want you to forget this 'Brother Ledbetter' stuff. I've never liked for people to call me 'Brother Ledbetter.' I want you to call me Henry." Him sayin' he wanted me to call him Henry reminded me of the time Ralph had stood beside the church piano and had asked me to call him Ralph instead of Mr. Rainey. At first I found it hard to call Brother Ledbetter by his first name: Henry. But after a while I got used to it. Sometimes when he come by the house I'd tease him. When he walked in the house I'd say, "Henry, are you horny?" And he'd say, "Yep, Beulah, I'm horny. Just call me Henry Horny."

Henry would come by the house much earlier than he'd come by the first time. The moment Ralph left he'd turn up. He'd park down the road and watch for Ralph to leave. By him comin' by earlier we could be together without me being late getting off to the cafe. More and more during these morning visits a side of Henry came out that I didn't know was there. You might say it was a soft side. Don't get me wrong. By "soft side" I don't mean a sissy side. What I mean is a side different from his preacher side. Or his pulpit side. Behind the pulpit he was stern. He was old John the Baptist come back to Jones County. He sounded like a summer thunder storm when he preached on the book of Revelations and on the second coming and when he preached by the authority of the blood. And time and again he'd go into a holy trance when the second blessing come over him. He'd get a holy look in his eyes and he'd lift his arms up over his head and chant over and over "bow before Mount Sinai and hold fast to Jesus."

When he acted like that he was Brother Ledbetter and I could feel a tingling sensation goin' up and down my spine. I felt I was in the presence of a special messenger sent down from God to New Jerusalem, Mississippi.

But when he came by the house early in the morning as soon as Ralph had pulled out of the driveway he was Henry. *Henry and Brother Ledbetter wasn't the same.* They was as different as night and day. Brother Ledbetter was stern. Henry was tender. Brother Ledbetter threw rocks. Henry didn't. Brother Ledbetter was bluster. Henry was quiet. Henry told me things I didn't know. He said he told me things he hadn't ever told nobody else.

I remember one morning we was laying next to each other on the bed and he had his arm around me and of all things he got to talking to me about Miss Sadie. I've told you about Miss Sadie and how she wears silly hats to church and won't look you straight in the eye and doesn't have no boobs. Henry said, "Beulah, I know people at the church make fun of Sadie. Behind her back they laugh about her hats. They complain about the way she sings off key in the choir. They talk about the way she turns her face to the right when she's talking to you or when somebody is talking to her. I know about all of this and there's nothing I can do about it. But I wish you could have known her back when I married her. Sadie the day I married her and Sadie today are not the same. The day I married her she was as cute as a kitten. That's right: she was as cute as a kitten. I say a kitten because she never was a big person. Neither was her mother or daddy. And she was sweet. She was as sweet as cotton candy. She and I got married and a year after we got married we had a child. He was a boy. I named him Christopher. I named him Christopher because I liked the way the name sounded. I didn't know what the name meant. The fact is I didn't know the name had a meaning. And then one day someone told me it was a name meaning 'bearing Christ.' I said, 'You've got to be kidding.' He said, 'I'm not kidding. Look the name up in a dictionary.' I went to the library in Hattiesburg and looked the name up in a name dictionary. And sure enough: the

dictionary said Christopher meant 'bearing Christ.' I couldn't believe it. Sadie and I were proud of Christopher. We were as proud as
parents can be. Back in those days Sadie was a happy wife and she was
a happy mother. Around the clock she had a smile on her face. She
kept on being happy until the day she drove to the dry cleaners to
pick up a dress she'd left there. She took Christopher in the car with
her. On the way to the cleaners Sadie was hit by a lady who was
ninety years old and was driving a Cadillac. She ran a traffic light and
smashed into the right side of Sadie's car. The lady driving the
Cadillac didn't get a scratch on her body. Not a single scratch. Not
a single bruise. After she'd rammed into Sadie's car she got out of her
Cadillac and said, 'Oh my goodness, I didn't see the traffic light. I
wasn't paying attention.' When she saw how the front of her
Cadillac was caved in she started crying. She cried about her car and
didn't give a hoot about Christopher. Christopher never had a
chance. They carried him to the hospital in an ambulance. He died
within an hour after they got him to the hospital. The doctors told
me his internal organs were damaged beyond hope. Within a month
after the wreck Sadie's hair turned gray. The way her hair turned gray
so quick beat anything I'd ever seen. Up until then she'd been a
brunette but overnight she became gray-headed the way she is now.
After Christopher's death she started acting strange. She was never
the same again. She blamed herself for the wreck. She'd say over and
over, 'Why did I feel I had to go the cleaners to pick up my dress?
Why couldn't I have waited?' Before the wreck she'd been a sexpot.
After the wreck she became a cold fish. Since then our marriage has
been downhill all the way. After all that happened should we have
split? I've asked myself that question a thousand times. Right or
wrong, I never tried to get a divorce. She'd been hurt enough and I
didn't want to hurt her anymore. I'm not proud of it but more times
than I like to admit I've wished she was dead. If Sadie died I could
start over again. I'd look until I found a woman who didn't wear silly

hats and could be lovey-lovey like Sadie was before the wreck."

That's what Henry told me while we was layin' next to each other on the bed. I didn't know about Christopher and the wreck. I didn't know about Miss Sadie changing on him. All of a sudden it hit me that Henry and me was singing out of the same song book and off the same page. His marriage wasn't happy and mine wasn't either. His marriage was a dead-thing-floating. When you stand on the bank of the Okatoma River ever so often you can see a dead-thing-floating. Like a dead fish or a dead turtle or a dead snake. They once had life in 'em but they don't have life in 'em anymore. That's the kind of marriage Henry was caged in. And it's the kind of marriage I had. I sometimes wonder how many people are locked into dead-things-floating marriages. Like Velma said, marriages are like shoes on your feet and tires on your car. All of 'em wear out with time.

After every time Henry and I made love we'd lay side by side on the bed and he'd tell me all kinds of things. He told me he wished he'd gone to college and to a seminary. I asked him what a seminary was and he told me it was a school for people who wanted to be preachers just like the Ole Miss law school is a school for people who want to be lawyers. He told me he was ashamed to be the pastor at his age of a church as small as the New Jerusalem Primitive Baptist Church was. He even told me he kept some of the peanut-brittle money for himself. The way he put it, "If I didn't keep some of that peanut-brittle money I wouldn't be able to make ends meet."

You might say me and Henry "found" each other. We was both hurting in the same way. Don't get me wrong. I'll admit it bothered me what me and the preacher was doin'. But I was lonely on the inside. Whether she's married or not, there's nothing worser than a lonely woman. And I think it bothered Henry what me and him was doin'. Maybe that's why he preached against divorce and adultery and was all the time talking about bowing before Mount Sinai. Velma says you can tell what's bothering a preacher by paying attention to what he's preaching against. If he's preaching against it, it's bothering him. At least that's what Velma says.

But then two weeks ago everything blew up. Or everything fell apart. Call it blowing up or call it falling apart. I don't care what you call it. All I know is two weeks ago all hell broke loose between me and Ralph and Brother Ledbetter. Pardon me for using the word *hell*. But I can't think of no better word to use. Two things happened which threw everything between me and Ralph and Brother Ledbetter into a tailspin. I'm gonna tell you about 'em. I'm gonna tell you about what happened during the revival at the New Jerusalem Baptist Church when it was my turn to feed the preachers. And I'm gonna tell you about what Ralph done to his mule.

Every year during the month of July we have a revival meeting at the New Jerusalem Baptist Church. A revival lasts a week. It used to be that revivals lasted two weeks but by the time two weeks was up everybody was wore out. So they've been cut down to last a week which as far as I'm concerned is long enough. I'm guessing you know what a revival is. The best way I know to explain a Baptist revival is to say it's kind of like a football pep rally. At the New Jerusalem High School they always have pep rallies before every football game. A pep rally gets you all excited about the New Jerusalem Crusaders playing another football team like the Salem Pirates. A revival meeting is to a church what a pep rally is to a high school before a football game. It's supposed to get you all pumped up about religion and it's supposed to bring you closer to the Lord.

Two weeks ago we had the annual July revival at the New Jerusalem Baptist Church. When you have a revival you always have a visiting preacher to do the preachin' and you have a visitin' song leader to lead the singin'. You bring in outsiders to liven things up. This year the visiting evangelist for our revival was Brother Baxter Claypool. They say Brother Claypool was born and raised in Kentucky. But he now lives in Waynesboro where he's the pastor of the

Waynesboro Primitive Baptist Church. Waynesboro is a county seat town east of Laurel. It's close to the Alabama line. Everybody says Brother Claypool is the best primitive Baptist preacher in southeast Mississippi. I'd guess Brother Claypool is around fifty years old. He's about the same age as Brother Ledbetter. When I stop and think about it him and Brother Ledbetter kinda look alike. Both of 'em are over six feet tall. Both of 'em wear dark suits all the time. The songleader for our revival this year was a man named Claude Fike. As it was explained to me, Claude Fike ain't a preacher like Brother Claypool is. Instead, he's a taxi driver in Meridian, Mississippi. He drives for the We Go Get Them Taxi Company. That's a nice name for a taxi company: We Go Get Them. So Mr. Fike makes his living drivin' a taxi but he's also a primitive Baptist who loves to sing. So on the side—kind of as a hobby—he leads the singing at revival meetings in primitive Baptist churches.

Brother Fike has a real low bass voice. And oh brother can he sing a solo. You ain't never heard a solo sung until you've heard one sung by Brother Fike. The solo he sung on the first night of the revival was "The Old Rugged Cross." I've never heard "The Old Rugged Cross" sung as pretty as the way Brother Fike sung it. The next night for a solo he sung "When They Ring Those Golden Bells for You and Me." The way he sung about them golden bells made tears come to my eyes.

Brother Fike not only knows how to sing solos. He really knows how to lead the singing. He got the folks in our church singing louder than they'd ever sung before. He led the singing in a way I've never seen anybody else do it. He had a trumpet, a bass drum and a pair of cymbals. The trumpet looked to me like it was made out of gold. Them cymbals was made out of brass. They was somehow fixed on a stand so that Brother Fike could clash 'em by pushing a foot pedal. That beat anything I'd ever seen—the way he could clash them cymbals with his right foot. You ain't gonna believe it but I'm tellin' you the gospel truth when I say that Brother Fike could blow his gold trumpet, pound his bass drum, and clash them cymbals at the same time. All three of 'em sounding together made you went to stand up and march and sing like you was a member of a heavenly choir.

The night the revival began I heard Brother Fike ask Ralph, "Ralph, they tell me you usually lead the singing here. What song do the folks like to sing the best?'"

Ralph said, "Give me a moment to think about that."

Ralph thought for a moment and then he said, "Brother Fike, our church loves to sing 'There's Pow'r in the Blood.' We sing that song most every Sunday."

When the time came for the singing to begin Brother Fike stood behind the pulpit and said, "Folks, Ralph Rainey tells me you love to sing 'There's Pow'r in the Blood.' He told me you sing it almost every Sunday. I want you to know something: I love that old song as much as you do. I want it to be the theme song of our revival and I want us to sing it every night."

Brother Fike went on to say, " This song has two words we need to shell down on when we sing it. You know what they are as well as I do. One of 'em is 'pow'r' and the other one is 'blood.' So as we sing this song tonight let's really shell down on 'pow'r' and 'blood.' Now then: while Miss Priscilla plays the piano let's all stand and sing this song together."

Everybody stood up. We started singin' and every time we got to either "pow'r" or "blood" we sang 'em as loud as we could. And every time we got to them two words Brother Fike would pound his bass drum and clash his cymbals and blow his trumpet. I can hear everybody in the New Jerusalem Baptist Church singin' it right now. Shelling down on "pow'r" and "blood."

"Would you be free from the burden of sin?

"There's POW'R in the BLOOD, POW'R in the BLOOD

"Would you o'er evil a victory win?

"There's wonderful POW'R in the BLOOD."

And then we sang the chorus:

"There is POW'R, POW'R

"Wonderworking POW'R

"In the BLOOD of the lamb;

"There is POW'R, POW'R

"Wonderworking POW'R

"In the precious BLOOD of the lamb."

I'm here to tell you that was real gospel music with everybody singing with all their might and with Brother Fike blowing his trumpet and pounding his bass drum and clashing them cymbals. That singing made you want to stand up and march all the way from New Jerusalem to the Jerusalem on the other side of the world.

After the song service was done with and after Brother Fike had sung "The Old Rugged Cross" for a solo it was time for Brother Claypool to preach. I'll say this about Brother Claypool: he knows how to preach. On the first night of the revival he preached about the serpent in the Garden of Eden. I can't remember his sermon word for word. But I sure remember his main point. I remember his main point because of what he done with a snake. Brother Claypool said the serpent in the Garden of Eden stood for temptation. The old serpent tempted Eve to go to the apple tree and eat an apple which the Good Lord had told her not to do. But she done it anyway. Brother Claypool went on to say that temptation always sneaks up on us just like the serpent sneaked up on Eve and got her to eat from the apple tree. Temptation comes when we're not lookin' for it or expectin' it.

Right when he was sayin' this Brother Claypool reached down behind the pulpit and picked up a big paper bag. He put that brown paper bag on top of the pulpit. He then said, "I want everybody in the congregation to look here at this brown paper bag." Which we done. We was all wondering what he was up to. While we was all staring at the brown bag he said, "Can anybody here tonight tell me what is in this paper bag?" He paused to see if anybody could tell him what was in the bag and of course nobody could because we didn't have the foggiest idea what was in there. But for sure we was all sure lookin'. Brother Claypool went on to say, "You don't know do you? Well, I'm goin' to show you what's in this brown paper bag. And I bet it's goin' to be a surprise." With that he opened the bag and put his hand inside it. Lo and behold he pulled a black snake out of the bag. I swear to god that snake looked to me like it was at least five feet long. Brother Claypool held the snake up high over his head. I mean he held it up real high so everybody could see it.

The snake was wiggling from left to right and from right to left. Brother Claypool kept on preaching while he was holding the snake. He said, "This snake is like the snake in the Garden of Eden. It stands for temptation and the way temptation comes on us when we least expect it. I asked all of you a few moments ago if you knew what was in the paper bag and not a single one of you knew. Absolutely nobody! I could tell you were surprised when I reached in the bag and pulled out this snake. That's the way temptation is. It always surprises us. And it comes on us when we least expect it."

All of a sudden Brother Claypool drew his arm back and threw the snake up in the air. It landed right in the middle of the congregation. You ain't never heard such screaming in all of your life as went on when he done that. Everybody jumped up. Including me. I jumped up like a jack-in-the-box. Mrs. Monroe and Mrs. Gunn got up and run completely out of the church they was so scared. Of course things settled down when everybody caught on it was a black rubber snake.

But it sure give everybody a scare. When things had calmed down and everybody had sat back down Brother Claypool explained he threw the snake to show how temptation comes at you real fast and when you ain't expectin' it. To my dying day I'll remember the time Brother Claypool scared the stew out of me with his rubber snake.

During the revival the ladies belonging to the peanut-brittle club take turns feeding the preacher and the song leader. Aunt Carrie and Uncle Sam fed Brother Claypool and Brother Fike on Monday night. Mrs. Monroe who ran out of the church when Brother Claypool threw the snake fed 'em on Tuesday night. My turn to feed 'em was on Wednesday night. I'd fed the visitin' preacher and song leader every year for the past three years. So this year wasn't the first time I'd done it.

When I knew for sure when my turn was comin' I sat down with Ralph at the kitchen table and I said, "We've got to decide on what we're gonna feed the preachers." Ralph had just finished his supper and was smoking a Swisher Sweet cigar. I said, "Why don't we do what we've always done? Let's have barbecue ribs and barbecue beans from the cafe. They'll be as good as anything."

Ralph belched and said, "Naw. We've done that for the last three years. We're gettin' in a rut. I think we oughta do something different this year."

I said, "Like what?"

He said, "Everybody knows preachers like fried chicken. So why don't we have that?"

Ralph belched again and said, "Let me get a pencil and a piece of paper and you and me can make a list of what we'll have." Ralph stood up and went to the bedroom and came back with a pencil and a sheet of white paper. Ralph sat back down and started making a list of what we'd serve the preachers. He said, "We'll have fried chicken. The tomatoes are real good in the garden this time of year so we can have lettuce and tomato salads for everybody. We ought to have some vegetables. Let's see. We can have creamed corn and lima beans and string beans. All three of them is good Mississippi vegetables. I

don't want any of this fancy out-of-California broccoli stuff. I think
we ought to have rice and gravy and potato salad along with
homemade rolls. Of course we'll want to have iced tea. And to top it
all off I think we ought to have pecan pie served with ice cream on
the top. How does all of that sound to you?"

I said, "It sounds fine but puttin' all that together is gonna be a
lot of work."

Ralph said, "I know it'll be a lot of work. But I'll tell you what:
the day we feed the preachers you stay home. Don't come up to the
cafe. Just stay here at the house and get it all ready." I could tell Ralph
was goin' all out for Brother Claypool and Brother Fike. Of course
Brother Ledbetter would come with 'em. I picked up the sheet of
paper Ralph had wrote on. There it all was: fried chicken, lettuce and
tomato salad, creamed corn, lima beans, string beans, rice and gravy,
potato salad, homemade rolls, iced tea, pecan pie, and ice cream. My
lord! To get all them things ready would take hours. But if this was
what Ralph wanted I'd give it all I had. I've always liked a challenge.

So last week I stayed home not only on Wednesday but I stayed
home on Tuesday too. Tuesday was the day Brother Ledbetter
usually paid me a visit but he didn't come by. I guess he didn't come
by because the revival meeting was goin' on. On Tuesday I give the
house a good cleaning from top to bottom. I took the vacuum
cleaner and cleaned every rug in the house. I really done a good job
on the living room rug. I dusted all the furniture in the living room
and the dining room. I took Ralph's best china out of the china
cabinet and ran all of it through the dishwasher so it'd all be clean
and fresh.

I went to town on both bathrooms. I got down on my knees and
cleaned the bathtubs and both commodes with Ajax. I scrubbed the
lavatories with Bon Ami. I put out fresh bars of soap and fresh
towels. I put rolls of expensive soft Charmin toilet paper in both
bathrooms in place of the sandpaper toilet paper we usually used. I

made sure everything was straight in all three bedrooms. While I was working from can to can't on the inside of the house Sumrall was working on the outside. He mowed the grass and took a water hose and washed down both the front and back porches. Sumrall said, "From the way all this cleaning and scrubbing is goin' on you'd think the king of England was about to visit you."

On Wednesday I didn't think about nothing but the dining room and the kitchen. Early in the morning I drove up to Laurel and did my grocery shopping at the Jitney Jungle Grocery. I bought several packages of Sanderson Farms fresh chicken, flour, three heads of lettuce, a jar of Hellman's mayonnaise, potatoes for potato salad, sweet pickles, Land O' Lakes butter, two big cans of Crisco shortening to fry the chicken in, and three bags of ice cubes. I had everything else I needed at the house. The vegetables I'd serve the preachers were in the deepfreezers on the back porch. On the way out of town I stopped at the Baskin-Robbins store and bought some French Vanilla ice cream. I needed it to put on top of the pecan pie which I was gonna have for dessert.

After doin' all this shopping I hotfooted it back to New Jerusalem. Believe you me I had my mind on my business. As soon as I got back to the house I unloaded the groceries and started gettin' things ready to feed the preachers. I had to have everything ready to eat at six o'clock sharp so the preachers could eat and get to the church by seven-thirty to begin the revival service. I made potato salad and sliced the tomatoes and cleaned the lettuce. I put all three of 'em in the refrigerator to get nice and cold. I couldn't believe how big and red the tomatoes were. They were fresh out of the garden. Sumrall picked 'em for me.

I knocked myself out baking two pecan pies. They were beauties. They were beauties because I went heavy on the pecans. The week before I'd drove down to Lumberton to the Bass Pecan Company to buy pecans for the pies. The Bass Pecan Company in Lumberton

sells the most beautiful pecans in all the world. Sumrall also picked
some green tomatoes out of the garden and brought them to the back
door. On the spur of the moment I decided to add fried green
tomatoes to what I was serving the preachers. I mixed the rolls so
they'd rise at just the right time. I covered the dining-room table
with a white linen cloth and set the table with china dishes and
silverware.

That silverware was something. You won't believe how pretty
and high-class it was. The only person in New Jerusalem who's rich
enough to have a complete set of silverware is Vanessa Perkins. Her
husband is named Roger and owns an auto repair business in Laurel
where he fixes and sells used cars. Vanessa is a Methodist. She don't
belong to the New Jerusalem Baptist Church. She's my friend. I've
known Vanessa all my life. She and Mama went to school together
when they was young. To make my supper for the preachers as pretty
and nice as possible I asked Vanessa to loan me her set of silverware.

On Monday I called her up on the telephone and I said,
"Vanessa, this here is Beulah. I'm about to ask you to do something
for me."

Vanessa said, "Beulah, I'll do anything you ask me to. There's
only one exception: I won't sell you my husband. But don't make the
offer for Roger too high because I might let you have him."

I chuckled. I then said: "Okay, Vanessa, here goes: day after
tomorrow I'm feedin' the revival preachers and I want everything to
be just right. I don't have no nice tableware. My forks and spoons are
a mess, and I'd like for the preachers to have pretty tableware to eat
with. So here's what I'm asking: will you loan me your set of
silverware? I promise you I will take care of it and I'll get every piece
of it back to you. That you can count on."

Vanessa said, "Land sakes, of course you can use it. I'll be glad for
you to. The only reason we have a set of silverware is because Roger
took it in as a down payment on a used car. But we never use it. All

it does is collect dust. So you come on over and get it."

Which is exactly what I done. On Monday afternoon I drove to Vanessa's house and picked up her set of silverware. It was in a wooden chest. Vanessa had this chest sittin' on her dining room table. I'd never seen anything like Vanessa's silver chest. I opened it and the forks were in one stack. The spoons were in another stack. So were the knives and spoons. There were all kinds of forks and spoons and serving pieces for meat and vegetables.

Vanessa told me the name of her silver pattern was Old Master. She told me, "It's been a long time since I've used this stuff. So you'd better wash it good in hot soapy water. Don't run it through an electric dishwasher. An electric dishwasher isn't good for silver." I didn't know you wasn't supposed to run silverware through a dishwasher.

I took the silverware home and handwashed every piece. I knew how to place it on the table because I'd gone to the public library in Laurel and checked out a book on etiquette. It was by a woman named Emily Post. From her book I knew to put the knife and spoon on the right side of the plate and I knew to put the dinner fork and the salad fork on the left side of the plate and I knew to place the linen napkins on top of the plates.

As you can tell, I was spinning around like a windmill in a wind storm. Right in the middle of all I was doin' the telephone rang. I started not to answer it but I did anyway. I was glad I did because it was Mrs. Lonnie Pittman. There ain't no nicer person on the face of the earth than her. She lives about a quarter of a mile down the road toward the church. Her first name is Sue.

When I answered the phone she said, "Beulah, this is Sue."

I said, "How's my favorite neighbor?"

She said, "Fine. I understand you're feeding the preachers tonight. Is that right?"

I said, "I sure am."

Sue said, "Could you use some roses to decorate your dining table with?"

I said, "Heavens yes. I'd love to have some." Raising roses is Sue's hobby. She has roses of every color you can think of.

Sue said, "I'll be right over with some roses for you to use."

And sure enough: fifteen minutes later Sue come driving up to the house with two buckets filled with the prettiest roses you ever laid your eyes on. Sue helped me and we arranged one bouquet to go on the dining room table and we arranged another bouquet to go on the coffee table in the living room. Some of Sue's roses was red. Some was pink. Some was yellow. A few was yellow in the middle and pink out on the edge. If I'd have bought all them roses at a florist in Laurel or Hattiesburg they'd have cost me a fortune. There ain't nothing better than nice neighbors like Sue and her husband Lonnie.

Late Wednesday afternoon I stopped working in the kitchen long enough to take a bath and fix myself up. I put on a pretty white dress with lots of lace around the neck that I'd bought six months earlier at Waldoff's Department Store in Hattiesburg. And I put on a pair of white shoes I'd bought at the same time from the Smart Shoe Store. Mr. Gurwitch who owns the shoe store helped me pick them out.

Ralph for once came home early from Laurel and took a shower. He put on his best blue suit. On the way home he'd gone by the feebleminded school in Ellisville and had picked up Oscar. Ralph said he wanted Oscar to be at the house when the preachers came by to eat supper with us. As he put it, "It ain't everyday you have preachers like Brother Claypool and Brother Ledbetter eatin' at your table. I want Oscar to be around 'em when they come." Frankly, I didn't want Oscar to be there. It's not that I have anything against Oscar. It's not his fault he doesn't have a dozen eggs in his basket. The reason I didn't want Oscar there is because he can't keep his finger out of his nose. I've told him over and over, "Oscar, don't pick your nose in public." But he does it anyway. I told Ralph I didn't want Oscar to come because he might pick his nose. But Ralph wouldn't budge. He kept sayin', "I want Oscar to be here."

It bothered Ralph that Oscar had never been saved and joined the church. That's why he wanted him to be around the preachers. He was hoping Oscar sooner or later would be saved. Every time someone tried to save Oscar you could tell he didn't get the point. One Sunday Ralph said to Brother Ledbetter, "Preacher, I want you to talk to Oscar about Jesus. And I want him to join the church." Brother Ledbetter said, "Ralph, I'll talk to Oscar this very day." The preacher got Oscar off in a corner all by himself and asked him, "Oscar, do you know Jesus?" And Oscar said, "Nope, I don't believe I do. Does he live in Ellisville?" Ralph didn't think Oscar's answer was funny. I thought it was.

The preacher for the revival last year was Brother Peter Snyder from Pascagoula. Ralph got him to talk to Oscar about Jesus. Brother Snyder after one of the revival services asked Oscar, "Have you found Jesus?" Oscar looked at Brother Snyder and said, "Nope, I ain't been lookin' for him." Brother Snyder said, "Oscar, that's not what I had in mind. I want to know if you've personally found Jesus? You really need to find him." Oscar said, "I didn't know he was lost." Answers like that really upset Ralph.

By five o'clock I was back in the kitchen cookin' full speed ahead. I was cookin' like I was Betty Crocker. I knew the preachers would turn up at the house at six o'clock. So I had to time everything to be ready by then. Gettin' everything to be ready at the same time wasn't easy. I started cooking the vegetables. I heated up the Crisco in the deep fry. I had a good deep fry to work with. It's a Frymaster—the same kind Ralph has in his cafe. There ain't no deep fry better than a commercial Frymaster. At the right time I started bakin' the rolls and frying the green tomatoes and frying the chicken. Believe it or not, by six o'clock I had everything cooked and piping hot on the stove. Everything from the rolls to the fried chicken to the creamed corn.

A whisker after six I looked out the front window and I saw the preachers driving up to the house. They drove up in a light blue Ford mini-van that belonged to Brother Claypool. Brother Claypool and his wife got out of the van first. Brother Fike the songleader got out next. Last of all Brother Ledbetter and his wife got out. Ralph and me went out on the front porch and invited all of them to come in which they done. As she always did, Miss Sadie had on a crazy hat. She had on a big straw hat which had a brim that went all the way around it. Miss Sadie had decorated the brim with cotton bolls. There was fourteen of 'em. I know there was fourteen because I counted 'em. Miss Sadie had stuck tiny flags into each one of the cotton bolls. Some of the flags was red. Some was green. Some of 'em was yellow. And one of 'em was a tiny United States flag.

I took a close look at the hat and I said, "Miss Sadie, that's a mighty cute hat you have on with all of those cotton bolls and flags." I didn't really think it was cute. I thought it looked stupid. But I was tryin' to be nice to her because I knew what was goin' on between me and her husband. And since I'd learned about Christopher and the car wreck and her hair turning gray overnight I'd had a different attitude toward Miss Sadie.

Miss Sadie said, "I call this my cotton patch hat."

I said, "Well, it's mighty pretty. And it sure is different."

I told everybody to have a seat in the living room while I put everything on the table. Mrs. Claypool said, "Let me help you." Miss Sadie said the same thing. But I said, "No. Just keep your seats. I can handle everything in the kitchen better by myself."

Which is what I done.

I hustled back to the kitchen and started taking up everything I'd cooked. I dished up the vegetables and the rice and gravy. I put them in pretty china bowls. I took the potato salad out of the refrigerator and I took the rolls out of the warmer. I put the fried green tomatoes and the fried chicken on platters. The last thing I done was to pour up eight tall glasses of tea. I made sure the glasses had a lot of ice in them. There's nothing worser than iced tea that's really not cold. I then put everything on the dining room table exactly where I wanted it to be. By each plate I put an individual lettuce and tomato salad topped with mayonnaise and a circle of bell pepper.

When I'd gotten everything in place I stepped back and took a good overall look. I was so proud of the way it had all turned out. The vegetables was piping hot and the rolls were golden brown. I was really proud of my fried chicken. You've never seen such brown and crispy fried chicken in all of your life. The reason it was so light brown and crispy is because I'd fried it in new Crisco shortening in our Frymaster deep fry. And right in the middle of the table between the fried green tomatoes and the fried chicken was the big bouquet of roses Sue had helped me to arrange. The Old Master silverware I'd borrowed looked beautiful. I was bustin' with pride. I'd planned and worked on this dinner for the preachers for days. It all looked to me like one of those fancy dinners you see painted on the cover of the *Saturday Evening Post* at Thanksgiving or Christmas.

I left the dining room and walked into the living room where everybody was sittin' and talking. I said, "Supper is ready. Let's all go to the dining room." I'm told that in some parts of the country the meal that you eat at the end of the day is called "dinner." That may be true. But here in south Mississippi the meal that you eat at the end of the day is called supper. That's why I said, "Supper is ready." Everybody got up and went into the dining room. Altogether there was eight of us. Ralph sat at one end of the table and Brother Ledbetter sat at the other end. On one side was Mrs. Ledbetter or Miss Sadie, Oscar, and Brother Fike the songleader. On the other side of the table was me and Brother and Mrs. Claypool. In the living room Brother Fike had already said he was sorry his wife wasn't with him. He explained that she worked for the telephone company and couldn't always get off to go with him when he led music in revivals.

After everybody had sat down Ralph said, "As the man of the house I am honored to have you men of God to come here and break bread with us. I'm goin' to call on Brother Claypool to bless this food before we partake." Every time we fed preachers Ralph said something like that.

Brother Claypool really lifted up a prayer. First of all he thanked God for the New Jerusalem Baptist Church and the wonderful revival we was having. He then thanked God for sending Jesus into this world to die on the cross so we could be washed in the blood. And he thanked God for us living in a country where there ain't no communists like there are in Russia. He just went on and on. He prayed so long I began to worry about everything getting cold. Thank goodness he finally got around to thanking God for the food set before us and the hands that had prepared it. Last of all he prayed, "Bless this food to the nourishment of our bodies and us in thy service. Amen." Every time we've had preachers to say grace before eating they always end their prayer by saying, "Bless this food to the nourishment of our bodies and us in thy service."

That's how you can tell when a preacher is getting to the end of saying grace when he prays about blessing the food for the nourishment of our bodies and us in thy service. What "us in thy service" means I don't exactly know.

As soon as Brother Claypool said "amen" at the end of his prayer Brother Ledbetter boomed, "Amen!'"

So did Ralph.

Not to be outdone so did Brother Fike the songleader. So did Oscar.

With the prayer and the amens done with, everybody started passin' the food around. I said, "Brother Claypool, why don't you start the fried chicken." And I said, "Miss Sadie, I'll ask you to start the fried green tomatoes and I'll start the potato salad." I wanted everything to go just right and to be as nice as possible. As the bowls and platters started goin' around I watched what everybody was puttin' on their plates. I was watching like a cat watches a mouse it's about to pounce on. Because I was watching so closely I couldn't believe what my eyes were tellin' me. Brother Claypool and his wife took huge servings of everything. And when I say huge I mean huge. When Brother Claypool started the chicken he took three pieces. I know he took three pieces because I counted them. He took a breast and a thigh and a leg. Mrs. Claypool dug into the potato salad like it was a pot of gold just shipped in from Alaska. Even Miss Sadie— as skinny as she is—was taking big servings. She took her fork and served herself six fried green tomatoes. That is what I said—six fried green tomatoes.

The thought that started goin' through my mind was: have I cooked enough vegetables? Have I fried enough chicken? Have I prepared enough potato salad? What about the rolls? Had I baked enough of them? I sure hoped I had. I knew that back in the kitchen I had seconds on everything. But I didn't have thirds and fourths. I hadn't taken two bites myself before I had to get up from the table and start taking bowls back to the kitchen to fill up again. I went back to the kitchen and served up more lima beans and more creamed corn and more fried green tomatoes. I refilled the fried chicken platter. I got more homemade rolls out of the warmer and put them on the table. I put on the table another stick of Land 0' Lakes butter. But where was all the food goin'? As soon as I put food on the table it disappeared like drops of rain evaporating on a hot tin roof. Brother Claypool and Brother Ledbetter was eatin' like hogs at the Jones County Fair. So was Mrs. Claypool who was on the plump side. You'd of thought none of them had had anything to eat for days. Of course you've got to understand that a lot of country preachers in Mississippi pride themselves on being able to eat a lot.

They like to brag about it. That's why so many of 'em have pot bellies and hanging jowls. For years in Jones County there's been jokes about preachers and how they can eat a lot of fried chicken. "Why does the rooster strut and crow? He struts and crows because he's got so many sons in the ministry."

I used to think that joke was funny. But after what I've been through the past two weeks I don't think it's funny no more. Velma says it's always struck her as odd that preachers can shell down so hard on somebody taking a snort of whiskey while they don't shell down on gettin' fat. She said that one day while she was in the beauty shop gettin' her hair worked on she read this article in the *Reader's Digest* that said there was seven deadly sins and that one of those sins was gluttony. Velma says gluttony means eating too much. If gluttony means eatin' too much and if it's a sin then I know a lot of Baptist preachers who're sinners.

While Ralph and the preachers was eatin' all that potato salad and rice and gravy they got to talking about blacks. How the subject of darkies come up I don't remember. But it did. Brother Claypool asked Ralph, "Ralph, I understand you have a cafe up in Laurel. Do you have many nigger customers?"

Ralph said, "Yeah, a few."

When Ralph said that I thought to myself: Ralph's crazy. That's a cockeyed answer. A lot of our customers are black. Not just a few but a lot. Maybe a third of our customers. If we didn't have our darky customers we'd be in trouble. Without them we couldn't pay our bills and make the payroll on Friday. And I sure ought to know. I ought to know because I keep the books and make out the checks to our suppliers like Sysco. Ralph don't let me sign the checks. But I make 'em out and then he signs them.

Ralph went on to say, "I don't particularly like 'em comin' into my cafe but there's nothing I can do about it."

I thought that was a cockeyed remark too. Ralph sure don't act like he don't like black customers. He cuts up with 'em. He tells 'em jokes. He knows every one of 'em by name. To be honest with you: Ralph likes anybody who comes into his cafe and spends a dollar. If a three-headed, bow-legged monkey came through the front door with a dollar bill in his hand Ralph would like him.

Brother Claypool asked, "You say you don't like 'em comin' into your cafe. Why do you let them come in?"

Ralph said, "Because I have to."

The preacher asked, "Why's that? You own the place."

Ralph said, "Because of the justice department. That's why. If I didn't let niggers into my cafe I'd have bureaucrats from the justice department in Washington on my neck before the sun went down. And I'd have the NAACP after me with a lawsuit. Nigger lawyers love to hit you with a lawsuit. That's the way they make a living. Sue the honkies and make 'em pay."

After they'd talked about colored customers at Ralph's cafe Brother Claypool and Brother Ledbetter started tellin' jokes. Why they got to tellin' jokes I don't know. But that's sure what they did. I bet they told at least a dozen. I don't want you to get me wrong. I don't have a thing in the world against jokes. The fact is I like a good joke. But what I didn't like was the way Brother Claypool and Brother Ledbetter told jokes with dirty words in 'em. I don't think preachers ought to tell jokes with dirty words in 'em. Particularly when in only a matter of minutes they'll be standing behind a pulpit preaching about the blood and the second comin' and the book of Revelations. But Brother Ledbetter and Brother Claypool used dirty words in their jokes like they was going out of style.

The first joke Brother Ledbetter told was his 'motherfucker' joke. He told about this colored church that was having a revival meeting. The first night of the revival the church was full of darkies. But they had a problem. The regular pianist was sick. And so the nigger preacher stood up and said, "Folks, we done hit a snag. It's time to start the service and our regular pianist is sick. Is there anybody here tonight who can play the piano?" From the back of the church somebody yelled, "Rastus can play the piano." The preacher said, "Rastus, you come on down here and play the piano for us." So Rastus got up and walked over to the piano and sat down on the piano stool. The preacher said, "Rastus, can you play 'Amazing Grace'?" Rastus said, "Let me give it a try." He hit a few notes of "Amazing Grace" but they was all messed up. So Rastus said, "I don't believe I can play it." The preacher then said, "Do you think you can play 'When the Roll is Called Up Yonder?'" Rastus said, "Let me give it a try." He hit a few notes but they was all messed up too. Rastus said, "I don't believe I can play it either." So the preacher said, "How about 'Revive Us Again?'" Rastus said, "Let me give it a try." He hit a few notes of 'Revive Us Again' and they sounded awful. Which is why Rastus said, "I don't believe I can play it." About that time somebody in the back of the church yelled, "Rastus is a motherfucker!" That made the preacher mad. It made him real mad. He yelled, "I want to know who it was who called Rastus a motherfucker. We ain't gonna allow that kind of language to be used in this here church. " The preacher was really hot. But nobody would tell him who yelled, "Rastus is a motherfucker!" Finally the preacher turned to the chairman of the deacons. His name was Othello. The preacher said, "Othello, what do you think I ought to do? I can't get nobody to tell me who called Rastus a motherfucker." The deacon chairman stood up and said, "Well, preacher, I'll tell you what I think we ought to do. Instead of spending a lot of time trying to find out who called Rastus a motherfucker, I think we ought to find out who the motherfucker was who said Rastus could play the piano."

Brother and Mrs. Claypool laughed. So did Ralph and Mr. Fike the songleader. Miss Sadie didn't laugh. I guess she'd heard the joke before. Instead of laughing, she took another big serving of potato salad. And another serving of rice and gravy. The question I was asking myself was: how can a skinny person like Miss Sadie eat so much? That was a puzzle.

After Brother Ledbetter had finished his "motherfucker" joke, Brother Claypool told one about a farmer's daughter. He said there was this farmer who had a good lookin' blond daughter who looked kinda like Marilyn Monroe. She got to goin' with a rich banker's son. This banker wasn't just rich. He was filthy rich. His son and the farmer's daughter dated and dated some more and one day she turned up pregnant. This made her daddy mad. So he grabbed his shotgun and drove into town. He went to the bank and marched into the banker's office and pointed his shotgun right in his face. The farmer said to the banker, "Your son has done made my daughter pregnant and I'm hot about it. The fact is, I'm mad as hell!" The rich banker done some quick thinking. He said, "Don't shoot! I'll tell you what I'll do. When the baby is born, I'll give your daughter a thousand shares of stock in this bank, five hundred acres of good farm land, and a new brick house to live in." The farmer said, "Could you say that again?" The banker said, "When the baby is born, I'll give your daughter a thousand shares of stock in this bank, five hundred acres of good farm land, and a new brick house to live in." The farmer put his shotgun down, scratched his head for a few moments, and said, "Well, let me ask you something. If she has a miscarriage, will you give her a second chance?"

Again everybody laughed. On and on it went like this. Everybody was swapping jokes about niggers and farmers' daughters and everybody was shoveling food into their mouths like they was gettin' ready for the seven years of famine you read about in the Old Testament.

Brother Claypool stood up and took off his coat. When he took his coat off you could see his red suspenders. I'd never seen suspenders that wide. I bet they was two inches wide at least. He had on a belt too. I wondered why he was wearing both a belt and suspenders. All the while I was hopping around like a jack rabbit. I bet I walked back and forth between the kitchen and the dining room a hundred times. I refilled the vegetable bowls. I put all the fried chicken I had on the table. I kept refilling everybody's iced tea glass. As I was doin' all of this it all of a sudden dawned on me that I was giving completely out of food. There wasn't no more fried chicken or potato salad or creamed corn or rice and gravy or rolls. I hadn't cooked enough. I had known there was gonna be eight people eating and I thought I'd fixed more than enough. But I hadn't. I hadn't expected them to eat so much. I could feel my face stinging I was so embarrassed. I began to feel like old mother Hubbard who went to her cupboard and found out nothing was there.

Brother Claypool looked at me with this big smile on his face and he said, "Miss Beulah, I want you to know I just love your fried chicken. I think it's the best fried chicken I've ever eaten. The people with Kentucky Fried Chicken ought to come here to New Jerusalem and study under you so they can learn how to fry chicken the way it ought to be fried."

Brother Fike said, "Amen brother. I'll agree with that."

Then Brother Claypool said something I wish he hadn't said. He said, "Your chicken is so crispy and tasty and delicious, I've got to have just one more piece. Just one more piece will delight my soul."

Brother Ledbetter broke in and said, "Beulah, me too. Just one more piece."

I could feel my face burning like I had fever I was so uptight. All I could do was say, "I'm sorry but there ain't no more. We've done ate it all up."

Ralph hit the ceiling when I said I was all out of fried chicken. I mean he hit the ceiling hard. That was always Ralph's biggest fault. Or you might say it was his biggest problem. He let little things fire him off like he was a firecracker on the Fourth of July. He made mountains out of molehills. Me giving out of chicken wasn't good but neither was it the end of the world. Ralph's face turned tomato red the way it always does when he's mad about something. He looked at me and snapped, "What do you mean there ain't no more fried chicken! There's got to be more!"

Ralph got up from the dining table and stormed back into the kitchen. I stayed in the dining room thinking about what I could say or do. But I couldn't think of what to say or do. I could hear Ralph in the kitchen banging around pots and pans. I heard him open and slam shut the stove door.

I heard him call me. He yelled, "Beulah! You come back here to the kitchen. You come back here right now!"

I left the dining room and walked into the kitchen. Ralph was a sight to behold. He was as mad as a rattlesnake with a bad toothache. He was acting like a crazy man. Which he can be when he gets upset. And which he can be because he's a Rainey. In Jones County the Raineys are famous for their tempers. Velma's first husband was a Rainey. So she knows the Raineys inside and out. One time she told me there's nothing to compare to "Rainey wrath." Them's the very words she used: "Rainey wrath." That's what I was lookin' at with Ralph knocking around pots and pans. I was looking at "Rainey wrath" in action. Ralph looked at me and barked, "Why didn't you fry more chicken?"

I tried to quiet Ralph down. I put my finger to my lips. I whispered, "Ralph, not so loud. The preachers can hear you."

He yelled, "I don't care whether they can hear me or not! I'm the man of this house! I call the shots around here!"

When he said that I lost it. Up to that point I'd tried not to cry. But all of a sudden I started crying. I cried like a baby. I was so upset I wanted my flesh to slide off my bones and crawl across the floor to a corner and hide behind the garbage can. For me feeding the preachers was turning into a nightmare. Before we'd sat down I thought the dining room table looked so pretty—especially with the bouquet of Sue Pittman's red roses sitting between the fried chicken and the fried green tomatoes. Now everything was all messed up. I stopped sobbing long enough to say, "I thought I'd cooked enough. They all ate more than I thought they would."

Ralph snapped, "Cryin' ain't gonna do no good, Beulah. What we need is not cryin' but more fried chicken and that's not gonna happen because there ain't no more."

He kept on lifting the lids off of the pots and pans on the stove. After he'd lifted them up he'd slam them back down. He snarled, "I see we're out of lima beans and creamed corn. And there ain't no more fried green tomatoes. Beulah, you've royally messed up."

What could I say? What could I do? This sure as heck wasn't the first temper tantrum I'd seen Ralph throw. I'd seen him throw them several times at the cafe—the worst one being when Mr. Nettles with the state tax commission came by to question Ralph about his sales tax payments. Every time we make a sale at the cafe we have to add sales tax which we send to the tax commission once a month. Mr. Nettles thought Ralph hadn't paid enough sales tax one month and so he came by to talk to Ralph about it. Ralph got so mad he took a meat cleaver and ran Mr. Nettles out of the store. He yelled at Mr. Nettles, "Don't you ever let me see your ass in this store again!" That was a bad mistake. You don't bully people with the tax commission. That afternoon Mr. Nettles turned back up at the store. He had with him two deputy sheriffs and a highway patrolman. The deputy sheriffs and the patrolman was wearing pistols. Each one of 'em looked to me like they weighed three hundred pounds. When Ralph saw Mr. Nettles and the deputy sheriffs and the patrolman walk into the cafe he wilted. He became humble in a hurry. Mr. Nettles looked at Ralph and said, "Mr. Rainey, I could have you arrested for what you did this morning. This time I'm going to let it slide by, but you threaten me again and I'm having you arrested and you're going to jail. Do you understand?" Ralph said he understood.

That's Ralph for you. When he has a temper tantrum he has a temper tantrum. There ain't no way to stop it. I knew the folks in the dining room could hear him rantin' and ravin'. There wasn't nothing I could do about that.

But I decided there was at least one thing I could do. I could apologize. So I said, "I'm gonna tell Brother Claypool and Brother Ledbetter and Brother Fike I'm sorry I ain't got no more fried chicken."

I was trying to make the best out of a bad situation. Or you might say I was tryin' to smooth things over. I wiped the tears from my eyes. I walked into the dining room. Ralph followed me. I said, "I want all of you to know I'm sorry we ain't got no more fried chicken. But we've done give out and that's all I can say."

But then Ralph had to get his two-bits in. He said, "I want to apologize too. Beulah has let us down."

It was awkward. I felt weak and helpless. To be honest with you I felt I was being pissed on. All of a sudden I remembered a bad dream I used to have when I was a little girl in grammar school and rode the school bus to the New Jerusalem Elementary School. I had this bad dream time and time again. In this dream I'd be standing beside the road in front of Daddy's house. I'd be waiting for the yellow school bus to come down the road and take me to school. In these dreams I'd always be naked. There I'd be—standing alone by the road without no clothes on. Without even a stitch. I'd see the bus coming down the road and it'd pull up to where I was standing. Everybody on the bus would look out the bus windows and they'd point their fingers at me and they'd laugh and snicker. And they'd scream, "There's Beulah Buchanan! There's Beulah Buchanan! Naked as a jaybird! Naked as a jaybird!" And they'd say, "She ain't got no clothes on!" When they'd come at me with those words I'd feel alone and helpless and weak. Why would I have a dream like that? I don't know. What I do know is that I had the same feeling of weakness and helplessness while standing in the dining room before the preachers and Miss Sadie and Mrs. Claypool. I felt naked as a jaybird.

While I was standing there in the dining room feeling naked as a jaybird both Brother Claypool and his fat wife were looking down at the table. I could tell they was avoiding looking Ralph in the eye. Mrs. Claypool had a fork in her right hand and was pretending to take another bite of her lettuce and tomato salad. Brother Ledbetter was looking down at the table and so was Miss Sadie and so was Brother Fike the songleader. I could tell they'd heard Ralph raising Cain in the kitchen and chewing me out and banging around pots and pans. The only person lookin' up was Oscar. He had a puzzled look on his face. He could tell something was wrong. He was picking his nose. That's why I didn't want him to come to eat with us. When Oscar picks his nose it turns my stomach. But Ralph had insisted that he come.

I didn't say nothing out loud when Ralph said, "Beulah has let us down." But the thought that was goin' through my mind was: like hell I have! I haven't let nobody down. On Tuesday I'd cleaned up the house better than it had ever been cleaned up before. I'd gotten down on my knees and scrubbed the bathroom floors and the kitchen floor with hot water. I'd seen to it that Sumrall had the yard mowed and raked. I'd spent all day Wednesday working on the supper—cookin' and fryin'. I'd worked so hard I was completely wore out. I felt like a twisted dishrag. And what did Ralph say. He said, "Beulah has let us down." Again I say: like hell I had.

As I stood there in the dining room I felt a head of angry steam building up inside of me against Brother Claypool. And against Brother Ledbetter. And against their wives—one of 'em as plump as a pregnant cow and the other one as skinny as a poker. For some reason or other I stared at Miss Sadie's cotton patch hat with its cotton bolls and tiny flags. Her hat made me want to go outside and puke. I looked at fat Mrs. Claypool and she made me want to puke too. I looked at Brother Claypool with his flopping jowls and red suspenders. I looked at Brother Ledbetter who'd come by the house between twenty to thirty times and told me how pretty I was while he was fucking my pussy. Both of them made me want to puke. The only two people sittin' at the table who didn't make me want to puke was Oscar and Brother Fike the songleader. He seemed like a pretty decent fellow. He hadn't stuffed himself like the others had. Who knows? Maybe a taxi driver can feel for others better than a preacher can. Brother Claypool and Brother Ledbetter both had tucked napkins under their collars so they wouldn't get nothing on their shirts or ties. Damn it! Why didn't they pull those napkins off and say something to Ralph to get him off my back? Why didn't they speak up so I wouldn't feel the way I felt when I was a little girl and had those bad dreams about standing naked beside the road while waiting for the school bus? Brother Claypool could have said, "Ralph, you're overreacting. I really didn't want another piece of chicken. I was just tryin' to make your wife feel good by complimenting her cooking." Or Brother Ledbetter could have said, "Ralph, you're shooting a snow bird with a shotgun. Calm down! I've had more than enough to eat and it was all mighty good." They could have said something like that. After all, they are men of God— set apart to do good. And to help people out who're in trouble—like the Good Samaritan done who found the man beside the Jericho road who'd been beat up by robbers. So why didn't they help me out? I'd spend the next day or two tryin' to figure that one out. Particularly since they'd eaten enough chicken and vegetables and rice and gravy and homemade rolls to feed the Confederate Army during the siege of Vicksburg. But they didn't say nothing. They just sat there like wooden Indians or stone monkeys. They let me swing in the wind like I was somebody who'd been hanged on the limb of a tree. And left there for the buzzards to eat.

Brother Claypool looked at his watch and cleared his throat. He said, "Oh my goodness! We'd better be going. It's almost time for the evening revival service to begin."

Brother Ledbetter said, "It sure is. We've got to scoot."

With that Brother and Mrs. Claypool and Brother Ledbetter and Miss Sadie and Claude Fike the songleader stood up and headed for the front door. They rushed out of the house like the house was on fire. I heard Brother Ledbetter say to Ralph, "Ralph, I'll see you at the church in a few moments."

Ralph said, "I'll be right behind you." Brother Claypool and Brother Ledbetter had said something to Ralph. But they didn't say nothing to me. Neither did their wives or Claude Fike the songleader. I was hopin' that someone would say, "Beulah, we really enjoyed the meal." Or "Beulah, your food was mighty good and we want you to know we appreciate it. Cooking a meal like that is bound to be a lot of work and take a lot of time." I was hopin' they'd say something like that. But they didn't. They just got up from the table and walked out the front door and got in Brother Claypool's minivan and away they went.

I walked out on the front porch and watched them drive off. Why I done that I don't know. The van stirred up a cloud of dust as it drove out the driveway. I had this big lump in my throat where I'd been cryin'. As the van was pulling away it hit me: I'd forgot to serve 'em their dessert. I'd forgot because I was so upset about givin' out of food. And I was upset about Ralph flyin' off the handle and making a fool of himself. Or at least I felt he'd made a fool of himself. That morning I'd baked two pecan pies. Them two pies was beauties. The reason some pecan pies ain't no good is because the person makin' them is stingy with the pecans. Pecans cost a lot of money. But I wasn't stingy with my pecans. I'd loaded those two pecan pies down with pecan halves I'd bought from the Bass Pecan Company in Lumberton. There ain't nobody in Jones County who can bake a better pecan pie than me when I turn my mind to it.

Looking back on it what I done was stupid. When it dawned on me that I'd forgotten to serve the pecan pie to the preachers, I ran down the front steps and I started yelling. I yelled as loud as I could. I bet you could have heard me all the way down to the Okatoma River. I yelled, "Brother Claypool! Brother Ledbetter! I forgot about the pecan pie! Come back and let me serve you a piece of my pecan pie!" But they didn't hear me. They kept on drivin' away. When they got down to the end of the driveway they turned right and headed down the road to the New Jerusalem Baptist Church for the Wednesday night revival service. I felt like kicking myself. Somehow I felt that if I could serve 'em a piece of my super pecan pie it would make up for me not having enough chicken and fried green tomatoes. Pecan pie wasn't the only thing I had for dessert. I'd bought a gallon of Baskin-Robbins French vanilla ice cream that I was gonna put on top of each piece of pie. And I was gonna offer everybody a cup of hot coffee to drink along with their dessert. But I couldn't do it because they'd all got in the van and drove off.

I turned around and walked back toward the house. I took my time walking up the front steps. I opened the front door and walked into the house. The first thing I noticed was that all the lights had been turned off. The second thing I noticed was Ralph. He was standing inside the house. There was enough light for me to tell he had a strange look on his face. It was a scowl look I'd never seen before. He was holding a Bible in one hand and in the other hand he was holding his black leather belt. Ralph looked at me and said, "Yelling about pecan pie ain't gonna do no good Beulah. What'll do you good is to hear the word of the Lord. I want you to listen to what I'm about to read out of the Bible."

Ralph turned on a floor lamp so he could see how to read from the Bible. When Ralph reads he has to wear glasses and so he put on his reading glasses. He cleared his throat and started reading from the Bible. Exactly where he was reading from in the Bible I don't know. You can take what I know about the Bible and put it in a thimble. All I know is it's a mighty important book. Brother Ledbetter says that every word in the Bible has been put there by God himself. Wherever it was that Ralph was reading from it had to do with wives and husbands. It said wives was supposed to submit to their husbands as to the Lord. After he'd read from the Bible about wives submitting to their husbands, Ralph looked right at me and said, "Beulah, you're a Christian woman and I'm a Christian husband. The time has come for you to submit to me in what I'm about to do."

By that time I was beginning to feel uneasy. I was beginning to be afraid.

I asked, "What are you about to do?"

He said, "I'm gonna give you a holy chastising."

I asked, "You're gonna do what?"

Ralph said, "I'm gonna give you a holy chastising."

I said, "A holy chastising? What's that?"

He said, "A holy chastising is a holy whipping."

I asked, "Why?"

Ralph said, "You know the answer to that question as well as I do. You've got to have a holy chastising because of what you didn't do today. Today we had two mighty men of God to come to our house to eat. They come here to break bread with us in the name of Jesus. And what is it you didn't do? You didn't fix enough for them to eat. We gave out of chicken and lima beans and rice and gravy and everything. I've never been so outdone and embarrassed in all of my life."

I couldn't believe Ralph was sayin' what he was sayin'. He was threatening me with a whipping because I hadn't fried enough chicken. But your ears don't lie to you.

I said, "My god, Ralph, they almost ate us out of house and

home. I didn't know they had stomachs that was bottomless pits."
Which is true. If I'd known how much they could eat I would have
fixed more. But I didn't know.

Ralph seemed to me like he was under some kind of hex. He
rambled on, "Brother Claypool and Brother Ledbetter are men set
apart to spread the word. Brother Ledbetter has the second blessing.
The reason I know he has the second blessing is because of the way
he can lift up a prayer and explain the book of Revelations. I think
Brother Claypool has the second blessing too. Them two men of
God comin' here tonight to eat with us was an honor but you went
and messed it up."

Ralph went on to say, "I was hopin' this would be the night when
Oscar got saved. But with all that's happened I can see this ain't
gonna be the night when Oscar gets right with the Lord."

I started to say, "Instead of Oscar gettin' right with the Lord
maybe the Lord ought to get right with Oscar. When you stop and
think about it: didn't the Lord screw Oscar by lettin' him be born
without all of his marbles? Because he doesn't have all of his marbles
he has to live in the home for the feebleminded in Ellisville. Who
wants to go through life being feebleminded? Who wants to go
through life not having any better judgment than to pick your nose
in public? Where was the Lord when Oscar was being put together?
Maybe he was watching the clouds instead of lookin' after Oscar."
That's what I started to say to Ralph but I didn't say it because I knew
it would make him madder than he was. A lot of people get screwed
by the Lord. But it's best not to think about that. If you thought
about it too much you'd go nuts. You might decide the world is a
crazy house like the crazy house at the Jones County Fair.

After he'd said what he said about Oscar gettin' right with the
Lord, Ralph pounced on me and grabbed my right arm and started
whipping me on my behind with his leather belt. It happened so fast
I didn't understand at first what was goin' on. Oh god but did it

hurt. Ralph's as strong as a bull. Every time he cracked his belt on my rear end he'd bellow, "I chastise you in the name of the Lord! I chastise you in the name of the Lord!"

I started screaming at the top of my voice, "No Ralph! Don't do this!"

He was beating me as hard as he could. As he was beating my rear end I started havin' flashbacks. Like claps of thunder I heard Mama's voice. I could hear her voice as clear as a bell on a cold winter day. I could hear Mama snapping:

"Ralph Rainey ain't no good!"

And: "Ralph is like a dime. He's got two sides. He's got a good side and he's got a bad side."

And: "Ruth Ann said that when he was at church Ralph was a lollipop but at home he was as mean as a rattlesnake."

And I could hear Mama saying: "One day Ruth Ann told me Ralph beat her with a belt and it felt like hot water mixed with iodine."

In the middle of it all I yelled, "Ralph! You're killing me!"

I done my best to break away from him but I couldn't.

And so I screamed, "Stop! You bastard! You sonuvabitch!"

But he kept on beating and bellowing, "I chastise you in the name of the Lord!"

Oscar started saying the same thing. He ran around the living room shouting, "I chastise you in the name of the Lord!" "I chastise you in the name of the Lord!" He shouted them words over and over.

I could tell Oscar didn't know what he was doin' or sayin'. He was as scared as I was. I kept on doing my best to break away from Ralph. But I couldn't. Like I just said, Ralph's as strong as a bull.

He finally stopped. I don't know how many times Ralph hit me on my butt with his belt. I didn't count 'em. All I know is when he stopped and turned loose of my arm I fell to the floor. I fell down like a limp sack of corn. The next thing I remember is blacking out. Or you might say I fainted. All I know is I fell on the floor and felt dizzy and weak as water. Then I didn't know nothing. I went out cold. I unfuzzed just enough to hear Ralph sayin', "You stay here. I'm goin' to the revival meeting. I don't want to be late." I remember Ralph sayin' something like that. Then I fuzzed out again.

I don't know how long I stayed blacked out. I stayed fuzzed out until I heard somebody callin' my name. I heard somebody sayin' "Miss Beulah! Miss Beulah!" The voice sounded far away. It sounded like it was comin' from across a lake. Or like it was comin' from the bottom of a well. Or through a long tunnel.

I lay still on the floor. At first I didn't recognize who it was who was callin' my name. I knew it wasn't Ralph. And I knew it wasn't Oscar. But I didn't know who it was.

Then the voice said, "Miss Beulah, it's me—Sumrall."

I opened my eyes. The room was as dark as a cup of black coffee. I said, "Who is it?"

He said again, "Miss Beulah, it's me—Sumrall."

Then he added, "Mr. Oscar come runnin' down to the house and said you was in trouble and needed help." Although I was groggy, Sumrall sayin' that got close to me. I'd never thought Oscar had enough eggs in his basket to do something like that. He'd run to Sumrall's house and told him I needed help. Sumrall lives in a shotgun shanty a quarter mile down the road.

Sumrall said, "Mr. Oscar says you're hurt."

I was comin' to my senses. I said, "Sumrall, turn on a light."

Which he done.

Sumrall took a look at me and asked, "Miss Beulah, what's happened to you?"

I said, "Ralph had one of his temper tantrums tonight and took his belt off and beat me up."

Sumrall asked, "Where's Mr. Ralph now?"

I answered, "He's gone to the revival meeting."

Sumrall took another look at me and said, "Miss Beulah, that floor's hard. You needs to be in bed. I know a nigger ain't supposed to touch a white lady, but would you let me help you get in bed?"

I said, "Sure. I wished you would."

Sumrall helped me get off the floor and stand up. I leaned on Sumrall and hobbled back to the bedroom. It seemed that every muscle in my body ached. When we got back to the bedroom I sat down on the edge of the bed.

Sumrall lifted my legs off the floor and helped me stretch out on the bed. He then turned on the ceiling light and took another look at me.

He said, "Miss Beulah, your right eye is swellin' like it's a balloon. You're gonna have a black eye."

He then added, "We'd better put some ice on it."

I said, "Sumrall, there's an ice pack on the top shelf of the bathroom closet. Please get it and put some ice in it for me. There's lots of ice in the kitchen." I knew there was lots of ice in the kitchen. I'd bought a bunch of bags of ice cubes at the Jitney Jungle Grocery so we wouldn't give out of ice for iced tea. I'd put them in a tin tub on the kitchen floor.

Sumrall said, "I sho will, Miss Beulah."

I heard Sumrall walk to the bathroom and get the rubber ice-pack. He then went to the kitchen and filled it with ice. He brought it to me and I placed it on my right eye. The ice began to numb the pain.

Sumrall said, "I'd better be goin', Miss Beulah. Mr. Ralph wouldn't like it if he knowed I was here."

Sumrall was right. One of Ralph's favorite sayings was, "You can't trust a nigger around a white woman."

And so I said, "You're right, Sumrall. You'd better be goin'. Ralph would blow his stack if he knew you'd helped me."

Before Sumrall left he turned to Oscar and said, "Oscar, you listen to me. Don't you tell nobody about me comin' here tonight. Do you understand?"

Oscar mumbled, "I ain't gonna tell nobody. As soon as I can, I'm goin' back to Ellisville. That's where I like to stay."

Sumrall turned to me and said, "Good night, Miss Beulah. I hopes you get to feelin' better. You're shore gonna be sore."

I said, "Good night, Sumrall. Thanks for what you done."

Sumrall said, "You're welcome." He slipped out of the house and walked away into the night. He faded into the night like a person walking through thick morning fog in the Okatoma Swamp.

5

I T'S A GOOD THING Sumrall left the house when he did. He
hadn't been gone out of the house five minutes before I heard
Ralph drive up in his pickup truck. He parked his pickup in the
garage and come on inside the house. Ralph would have gone crazy
mad if he'd known Sumrall had come inside the house and helped
me to my bed. You ain't gonna believe this but Ralph come into the
house singing. He was singing "Amazing Grace."

He was singing so loud you could have heard him all the way to
Laurel. If I didn't know better I'd of thought he was drunk the way
he was belting out "Amazing Grace."

"Amazing grace! how sweet the sound,

"That saved a wretch like me!

"I once was lost, but now am found,

"Was blind, but now I see."

That's what Ralph was singing at the top of his voice. I thought
to myself how odd that was. Or maybe I ought to say weird. An hour
or so before he'd beat the stew out of me with his belt. And now he
was walking around the house singing a gospel song like nothing had
happened.

When I heard Ralph come in I didn't move. I stayed on the bed
where I was. I still had on a dress—the white one with lots of lace
which I was wearing when Ralph whipped me. Or as he put it,

chastised me. I was hoping Ralph would come back to the bedroom where I was and say something to me. I was hoping he might say, "Beulah, I want to apologize. I shouldn't have done what I did. Sometimes I fly off the handle when I shouldn't. So I ask you to forgive me." Why I hoped he might say this I don't know. When you stop and think about it, why would I want a man who had just whipped me to say anything to me? That doesn't make sense. But Ralph didn't come back to the bedroom where I was. He stayed away from me like I had leprosy or some other kind of gosh awful disease. I heard him take a leak in the bathroom. After he'd taken a leak he flushed the toilet and brushed his teeth.

I heard him walk to the front bedroom and take off his shoes. I heard 'em hit the floor. That's the way Ralph does. He takes his shoes off one at the time and drops 'em on the floor. He slept that night in the front bedroom. It didn't take him five minutes to go to sleep. I know what I'm talking about because I heard him start to snore. Ralph got up real early Thursday morning. I heard him wake up Oscar who'd slept on the sofa in the living room. I heard Ralph say, "Wake up, buddy, we gotta go." Before he left the house he still didn't say nothing to me. He didn't come to the bedroom where I was. He just got up, dressed, and left in his pickup truck. He took Oscar with him. My guess was he was taking Oscar back to the feebleminded school in Ellisville. Ellisville and Laurel are not but five or ten miles apart.

Ralph went to work but I didn't. I stayed home. I'm talking about Thursday of last week. I was too sore to go to work. I was sure enough sore on my back and rear end where Ralph had whipped me. And besides being sore on my back and rear end my face was a mess. It was a real mess. Somehow when Ralph was whipping me he hit my right eye. I remember him hitting my right eye with his elbow when I was fighting like a tiger to get away from him. I'll say one thing for me: I fought back. I let Ralph know what I thought. Which is why

I called him a sonuvabitch. I did my best to scratch his face but I
didn't have any luck. I went into the bathroom and looked in the
mirror at my face. I had a blackeye. Sumrall had said I'd have one.
And I sure did. My eye looked like somebody had taken a paint
brush and painted it with black paint. Or with chimney soot. What
I did most of Thursday was keep an ice pack on my black eye.
Another thing I done was soak in the bathtub in warm water. I let
more water in the tub than I usually did. I found out when I sat real
still in warm water I didn't hurt so bad. And I took me a lot of
Tylenol to help ease the hurting.

When Ralph got home that evening after work he came back to
the bedroom. I was laying on the bed. I took the ice pack off of my
eye and showed him my black eye. I said, "There wasn't no need of
you doin' this to me."

He looked at me and said, "Whom the Lord loves he chastises."

Ralph then added, "That's straight out of the book of Hebrews
and the book of Hebrews don't lie."

After he'd said that he turned and left the room. That night and
for the next two or three days Ralph acted real cold to me. That's the
way he can be. He can be as cold as ice and as sharp as an icicle. Or
a razor blade. He was actin' the way Mama acted when Ralph and me
got married. He didn't have nothing to say to me. He went his way
like I wasn't around. Or wasn't alive. On Thursday and Friday
nights he kept on goin' to the revival at the church. The revival with
Brother Claypool from Waynesboro and with Brother Fike the
songleader ended on Friday night. I couldn't help but wonder if
Brother Claypool pulled any other stunts like he done when he
threw the snake out in the congregation and scared everybody to
death. But I didn't ask nobody whether he did or not.

On Friday and Saturday I stayed home like I did on Thursday. I
kept on using an ice pack and I kept on sitting in the bathtub with
a lot of hot water in it and I kept on taking Tylenol. In a way I felt

like I was turning into a Tylenol capsule. I was all by myself
Thursday, Friday, and Saturday. Being by myself for three days gave
me time to do a lot of thinking. And believe you me I did a lot of
thinking. I did a lot of thinking about Brother Ledbetter. Or as I'd
come to call him when it was just me and him by ourselves: Henry.
Like I've told you, Ralph thought Brother Ledbetter hung the moon
up in the sky. He thought he was the cherry on top of the sundae and
the white icing on a chocolate cake. I wondered what Ralph would
say if he'd known about what had been goin' on between me and
Henry. Brother Ledbetter sure looks dignified when he stands
behind the pulpit on Sunday morning all decked out in a black suit
with his diamond stickpin sparkling on his red tie. He stands tall
behind the pulpit and preaches on the book of Revelations explaining what all of them candlesticks and trumpets mean. But he looks
like any other man when he takes his pants off. I know because I've
seen him take his pants off dozens of times. He always has on two
kinds of underwear shorts. One kind he wears is white with little red
dots. The other kind he wears is white with little blue dots. His
underwear shorts was always a puzzle to me. I wondered where he'd
bought them. But I never got around to asking him.

As I was laying there on the bed trying to figure out what to do
about Henry there was one thing I still couldn't get around. I've told
you before and I'll tell you again: I couldn't deny Henry had woke up
inside of me feelings I didn't know was there. Those feelings had
been sleeping. Henry woke 'em up. Before goin' to bed with Henry
I'd never enjoyed having sex. To be up front with you: I didn't know
a woman could enjoy havin' sex with a man. With Ralph sex was just
meat rubbin' against meat. But Henry taught me sex can be lots of
fun if its done right. We'd French kiss. By that I mean we'd stick our
tongues into each other's mouths. He'd kiss and fondle and suck my
boobs making my cherry tingle. All the time he'd be sweet talking
me. On his fourth visit Henry asked me, "Beulah, have you ever had

oral sex before?" I said, "What's that?" He said, "You lovin' me with your mouth." I said, "No, I ain't never done that." He said, "Would you like to try it?" I said, "Sure, but I'm not sure I know how to do it." Henry said, "Put my dick in your mouth and go up and down like it was your pussy." I said, "Okay, I'll give it a try." Which is what I done. I got to where I could go up and down on Henry's dick until he jacked off. He told me that doin' it that way really felt good. It felt good to me when he put his tongue on my clit and loved me that way.

What I think it all boils down to is we was both lonely and love starved. Henry was starved from being married too long to Miss Sadie who has a figure that looks like a broom stick. I was love starved from being married to Ralph who has teeth like a horse and who always smells like Swisher Sweet cigars and onions and barbecue sauce. I'd convinced myself that Henry loved me. That's what he told me time and time again. Being loved by Henry who was also Brother Ledbetter made me feel important. It made me feel special. Nobody had ever talked to me the way Henry did. And believe it or not: I didn't feel what me and Henry was doin' was sinful. Given what he was up against and given what I was up against, I didn't feel like we was sinnin' against Mount Sinai when we loved each other. I didn't feel what we was doin' was adultery. I felt it was love between two people who understood each other and was fightin' the same battle in different ways.

And it's because I loved Henry and because I thought he loved me that I couldn't understand why he acted the way he did when Ralph got to yellin' at me about not cookin' enough fried chicken. I felt let down. If Henry really loved me wouldn't he have done something? Wouldn't he have come to my aid some way or other? Maybe he could have said, "C'mon, Ralph, let up. You're being too hard on Beulah. She's done a good job of fixing our supper and me and Brother Claypool has had enough to eat." He could have said something like that. But he didn't. He wouldn't take on Ralph. And I think I know the reason why. It's because Ralph gives a lot of money to the New Jerusalem Baptist Church. One time Ralph said to me, "You know something, Beulah, they ought to name me Deacon One-Third." I said, "Why in the world do you think they ought to name you Deacon One-Third?" Ralph said, "I know what our church budget is. I know how much money comes into our church every year. And you know what? One out of every three dollars that comes into the New Jerusalem Baptist Church every year comes out of my pocket. That's right. I give one out of every three dollars that's given to our church. That's why they ought to name me Deacon One-Third." Brother Ledbetter wasn't about to take on Deacon One-Third. He knew which side his bread was buttered on. If he'd said something in my favor Ralph might have creamed his ass. A preacher doesn't ever want to cross swords with somebody who loads down the collection plate. That would be bitin' the hand that feeds you.

Where did all of this leave me? I'll tell you where it left me. I came to see something I didn't want to see. By the way he didn't stand up for me I could tell Brother Ledbetter didn't have no backbone. Or if he had one it was made out of Jello. Or vanilla puddin'. Brother Ledbetter in his sermons was all time talking about things being sacrificed on altars. Well, the way I figure it he sacrificed me on an altar named Ralph. Which is why I felt I'd been had. All that whispering he did to me on the bed about how much he loved me was so much gobbledegook. Or as Velma would have put it: it was perfumed bullshit. And so by god I reached a decision. It was all over between me and Henry. Or maybe I ought to say Brother Ledbetter. I decided that if he ever came by the house again early in the morning I'd look him right in the eye and I'd say, "Listen, Henry, you've got a backbone made out of jelly. How do I know this? When Ralph was yellin' at me and treating me like the scum of the earth because I hadn't cooked enough you didn't say or do nothing. You acted like a mouse. Because you didn't say or do nothing you double-crossed me. So you get in your peanut Pontiac and be on your way. If you need sex go fuck your fist."

While I was comin' to this decision I found myself doubting whether or not he had the second blessing. The night Brother Ledbetter ate with us he told a motherfucker joke. If somebody has the second blessing is he gonna tell a motherfucker joke? How can someone who has the second blessing be at one moment tellin' a motherfucker joke and then a little while later be at the New Jerusalem Baptist Church prayin' and singing about Jesus at a revival meeting? Pardon me, but somehow I don't get it.

Deciding to break it off with Brother Ledbetter wasn't the only thing I decided. More important—much more important—I also decided it was all over between me and Ralph. The time had come for me to get out from under his thumb where I'd been stuck for six years. For six long years I'd been his wife and time and again he'd been sharp with me and hurt my feelings. My gut told me to stop bein' Mrs. Ralph Rainey and to go back to bein' Beulah Buchanan. I'd been thinking this way off and on for a long time. But thinking about doin' something and then doin' it is two different things.

Some husbands are sweet to their wives and help them out. In the morning they bring their wives coffee to the bed. They take out the garbage can on trash day. They take their wives to nice restaurants and give them flowers on their birthday. But all husbands are not like that. Let's face it: some husbands are mean. That's the way they're wired. Maybe they can't help it. Maybe they don't even know they're mean. Sometimes you have to live with 'em for a long time before you can come to see what they're really like.

Some husbands you'd never suspect of being mean are mean. You take Dr. Kemper. His full name is Dr. Joel Faulkner Kemper. Dr. Kemper is a stomach and intestines doctor. My daddy has gone to him for years. He's the kind of doctor you go to if you have trouble digesting your food or if you have blood in your bowel movements. Around Laurel there's nobody more highly thought of than Dr. Kemper. He's the only person in Laurel who drives a red Mercedes convertible. He's a member of the Episcopal church. He used to be a Presbyterian. He told my daddy he became an Episcopalian so he could sip a Manhattan every evening when he got home from the hospital. Episcopalians can drink. Presbyterians can't. I asked Daddy what a Manhattan was and he said it was some kind of drink made with whiskey. Dr. Kemper belongs to the country club and he and his wife live in this plush subdivision north of Laurel called Canebrake. Canebrake is a subdivision built around a lake. All the homes are brick mansions. What's my point? There's nobody in Jones County fancier than Dr. Kemper.

Month before last Dr. Kemper came drivin' up to the emergency entrance of the hospital in Laurel. He was in his red Mercedes. His wife was slumped over in the seat beside him. Her name is Tammy. Dr. Kemper jumped out of his car and yelled, "Tammy's been hurt." They rolled her into the emergency room. The reason I know about all of this is because my cousin works in the emergency room. She's also an operating room nurse. I'm talking about Molly, Uncle Alonzo's daughter. Molly told me that Mrs. Kemper was a mess. It turned out she had three broken ribs and a sprained right arm.

They took her to the operating room to get her fixed up. Molly happened to be on duty. They put Mrs. Kemper to sleep so they could work on her ribs. After she'd been put to sleep she started talking. Molly says this happens all the time. They put people to sleep and they start talking like ladies talking in a sewing club. Molly says they'll even carry on a conversation with you. The doctor working on Mrs. Kemper was Doctor Gibson. His first name is Fred. Out of the clear blue sky Dr. Kemper's wife blurted out, "Joel Faulkner Kemper is a sonuvabitch."

Dr. Gibson said, "Now Tammy, you don't believe that. Your husband is a nice fellow."

Tammy Kemper said, "Like hell he is." She then asked, "Who're you?"

Dr. Gibson said, "I'm Fred Gibson. You and I know each other. We've known each other for years. We both belong to the Episcopal church."

Mrs. Kemper said, "Hi Fred. You know Joel, don't you?"

Dr. Gibson said, "Sure I do. We've been on this hospital staff together for over twenty years."

Mrs. Kemper said, "Then you know as well as I do that Joel is a sonuvabitch."

Dr. Gibson said, "Tammy, let's change the subject. Your husband told us you hurt yourself when you fell off of a ladder. What were you doing on top of a ladder?"

Mrs. Kemper said, "What ladder?"

Dr. Gibson said, "The ladder you fell off of. Joel said you hurt yourself when you fell off of a ladder."

Mrs. Kemper said, "Joel is full of horseshit. I didn't fall off of a ladder."

Dr. Gibson asked, "You must have. You've ended up with a bunch of broken ribs."

Mrs. Kemper said, "I got these broken ribs from Joel kicking the shit out of me."

Dr. Gibson asked, "Did you say Joel kicked you?"

Mrs. Kemper said, "He sure did. He kicked me over and over."

Dr. Gibson asked, "Why did he do that?"

Mrs. Kemper said, "Because I couldn't find the keys."

Dr. Gibson asked, "What keys?"

Mrs. Kemper answered, "The keys to his Winnebago. He wants to drive this weekend to Gulf Shores to go fishing and when he goes fishing he likes to drive his Winnebago. When I couldn't find the keys he got as mad as the devil and threw me down on the floor and started kicking me. He yelled at me, 'Goddamnit, Tammy, I've told you to always know where the Winnebago keys are and goddamnit you can't find them.'"

Molly said Dr. Gibson and Mrs. Kemper kept on talking like this all the time she was in the operating room. Mrs. Kemper said people in Laurel would be surprised if they knew what an asshole her husband was. Five people in the operating room heard what Dr. Kemper's wife said. But they didn't do anything about what she said. Dr. Kemper is on the hospital's Board of Directors and so everybody figured the best thing to do was to say nothing. What I'm sayin' is some husbands you'd never suspect are mean to their wives. The way they act outside their homes is different from the way they act inside their homes. Inside their homes they're somebody different.

That's the way it was with Ralph. Outside the house he was jolly Ralph Rainey. He's a good old boy from Jones County who loves to go fishing and coon hunting at night. During the deer season Ralph always took off one day to go deer hunting with his buddies from the Rainey clan or with his buddies in his hunting club. During the turkey season he always took off one day to go hunting for a gobbler. He never killed a deer and he never shot a gobbler. His cousins told me he's not worth a hang when it comes to shooting a rifle. But that didn't bother Ralph. He'd say "I enjoy bein' with the fellows." When a customer came into his butcher shop he was all smiles 'n spice. I can hear him now. "Good afternoon, Mr. Runnels! It's good to see you! What can I fix you up with this afternoon? How about some ground round? Or how about some pork chops?" And when the customer leaves the butcher shop I can hear Ralph sayin', "Mr. Runnels, I really appreciate your business. Please come back to see us." And when customers came into the cafe he'd sweeten 'em up. "Come right in! What would you folks like today? How about some of our pork ribs? I've got the best ribs in Laurel. There's no doubt about that." All the time Ralph will be smiling and when the customers leave he'll say, "Have a nice day!" It doesn't matter what the weather is outside. It can be raining cats and dogs. Or it can be as hot as boiling water. Or as cold as a block of ice. And what will Ralph say? "Have a nice day!" I bet he spoke them four words a thousand times every day. Customers leave the cafe thinking, "Ralph is a nice guy." The same goes for people who belong to the New Jerusalem Baptist Church. Like I've told you, the first thing he did when he got to church was to turn on the lightbulb beside his name on the "Let Your Light Shine For Jesus" board. Every Sunday he led the singing and helped take up the collection. Last year he was chairman of the piano committee which raised enough money for the church to buy a new piano. I'll say one thing: the church needed a new piano. The old upright one we had was shot. You couldn't keep it in tune if your life depended on it. The church raised enough money to buy a brand new upright Baldwin piano from the Roseberry Piano Company in Hattiesburg. So around the church Ralph was as nice as boiled custard. And he was as sweet as homemade ice cream.

But around the house—when there was nobody there but him and me—his mean side could explode. His mean side scared me in the past. It's scared me a lot of times. But I ain't never been as scared of Ralph's mean side as I was this past Saturday night. I'm now gonna tell you what Ralph did this past weekend to his mule. What he done to old JR pushed me into swallowing something I didn't want to swallow and that is: Ralph was a psycho. Someway and somehow he had a loose screw. You're not gonna believe what Ralph done to JR. If you don't believe what I'm about to tell you, you can ask Sumrall and he'll back me up. He'll let you know I'm tellin' the truth, the whole truth, and nothing but the truth. Nobody knows exactly how old JR was. Sumrall said JR was the oldest mule in Mississippi. And that might be true. Ralph came home from the cafe last Saturday night and got to the house right before sundown. He parked his pickup truck in front of the barn. When he got home he didn't say nothing to me. The last time he'd spoken to me was when he said, "Whom the Lord loves he chastises." Or something like that. Ralph went out to the barn and hitched up old JR to a plow. He decided to plow some in his garden. Why Ralph decided to do this as late in the day as it was I don't know. But he did. I thought it was dumb. Ralph led JR out to the garden and started plowing. By then it was almost night. Old JR wasn't in a very good mood. He didn't want to plow. My guess is he thought it was stupid to plow when it was almost night. He started givin' Ralph a hard time. He wouldn't do what Ralph told him to do. When Ralph told JR to move he wouldn't budge. I heard Ralph yell, "C'mon JR, let's go!" It didn't make no difference what Ralph yelled or did. Old JR, bless his heart, just stood there like a statue made out of Birmingham iron. JR acting the way he was acting made Ralph really mad. So what did Ralph do? He dropped the reins and ran to his pickup truck. He reached in the back of his truck and picked up a can of gasoline. Ralph always keeps a ten-gallon can of gasoline on his pickup. He keeps it full of gas. The reason Ralph does this is because he's afraid he might be off somewhere and give out of gasoline. Ralph took his can of gas and ran to the garden. He poured those ten gallons of gas all over JR. He poured gas on JR's back. And on his head. And on his legs. All the time he was doin' this he was screaming, "By god JR I'll show you!" After he'd emptied the can he threw it over the fence. He then stood back and took out a match. Ralph always had matches on him to light his Swisher Sweet cigars. Ralph struck a match and set JR on fire. The burning gasoline made him look like a fireball. JR burning like a torch started running all over the garden. He was pulling the plow behind him. I can't describe the sound JR was making. It was terrible. It was horrible. I'd never heard a sound like it. And I hope I never hear a sound like it again. If you can say a mule knows how to scream, JR was screaming. And running and screaming and running and screaming. He knocked over Ralph's tomatoes and his corn and his butter beans. He ran into the fence. All this made Ralph furious. He started yelling at JR. He yelled, "Stop, you bastard! Stop I say!" And he screamed, "You're ruining my garden!" But JR was on fire and in agony and he wouldn't stop running. Ralph ran to his pickup truck and took out his automatic shotgun. Ralph always had an automatic shotgun on a gun rack in his truck. Ralph started shooting at JR. The first two shots missed. But the third shot hit JR in the head and took him out of his misery. Ralph stood over JR's body and pumped two more shots into him. He yelled, "You four-legged bastard! This serves you right!" I watched all that was happening between Ralph and JR from the backporch. I thought to myself, "If there is a hell this must be what it's like." I wanted to scream. I wanted my screams to mix and mingle with JR's screams. But I didn't scream. What good would it have done? I just stood on the back porch like a mummy and took it all in.

The next day—this past Sunday—Ralph got Sumrall to borrow Mr. Seller's backhoe and dig a hole in the pasture and bury what was left of JR. About all that was left were his bones. Ordinarily Ralph don't let Sumrall do no work on the Sabbath day. But he told Sumrall since the ox was in the ditch it'd be okay for him to work on Sunday. The smell from JR's body was awful. I ain't never smelled nothing that bad. What got my goat was the way Ralph went on to church the next day as though nothing had happened to JR. I didn't go to church. I stayed home like I'd done since Thursday. But I'll bet you a silver dollar on top of a pancake that the first thing Ralph done when he got to church was to turn on the lightbulb beside his name on the "Let Your Light Shine For Jesus" board.

6

I
F I LIVE TO BE ten thousand years old I'll never forget watching Ralph set old JR on fire and then shooting him in the head with his shotgun. He gunned him down like he was a mad dog with rabies. Or he shot him like he was a big rattlesnake about to strike. And then he stood over JR and called him a four-legged bastard. Old JR didn't deserve that treatment and he didn't deserve those words. JR never hurt a flea. He plowed Ralph's gardens for almost twenty years. And what did he get? He got burned alive. In my ears I can still hear JR screaming. And in my mind I can still see him running around and around in the garden. He was pulling the plow and running around like a crazy man on fire. What Ralph did to JR showed me once and for all that he was sick. When I say Ralph was sick I don't mean being sick in his body like having fever or some kind of stomach trouble. I'm talking about sickness in his heart and soul. Only someone who is sick in his soul would take a ten-gallon can of gasoline and pour it all over a helpless old mule and then set the mule on fire. Particularly a mule like JR who never gave nobody no trouble.

So the time had come for me to clear out and I knew it. Or to put it another way: it was time to crap or get off the pot. But deciding how to crap wasn't easy. I didn't have no money. Once I left Ralph

I wouldn't have a job or a place to eat and sleep. I wasn't goin' back to my daddy's house. If I did that I'd have to live with Mama and she hadn't been sweet to me since I'd married Ralph. My baby sister Earline wasn't there no more. She'd gotten married and moved to Laurel. Her husband Sammy works for a janitorial service. Earline has become a beautician. Everybody says she's really good at it. She's got more customers than she can handle.

I ain't proud of it but I had a mean thought: wouldn't it be nice and solve all my problems if Ralph died? I imagined getting a telephone call with somebody sayin', "Is this Mrs. Ralph Rainey?" And I'd say, "Yes it is." And then they'd say, "Mrs. Rainey, this is the sheriff's office. I've got terrible news for you. Your husband has been killed in a bad automobile accident." A call like that would solve my problem. If Ralph was dead I wouldn't have to figure out how to get rid of him. But—so I thought—Ralph wasn't about to die. He wasn't good enough to go to heaven and he was too mean to go to hell. The old devil would say, "Ralph, I've got troubles enough as it is. I'm not about to let you in here."

Being all undone as I was what I needed was advice. I needed to talk to somebody who'd give me directions and help me figure out what to do. And all of a sudden it hit me: *Go see Velma.* Get her to give me advice. I've told you who Velma is. In case you've forgotten I'll remind you. Velma is my cousin. She's Uncle Sam's and Aunt Carrie's daughter. She's older than me but we've known each other all our lives. When I was a little girl Velma would help me chase lightning bugs at night. We'd catch 'em and put 'em in a jar. When Mama wouldn't have anything to do with my wedding Velma and Aunt Carrie stepped in and helped me have a nice wedding. I'll always appreciate them doin' that. In some ways—when I stop and think about it—Velma and I have gone down the same path. When she was sixteen years old she got married. That's what I did. She married a Rainey and so did I. She married Chester Rainey who is one of Ralph's cousins. Chester was in the loggin' business and that's what he's still doin'. He owns a bunch of trucks and has crews of blacks who work for him. Chester goes out and buys timber from farmers in Jones and Forrest and Stone counties. He'll get his crews to cut it down and they haul it to the sawmill in Wiggins. I'm told Chester is one of the biggest timber buyers in south Mississippi. But he gave Velma a hard time just like Ralph has done me. Velma got a belly full of Chester. So one day she packed up her clothes and moved out on Chester. She got a divorce. She moved to Hattiesburg and went to work at the Confederate Truck Stop. She started out as a waitress in the coffee shop. The truck stop was owned by a bald-headed man named Edmond Norton. His wife had died two years earlier from lung cancer. She was addicted to Chesterfield cigarettes. She smoked two packs of Chesterfields every day. That's why people said she dug her grave not with a shovel but with Chesterfield cigarettes. After Velma had worked at the truck stop for a year she and Edmond started dating. She told me that one day Edmond came up to her in the coffee shop and said, "Velma, I believe you're off tomorrow. Is that right?" Velma said, "Yep. Tomorrow is my day off. I won't come back in until day after tomorrow." Edmond said, "In that case would you let me take you out tomorrow night for dinner?" Velma was flabbergasted. She wasn't expecting Edmond to ask her for a date. She said, "Why of course. I'd love to. Where did you have in mind?" He said, "I'll take you to the Purple Parrot." That's an odd name for a restaurant but the Purple Parrot is the nicest restaurant in Hattiesburg. To eat there costs you an arm and a leg but everybody says it's worth it. The next night Edmond took Velma to the Purple Parrot and three months later they got married. Edmond is older than Velma. I've heard Velma say, "I know Edmond is not hand-some but he sure is sweet and good to me. What else could I ask for?" Everybody says Edmond is a fine man and that he's made a lot of money out of his truck stop. He runs the truck stop side of the

business and Velma runs the coffee shop side. The Confederate
Truck Stop is a sight to see. It's open twenty-four hours a day and
seven days a week. It's just north of Hattiesburg on U.S. 49. It does
a land-office food and gas business. Any time you go there there'll be
between twenty and thirty eighteen wheelers parked around it. All
the way up and down U.S. 49 between Jackson and the Mississippi
Gulf Coast they have big billboards that read, "Stop at the Confederate Truck Stop. We serve the best food in the Deep South. Free
coffee around the clock for men driving eighteen wheelers." The
billboards also read: "Free Beer Tomorrow."

Customers at the truck stop like Velma. They think she's great.
She gives all of 'em the royal treatment. But Brother Ledbetter and
most of the members of the New Jerusalem Baptist Church ain't got
no use for Velma. The church has a lot of Raineys in it. They say she
done wrong in gettin' a divorce from Chester Rainey and then
marrying Edmond. Brother Ledbetter is all time preaching against
divorce just like he preaches against lipstick and cuttin' your hair.
I've heard him say a hundred times that if a man marries a divorced
woman they both are living in sin. They're living in adultery.
Brother Ledbetter says that's what the Bible teaches. When Velma
married Edmond she was a member of the New Jerusalem Baptist
Church. But she ain't no more. Like I've told you, the church held
a business meeting one night soon after Velma and Edmond got
married and they voted her out of the church. At the business
meeting Brother Ledbetter said they had to vote Velma out of the
church because she was a divorcee who married again and was living
in adultery. I know what Brother Ledbetter said about Velma
because I was there and took it all in. I told Velma what Brother
Ledbetter said: that she and her husband was living in sin. Velma
told me, "The next time you see the preacher you tell him I said for
him to kiss my ass." Since Velma got voted out of the church she
don't go to church no more. She says Baptists are the meanest people

on this earth. Since getting voted out of the church she's changed. She now goes regularly to a beauty shop and has her hair cut short. She wears makeup like lipstick and eye shadow. When she ain't workin' at the coffee shop she wears real nice clothes and high-heel shoes. On top of all of this she drives a four-door Cadillac. Velma's Cadillac is the prettiest car I believe I've ever saw. Its color is baby blue and on the inside it has cream-colored leather seats that are so soft you'll go to sleep just sittin' on them. Once a week Velma drives in her blue Cadillac from Hattiesburg up to New Jerusalem to visit her mama and daddy. She does this every Wednesday. Velma has done her best to get Aunt Carrie and Uncle Sam to move down to Hattiesburg where she can keep a closer eye on them and look after them better. But Aunt Carrie and Uncle Sam don't want to move to Hattiesburg. They say it's too big and has too much traffic. They say, "As long as we can hobble around we're staying right here in New Jerusalem where we know everybody and everybody knows us. We feel safe here and here is where we belong." Aunt Carrie and Uncle Sam don't know about the mean things the Raineys in the New Jerusalem Baptist Church say about Velma. They say things like, "Velma thinks she's something on the end of the stick. You can tell that by the way she wears high heels and drives around in her big blue Cadillac. She ain't nothing but a redneck who wears lipstick."

But I've never felt that way about Velma. For some reason or other I've always liked her. I think she has spunk. She's bound to have spunk the way she walked out on Chester Rainey and took off on her own. And I've always thought of her as being my friend.

So last Sunday after Sumrall had buried JR and after Ralph had left the house to go to church I put on some clothes and got in Ralph's car and headed south for the Confederate Truck Stop. I was still sore but I wasn't as sore as I had been. I could get around without feeling like I was ninety years old with one foot in the grave. I left Ralph a note on the kitchen table. I wasn't about to tell him I was goin' to find Velma. The note I left him read like this: "I've gone to buy some more Tylenol. I'll be back later this afternoon."

I got to the truck stop a little after twelve. I bet there was forty eighteen wheelers parked around the place. On Sunday Velma serves a blue plate special which features a T-bone steak which truckers really go for. I parked on the side and got out of my car and looked around. I spotted Velma's blue Cadillac and that told me she was there. I was glad for that. She and Edmond could have been out of town.

I walked into the coffee shop. I think every booth and table was filled with customers. They was all jabbering with one another. The jukebox was playing a Dolly Parton song. Velma was standing behind the cash register and was counting a stack of one dollar bills. By the way she was doin' it you could tell she'd done it a million times before. She looked up from her counting and recognized me. A big smile came on her face and she said, "Lordy, lordy, if it's not Beulah Rainey!"

She put her arms around me and give me a big hug. She said, "Beulah—bless my wicked bones—it's good to see you! When was the last time we saw each other? I guess it was a year ago at Uncle Henry's funeral."

I said, "Yep. I believe that was the last time we was together."

I could tell Velma was working the cash register. Customers were coming up and paying their checks. Velma was real nice to all of 'em. She'd say things like, "Thanks, Charley. Was everything okay?" Charley said everything was okay and Velma said, "That's great. I'll see you next Sunday." Between customers paying their checks Velma and I done some small talk. We talked about the new roof that was goin' on her mama and daddy's house. She said that she and Edmond was paying for the new roof. "Since we're paying for it I want the job done right. You don't shell out two thousand dollars unless you know you're getting your money's worth." She wanted to know if it was true that Sam Applewhite had resigned from being school principal at the New Jerusalem School. I told her that was true. She said, "Sam is a good man. He is going to be hard to replace." We then talked about Polly. Polly is Velma's daughter from her first marriage. She said, "This fall Polly is entering Ole Miss to study to be a pharmacist. I don't want her to have a thing in the world to do with the restaurant business. This is a hard way to make a living and I want Polly to have an easier time of it than I've had." She said I ought to know the restaurant business is tough since Ralph and I ran a barbecue cafe.

Up to this point in my conversation with Velma I'd put a big smile on my face. That's the way I've acted a lot lately—smiling on the outside while hurting on the inside. I quit smiling and said, "Velma, have you got a few moments you could spare me? I need to talk to somebody like you. That's the real reason I've come by. I can tell you're busy but I need some advice."

Velma looked at me with a puzzled expression on her face. She could tell I had something on my mind. She said, "Beulah, if you want to talk to me then I say let's talk. I've got two ears and I know how to listen."

Velma pointed to a table in the corner by a window. She said, "You see that table by the window? Let's go over there so we can be off by ourselves as much as possible." Velma then turned and called to a waitress who was a little on the chubby side. She said, "Joyce, keep an eye on the register for me. I've got to leave it for a few moments." Joyce smiled and said, "I'll take care of it."

Velma looked at me and asked, "Beulah, would you like to have some coffee while we talk?"

I said, "I sure would."

She said, "Do you take cream and sugar?"

I said, "I just take cream. No sugar."

Velma then said, "I'll drink some coffee too. I haven't had any since early this morning. You go ahead to the table and I'll be right behind you."

I walked across the dining room to the empty table by the window. I sat down and looked out the window. I could tell the sky had gotten dark. An early afternoon thunderstorm was comin' down. I could hear it thundering outside. The coffee shop was still loaded with customers and the jukebox was still playing. This time it was playing a Tammy Wynette song.

Velma went behind the counter and poured up two cups of coffee. She put them on a tray and brought them to the table where I was sitting. Velma put the cups on the table and said, "Here's a cup for you and here's a cup for me." By then the thunderstorm outside was gettin' worse. The rain started comin' down in sheets. Because of the rain I could hardly see the cars and eighteen wheelers parked outside. Velma sat down and looked out the window and said, "I love a Mississippi thunderstorm. It makes the air smell clean. And it settles the dust."

We both put cream in our coffee and stirred the cream with spoons. Velma ain't a person to fool around and waste time. She's a straight shooter. So after she'd said she loved a thunderstorm she looked at me and asked, "Beulah, what's on your mind? You said you needed to talk to me about something. What's up?"

I said, "If I tell you will you promise you won't tell nobody?"

I don't know why I didn't want Velma to tell nobody. Maybe it was because I was embarrassed over what I was about to tell her. Or maybe I was worried about what other people would think if they knew about my situation and what I was thinkin' about doin'. I've always worried about what other people think.

Velma said, "Listen, Beulah, you don't have to worry about me not being able to keep a secret or not being able to keep my mouth shut. There's not a week that goes by without somebody telling me something they don't want other people to know about. Right now one of my waitresses is as pregnant as an alley cat. She's not showing yet but she'll be showing soon. She let her boyfriend do her up and now the skinny asshole won't have anything to do with her. I'm tempted to hire somebody to cut his prick off. Two weeks ago she told me what her situation is and Edmond and I have worked it out so she'll leave next month for New Orleans to enter a home for unwed mothers run by the Catholic church. I've not mentioned her situation to anybody here at the coffee shop. And I'll never tell you or anybody else who she is. So you can trust me. Tell me anything you want to and I'll keep it to myself."

When Velma said that I took a sip of coffee and then I started talking. I talked like a tape recorder that's out of control and that's goin' full speed ahead. While I was talking and pouring my heart out Velma didn't say nothing. She just sipped on her coffee and listened to me. I got so busy talking I forgot about the cup of coffee in front of me. I told Velma the reason I wanted to talk to her is because she and me had something in common and because of that I felt she'd understand where I was comin' from. I said, "Velma, you and I both married when we were sixteen years old. Lookin' back on it I don't think we were old enough to get married. We didn't have sense enough to understand what we were doin' and what we were gettin' ourselves into. We both married Raineys. You married Chester. I married Ralph. My marriage to Ralph has gone to pot. It's like a dead corpse." I told Velma how being married to Ralph was all work and no play. Six days a week I worked like a Chinese coolie in his cafe and butcher shop. And I worked like a Chinese coolie taking care of his garden and putting up enough butter beans and okra to feed all the people in Chicago. I told her about Ralph's temper and about how he wore me out goin' Sunday after Sunday to the New Jerusalem Baptist Church.

At this point Velma interrupted and said, "So you can let your light shine on the Jesus board."

I said, "That's right. Ralph always insists I flip the switch beside my name on the 'Let Your Light Shine for Jesus' board."

Velma said, "I think that board is silly. I think it's the last word in poor taste. I don't understand why somebody doesn't slip into the church some night and take the damn thing out and tear it up or burn it. I've interrupted what you were saying. Keep on going. I'm listening with both ears."

I told her I didn't get no joy out of our love life because all Ralph done was jack off and go to sleep. I went into detail telling about me fixing supper for the preachers during the revival and how Ralph exploded over me not fryin' enough chicken for the preachers. I told her about the whipping. I showed her what was left of my blackeye. I told her about Ralph setting JR on fire and how poor old JR ran around the garden screaming because he was in so much pain.

Velma said, "If Ralph did that he's a sick man."

I said, "I think he's sick too. That's why I've almost decided to divorce him and strike out on my own. But I'm having a hard time bringing myself to do it. I'm worried about what people in New Jerusalem will think if I divorce Ralph. You know good and well the Raineys will blame me for our marriage falling apart. On top of that, I don't have no place to go. And I don't have a thin dime to my name. Ralph never paid me nothing. He always said it was my duty to work for him free since I was his wife. But I know you upped and did what I want to do. You packed up and walked out on Chester. What I want to know is: how did you find the guts to do it?"

That's the real reason I'd gone to see Velma. I wanted to know where she got her guts from. Tellin' her all I told her took almost an hour. Velma heard me out. The words rolled out of my mouth like water comin' out of a faucet. It didn't feel good while I was telling Velma everything I had to say. When I think back on it, I felt like you do when you're vomiting up rotten stuff you need to get out of your stomach. Vomiting is no fun while you're vomiting, but when it's over with you feel a lot better. You know you've gotten out of your system some stuff that needed to come out. Just tellin' my troubles to Velma made me feel better. By the way, I didn't tell her about the affair I'd had with Brother Ledbetter. I kept that to myself. What I was tryin' to do was to concentrate on Ralph.

The thunderstorm had passed over by the time I got through tellin' Velma everything. The sun came out real bright through the clouds. Up north toward Collins was the biggest and prettiest rainbow up in the sky I think I ever saw. It stretched from one side of the horizon to the other side. I couldn't help but think about the story I was told when I was a little girl that at the end of the rainbow is a bunch of fairies dressed in green costumes along with a big pot of gold.

When I was through Velma said, "Well, Beulah, you've been through the mill. Or maybe I ought to say you've been through a meatgrinder. If even half of what you've told me is true I don't see how you've held up without going nuts. But you're a Buchanan and Buchanans are known for their toughness. There's the old Jones County saying: you can get a Buchanan down but you can't keep a Buchanan down."

She went on to say something I wasn't expecting her to say. Velma said, "Frankly, Beulah, some of us have been worried about you. For a long time you've had a kind of sad or forlorn expression on your face. My mother and I have talked about it. I've discussed you with your sister Earline. By the way, Earline has really got a good reputation in Laurel as a beautician. I've been driving up every two weeks to let her do my hair. Earline has told me she's been worried about you and Ralph. You're right about us marrying too young. No woman ought to get married when she's sixteen years old. When you're sixteen you're still a little girl. You haven't lived long enough to get your bearings. When you and I were sixteen and living in New Jerusalem we were both rotting in what I call the *rural rut*. We didn't understand we were rotting in it but we were. What do I mean by rotting in the rural rut? I'll tell you. Rotting in the rural rut is doing what country girls in Mississippi were expected to do when you and I were sixteen. It was simple. You got married at age sixteen to a redneck who lived one or two miles down the road and whom you'd known all your life. Next of all you moved into a mobile home set up on his daddy's land and you started having babies like you were a rabbit. Neither your daddy nor your husband nor your father-in-law thought you were to have an education and prepare yourself to do anything in life except fuck, have babies, and cook cornbread. You became a grandmother in your thirties and at the same time you became a grandmother you became an unpaid babysitter for your grandkids. You became a great-grandmother in your late forties or fifties, your skin became as rough and wrinkled as a washboard, and the most exciting thing you ever did in life was bake a spiked fruitcake at Christmas or go to the Jones County Fair in Laurel so you could eat a candied apple. That's what I mean by rotting in the rural rut and both of us were up to our knees in it and didn't know it. So what did both of us do? We crapped in our pants by marrying a Rainey. I married Chester and you married Ralph. Say what you want to about the Raineys they aren't lazy. Chester hit the floor every morning before five o'clock to run his logging business and most days I didn't see him until after the sun had gone down. In the summer he would come in covered with perspiration from head to toe. But the Raineys are hard. All of them are as hard as a steel ball. They don't have a soft side. They don't know other people have feelings and can be hurt. Worse than that, they have hot tempers. When they get mad they explode on you like gunpowder. They're okay to be around occasionally, but they're hard to live with day after day and year after year. They get on your nerves. I took garbage off of Chester for years before I finally decided I'd had enough and that it was time for me to leave. So by god, I left. And I'm glad I left. If

I'd hung on as Chester's wife—thinking I had no choice in life but to be Mrs. Chester Rainey—I believe I'd be six feet under by now. Either the Moore or the Hulett-Winstead Funeral Home would have put me in my grave. Or else I'd be in the loony barn at Whitfield." In case you don't know, Whitfield is Mississippi's insane asylum. It's located a few miles east of Jackson. And Hattiesburg has two funeral homes. There's the Moore Funeral Home on Hardy Street and the Hulett-Winstead Funeral Home in downtown Hattiesburg on Bay Street.

Velma stopped talking for a moment. She took a package of Lifesavers out of her pocket and put one in her mouth. She asked me, "Would you like to have one?"

I said, "No thanks."

Velma started talking again.

She said, "You asked me a few moments ago how I found the guts to walk out on Chester. Do you really want to know?"

I said, "I sure do."

Velma said, "Okay Beulah, if you want to know I'll tell you. It's very simple. I found the guts to walk out on Chester when I decided one day that from then on I was going to paddle my own canoe instead of letting others paddle it for me. I decided I'd paddle my canoe where I thought it ought to go. And more important: I decided not to give a damn any longer about what others thought about me and what I did. I was going to do what I thought was best for Velma and if other people didn't like it that was just too bad. They could go hang it up. I got so low—so fed up with Chester's tart tongue and being his doormat—that I didn't care what people would say or think if I left Chester. That included Mama and Daddy. Bless their hearts, I love them to death. But they were horrified when I told them I was going to divorce Chester. I remember my daddy saying, 'Velma, Chester makes a lot of money in the logging business. You're stupid to walk out on a man who makes his kind of money.' And they were embarrassed when I came down here to Hattiesburg and moved into a house trailer with my daughter and started working here as a truck-stop waitress. But I didn't care what they thought. I didn't care what they thought even though I loved them. And I didn't care what other people thought either. Since I didn't care, I was free. As long as you care about what other people think, you're like a canary locked in a cage. But when you don't care any longer about what happens to you or about what other people think, you're free. Who gives a damn what other people think? To hell with them. It's when I developed this I-don't-care-anymore spirit that I found the guts to walk out on Chester. Believe you me, walking away wasn't easy. It made Chester livid. The very day I told him I wanted a divorce he canceled my credit cards and removed my name from our checking account. I became as poor as a field mouse and had to crawl. But I felt I knew what I was doing. I was paddling my own canoe in the direction I wanted it to go. I'm proud of myself for doing what I did. I'm a heck of a lot better off today than I was the day I divorced Chester. And can you believe this? Chester and I now speak to one another. We have a civil relationship. It's because of Polly. Chester never missed a month paying child support. Last week he came in here and drank a cup of coffee and told me he wanted to pay her tuition to go to Ole Miss. He said he thought Polly becoming a pharmacist was a great idea."

About that moment the chubby waitress who had been handling the cash register walked over to the table where Velma and I were sitting and she said, "Miss Velma, I'm givin' out of change. I need some more dimes and quarters."

Velma looked at me and said, "Give me a moment. I've got to open the safe and get out some more change. I'll be right back."

She got up and disappeared through a swinging door into the kitchen.

Ten minutes passed. Velma reappeared and walked over to the

cash stand with rolls of coins in her hands. She handed them to the chubby waitress. She then bent over and removed something out of the display case under the cash register. At the time I didn't know what it was. But whatever it was she put it in her pocket. She then walked back over to the table where I was sitting. She sat down.

She got back on the subject of me and Ralph.

Velma said, "You said a few moments ago you were afraid to leave Ralph because you didn't have any place to go and you didn't have any money or a job."

As she was saying this Velma reached into her pocket and took out what turned out to be a truckstop key ring. I'd never seen one like it before.

Velma said, "You see this key ring? I've just taken it out of the display case. Take a good look at it. This key ring is made out of Alabama iron. I have them especially made for us at a metal shop over in Bessemer. Look at this metal tab. On it are five words: 'Confederate Truck Stop—Hattiesburg, Mississippi.' We give them away as souvenirs to our regular customers. Truckers like them because they're big and strong."

Velma then looked me in the eye and said, "Beulah, I'm giving you this key ring. I want you to put it in your purse. What is a souvenir? A souvenir is a reminder. I want you to keep it as a reminder of what I'm about to say to you. If you decide to leave Ralph I want you to know you've got a job waiting for you right here in this coffee shop. I stay open around the clock. My biggest headache running this place is finding people who want to work. A lot of people don't want to work anymore. They go on welfare and let the rest of the world support them. With your food experience you have a job any time you walk through the door of this coffee shop and tell me you want to go to work. And don't worry about a place to stay. Edmond and I have a lot of rental property and we always have an apartment that's empty. You can live in one of my apartments. Us rebels and renegades from New Jerusalem have got to stand by each other."

She then stood up and kissed me on my forehead. She whispered in my ear and said "You've got what it takes. Paddle your own canoe and don't worry about what others think. You're too sweet and smart to be dumped on."

I wasn't expecting Velma to say all that she had said. I started cryin'. I couldn't help it. Velma—the person Ralph called an asshole on high heels—was the first person I'd met in a long time who was giving me a push instead of a kick. I'd talked a time or two to my folks about leaving Ralph. Daddy told me he didn't want to talk about it. The last time I mentioned to him what I was thinking about doin' he took his cigar out of his mouth, farted, and said, "If you leave Ralph, you're a damn fool."

7

BELIEVE YOU ME my middle-of-the-day visit on Sunday with Velma at the Confederate Truck Stop in Hattiesburg perked me up. I felt like a new person. I quit crying. I put my arm around Velma and hugged her as hard as I could. I said to her, "This may be the turning point of my life." I got in my car and left the truck stop and drove back home. On the way out of Hattiesburg I stopped at a drug store and bought two bottles of Tylenol. I done that because I'd left Ralph a note saying I was going off to buy some Tylenol. I was covering my tracks. I drove home and got out of the car and went to the back bedroom.

Later that evening—that was four days ago—things took a turn I wasn't expecting. For days—ever since he gave me a whipping— Ralph hadn't had anything to do with me. He didn't talk to me. All he done was pout and walk around like a zombie and give me the silent treatment. Ralph broke his pouting and his giving-me-the-silent treatment by walking back to the back bedroom where I'd been hibernating since my whipping on Wednesday night. I was listening on the radio to some country music out of Nashville. As far as music is concerned I believe Nashville music is the best music there is. The thing I like about Nashville music is they sing about life as it really is and not as it ought to be. Nashville music is different from gospel music. Gospel music sings about life as it ought to be. Nashville music sings about life as it is.

Ralph walked in the bedroom where I was and asked, "Do you think you can come to work tomorrow? I'm gonna be short of help."

I asked, "Who ain't gonna be there?"

Ralph said, "Eb ain't. He's got to go to a nigger funeral in Lumberton. His sister died."

"Eb" is short for "Ebenezer." Eb don't work in the cafe. He works in the butcher shop. He's our colored butcher. I've heard Ralph say, "If I didn't have Eb, I'd close my butcher shop down. He's the best butcher in Jones County." Eb learned how to butcher when he was in the army. He was stationed for ten years at Fort Knox in Kentucky where he worked in the food commissary and learned all about meat and how to cut it.

My black eye didn't look too bad no more. So I said, "I guess I can go back tomorrow."

Ralph said, "I'll need you more in the butcher shop than in the cafe."

That was okay with me. I knew more about the cafe than the butcher shop. But I knew enough about the butcher shop to make do.

Ralph said, "The Sanderson Farms truck is comin' early in the morning to deliver some chickens. So I'm gonna leave the house earlier than I usually do. Can you be at the store by eight o'clock?" Sanderson Farms is the chicken processor we buy our chickens from. They bring 'em to us iced down in cardboard boxes.

I said, "Yeah, I'll be there."

With that Ralph turned and walked out of the bedroom. He didn't ask me how I was feeling. He didn't say he was sorry about what happened Wednesday night when I fed the preachers. He didn't say nothing about JR. He just turned and walked away. Ralph can be an iceberg on legs when he wants to be.

After Ralph walked out of the room I turned off the radio and got out of bed. I went to the kitchen and fixed me a sandwich to eat. I fixed me a bacon and tomato sandwich. That's my favorite kind of sandwich. There ain't nothing better than a bacon and tomato sandwich when it's fixed right. And by fixed right I mean when it's made with tomatoes fresh off the vine, lots of bacon, and light bread with mayonnaise. You need the tomatoes cold and the bacon crisp. The crisper it is, the better. I poured me up a Coke to go along with my sandwich.

I sat down at the kitchen table and ate my sandwich and drank a Coke. I was by myself. I heard Ralph get in his pickup and drive off. Since it was Sunday evening my guess was he was goin' to church to hear Brother Ledbetter rant and rave about the book of Revelations—explaining all of them seals and trumpets.

After eating my sandwich I washed off my plate and tidied up the kitchen. I then went out on the back porch and sat down in the porch swing. I started swinging. I didn't swing big. I took little swings. From the swing I could see JR's grave out in the pasture. It looked so lonely and out of place. JR's grave put a lump in my throat. While I was swinging I thought real hard about all the things Velma had said to me earlier in the day at the Confederate Truck Stop. I thought about her finding the guts to leave Chester the moment she stopped caring about what people thought about her and what she did. As long as you worry about what other people think and let them live your life for you you're like a canary in a cage. You're not free to fly on your own. I thought about her deciding to paddle her own canoe. All of a sudden I stopped swinging. I got out of the swing and I stood up. I stood up as tall as I could. I put my hands on my hips and I took a deep breath. Right then and there I reached a decision. As they say here in Jones County, I decided to let the shit hit the fan. *I decided to become another Velma*: somebody who'd grown up and paddled her own canoe and who didn't worry about what other people thought. That was a big mistake I'd always made. In the past, I'd worried about what other people might think. What would members of the New Jerusalem Baptist Church think if I dumped Ralph? What would the ladies in the peanut-brittle club think? What would our cafe customers think? What would Ralph's folks think?

I decided not to worry about those questions no more. They were all water under the bridge. I decided that from that moment on I was gonna do what was best for Beulah and screw the consequences. Becoming another Velma meant I'd get off my ass and push through my divorce from Ralph. I wasn't gonna hang on to him no more. Some women will do anything to hang on to a husband. It don't matter how mean their husbands are, they'll hang on to 'em like a hat hanging on a nail.

That's what Luella has done. Luella is my sister-in-law. She's married to Ralph's brother named Harold. Harold's nickname is "Lucky." Everybody calls him "Lucky" because one time he won ten thousand dollars in the Louisiana lottery. Over the years Lucky has been as mean to Luella as Ralph has been to me. Luella and Lucky have twin daughters named Susie and Patricia. Luella and Lucky got into a big squabble years ago when Susie and Patricia was six months old. They got into an argument because Luella found out Lucky was runnin' around on her. Lucky got as hot as a hornet. He told Luella he was leaving her and the babies for good. Lucky said, "I'm tired of you tryin' to put a harness on me." He started loading his stuff into his truck. Luella started cryin'. She started beggin', "Lucky, please don't leave us." Lucky said, "I've made up my mind. I'm goin' and I ain't comin' back."

So what did Luella do? She took her twin babies out to Lucky's truck and put Susie in front of the right front tire and she put Patricia in front of the left front tire. Luella then lay down in front of the truck herself. She screamed, "Lucky, when you leave drive over all

three of us. With you gone I'd rather me and the babies be dead."
Her sayin' that caused Lucky to change his mind. So he didn't leave.
But he still treats Luella like she's a dog. And she takes it and hangs
on to Lucky like he was Prince Charming. She tells me she does it for
Susie and Patricia. That's what a lot of wives do. They take crap off
their husbands and then say they're doin' it for their kids.

If that's what Luella wants to do, that's her business. But as far as
I'm concerned, to stay in a marriage that's dead is like keeping a
corpse around the house after the person has died. Getting rid of the
corpse would make things better. A divorce ain't nothing but gettin'
rid of the corpse of a dead marriage. The next question I had to face
was: when was I gonna tell Ralph it was all over between him and me?
I decided not to put it off. I was hot to trot. Putting off telling Ralph
I was leaving him wouldn't do no good. I decided to tell him the very
next day. Which was Monday—three days ago. I'd go to work on
Monday like he wanted me to—pinch-hitting for Eb who was goin'
to a nigger funeral. And then sometime during the day I'd tell Ralph
I was leaving him. I figured it would be better to tell him at the store
than to tell him at the house.

Since I had finally once-and-for-all made up my mind to leave
Ralph, I decided to pack up some of my stuff to take with me. So I
left the back porch and went to my bedroom. I took some of my
clothes out of my closet. I carried 'em outside and put 'em in the
trunk of my car. I call it my car because I drive it. But it don't belong
to me. It really belongs to Ralph. As does everything else we have.
I've heard him brag over and over about everything he owns being in
his name and in his name only. Clothes wasn't the only thing I put
in the car trunk. I got me a cardboard box and put all my medicine,
a hand mirror, and four pairs of shoes in it. I put this box in the trunk
along with my winter coat, an umbrella, and a raincoat. I didn't have
no cosmetics to pack. Women like me who belong to the New
Jerusalem Baptist Church don't use no cosmetics. One of the things

I was looking forward to after leaving Ralph was using cosmetics. I
don't see nothing wrong with a woman using powder and lipstick. I
knew that if I ever started using powder and lipstick I'd get voted out
of the New Jerusalem Church. But that didn't matter. They'd vote
me out for leaving Ralph. I figured I could find me another Baptist
church to join. Or maybe I'd just stop goin' to church. That's what
Velma has done. She don't go to church no more. She don't seem to
be no worse off for it. I heard her say one time she didn't want no
suspenders-snapping Baptist preacher tellin' her what to do no
more.

Before I went to sleep I opened my purse and took out the key
ring Velma had give me. I read the tab: "Confederate Truck Stop—
Hattiesburg, Mississippi." I held the key ring up to the light. When
I did that it shined like a new silver dollar. Just holding the key ring
in my hand gave me strength. It was like a lifeline you throw to a
person who's drowning in water over his head. It gave me something
to hold on to. And that was knowing Velma had a job waiting for me
anytime I wanted it. I'd learned a lot about the food business while
working at Ralph's barbecue cafe. I went to sleep thinkin' about how
hard I was gonna work for Velma at the Confederate Truck Stop. I
was gonna be the best help she'd ever hired. I'd work circles around
everybody else. That's what I've always done. And I'd keep on doing
it. When I stop and think about it, work is all I've ever known.

8

WHEN I WOKE UP day before yesterday, Ralph had already left the house for work. I knew he'd left early so he could go meet the Sanderson Farms chicken truck. He'd told me the night before he wanted me to be at the store by eight o'clock to hold down the butcher shop and take care of early customers. So I got out of bed, got dressed, and fixed me some breakfast. For breakfast I ate me a bowl of Kellogg's corn flakes and two pieces of whole wheat toast. I drank two cups of coffee. By half past seven I was in the car and on my way to Laurel. Nobody but me knew I had the car's trunk packed full with my best clothes and shoes and odds and ends. And nobody but me knew that before the day was over I was gonna tell Ralph I was leaving him for keeps. Knowing I was about to be free from Ralph made me feel giddy. While I was driving to Laurel I changed my mind about how and when I was gonna tell him I was divorcin' him. I'd thought earlier I'd tell Ralph at the store. But I changed my mind. I decided the best way to tell him it was all over between me and him would be over the telephone. I figured that some time during the day I'd leave the store and call Ralph from a pay telephone. Over the phone I'd tell him it was all over between him and me. If he got mad, at least I wouldn't be where he was. And he wouldn't know where I was. Maybe after callin'

Ralph I'd go to Earline's house in Laurel or maybe I'd go to the Blue Gables Motel and rent a room and hide out. The Blue Gables is a motel north of town on the highway toward Meridian. Or maybe I'd go on down to Hattiesburg to the Confederate Truck Stop. It made me feel good knowin' I wasn't gonna spend another night under the same roof with Ralph Jefferson Davis Rainey. He could smoke his Swisher Sweet cigars and pick his gold tooth all by himself for the rest of his life.

Another thing that made me feel good was thinking about how I didn't care no more what other people thought. That was like a ten-ton load lifted off my shoulders. So what if Ralph got mad? So what if my mama and daddy didn't think I ought to leave Ralph? So what if the members of the New Jerusalem Baptist Church and the peanut brittle society gossiped about me walking out on Ralph and goin' to work at the Confederate Truck Stop? I didn't care what none of 'em thought no more. They could all kiss my foot. I bet last Monday morning I said "I don't care no more" to myself at least a hundred times while I was driving from New Jerusalem up to Laurel.

When I got to the store the colored help welcomed me like I was the Queen of England. Or like I was the Queen of Sheba. I hadn't been at the store for four days. So they said things like, "Miss Beulah, we have sure been missing you." "Mr. Ralph says you've been under the weather." From what the help said I could tell Ralph had told 'em I'd been sick. Which was true. What he didn't tell 'em was I'd been sore from head to toe because he'd beat the shit out of me. Or as he put it, chastised me in the name of the Lord for not cookin' enough chicken for a bunch of pot-bellied preachers.

Ralph was busy puttin' chickens on the grill and brushin' them with barbecue sauce. He told the help, "Since Eb ain't here today, Beulah's gonna work mainly over in the butcher shop." He looked at me and said, "Eb packaged a lot of meat before he left last night. I don't think there'll be much cuttin' for you to do."

I could tell Ralph was being nice to me in front of the help. Ain't it odd or weird that a husband will be nice to his wife in public and then treat her like a stray dog when they're by themselves? But to be honest with you, I felt above it all. I felt like a canary let out of a cage. Ralph didn't know about my conversation with Velma. He didn't know about the Confederate Truck Stop key ring I had in my pocket. And he didn't know that before the day was over Beulah was gonna tell him to go fly a kite. And kiss her fanny.

Monday—most of the time—is the slowest day in the week. I've heard Ralph say that if it wasn't for his regular customers, he'd stay closed on Mondays. About all you do is make payroll and expenses. But this last Monday was different. Believe it or not we done a land-office business. Business was heavy because of some kind of labor meeting or vote they was having all day at the Masonite plant. The barbecue business was so heavy I ended up working more in the cafe than in the butcher shop. That's what you call the squeaking wheel getting the grease. I'd planned to leave in the afternoon around two or three o'clock and go to a pay phone and call Ralph and tell him what I'd decided to do. But business was so hot and heavy all afternoon and there was so much to do—making barbecue sand-wiches and more potato salad and baked beans—I felt it wouldn't be right to leave. I suppose you think it was silly for me to feel that way since it was the day I was walking out on Ralph. But that was the way I felt. I hung in there all day for the colored help, not for Ralph. They was all workin' their tails off. So all day Monday I shifted back and forth between the barbecue cafe and the butcher shop. I stayed—can you believe it—to closing time and by then I was dog tired. I was so tired I was ready to drop.

After closing down the store, Ralph looked over the display case in the butcher shop and he said, "Before I go home, I'd better package up some meat. If I don't, Eb is gonna be in a bind when he opens tomorrow." What Ralph was saying made sense. He's got some early customers who turn up every morning ready to buy meat. Ralph went on to say, "When I get through packaging some meat there's something I want to talk to you about." Him saying that surprised me and got my curiosity up. Ralph usually don't talk to me about nothing.

If I'd had any sense, I'd of said, "Ralph, I think I'll be on my way. I'll see you at the house." I admit that would have been a barefaced lie. I never intended to go back to Ralph's house again. Instead, I was gonna go to a pay phone and call him on the phone and tell him what I'd decided to do. I'd decided early that morning which pay phone I was gonna call Ralph from. I was gonna use the pay phone in front of Andy's Texaco Station. It's in a phone booth right next to the street. Nobody could have heard what I said.

But I didn't do that. Instead, I stayed at the store. I didn't leave because Ralph had said he had something he wanted to talk to me about as soon as he finished packaging the meat. I thought maybe he wanted to apologize to me for him acting like a horse's ass. So I let my curiosity get the best of me. Which I shouldn't have done. I should have remembered the old saying about curiosity killing the cat.

Ralph always bought his red meat from the Superior Meatpacking Company in Meridian. They run a truck through Laurel three days a week—on Monday, Wednesday and Friday. They package ground round and ground sirloin and hamburger meat in plastic tubes. Them tubes look like big hot dogs. They're long and round and shaped like a toy blimp. They come frozen—each one of 'em weighing ten to twenty pounds. All Ralph or Eb has to do to make individual packages of ground beef for customers is dip the meat out of the tube, put it on a plastic tray, and wrap it in PVC film.

Since I was as tired as a dog I sat down in a chair. I opened me a Barq's root beer and started sipping away on it. I watched while Ralph stepped inside the walk-in freezer and took out two tubes of frozen hamburger meat. I want you to listen carefully to what I'm about to tell you. I know I'm tellin' you the truth when I say Ralph took out of the freezer two plastic tubes of hamburger meat. It wasn't ground sirloin he took out. It wasn't ground round he took out. It was hamburger meat he took out. And I say H-A-M-B-U-R-G-E-R and that spells "hamburger." That don't spell "sirloin." And it don't spell "ground round."

He put one of the tubes in the sink and ran hot water over it. He did that so the meat would thaw. After the meat had thawed, he started dipping it out of the plastic tube and putting it on five-by-six-inch trays. After he'd put hamburger meat on one of the plastic trays, he'd wrap it in PVC film and weigh it. Then he'd put a sticker on the package showin' how much it weighted and what the price was. I've seen Eb do this a thousand times. So I didn't pay no real attention to Ralph when he was doin' it. Me goin' out of my way to pay close attention to Ralph packaging meat would be like a carpenter goin' out of his way to watch a hammer drive a nail into a piece of wood. He just wouldn't do it.

After he'd made up several packages, Ralph said, "Beulah, I'm goin' back to the john and take a leak. How about puttin' these packages in the display case." Which I was glad to do. I walked over to the work table where Ralph had stacked up the packages of hamburger meat. There were ten or twelve of 'em—all of 'em weighed, priced, and wrapped in PVC film. It was then and there I made a mistake. I say it was a mistake. Maybe it wasn't a mistake. Maybe it was just one of those things that boomerangs on you in a way you couldn't expect. I picked up one of the hamburger packages and I put it on the scales. Why I done that I don't know. The sticker Ralph had put on the package read it weighed one pound and eight ounces. I looked at the scales and they didn't read one pound and eight ounces. The scales read one pound even. I took another look at the package. Ralph had stuck on it a red, white, and blue label that read "Ground Sirloin." I could look at the meat and tell it wasn't no ground sirloin. The meat had too much fat in it to be sirloin. It was plain, as-obvious-as-the-nose-on-your-face hamburger meat with a lot of fat in it. Just to be certain I was right I went to the trash can and took out the plastic tube I knew the meat had come out of. The tube had "Hamburger Meat" printed on it in big blue letters.

I picked up another package and put it on the scales. The scales read one pound and two ounces. But the sticker Ralph had put on it read one pound and nine ounces. Again the package wasn't nothing but fat-loaded hamburger meat. Yet Ralph had put on it a red, white, and blue label that—you guessed it—read "Ground Sirloin."

One by one I put every one of Ralph's packages of meat on the scales. All of 'em were over-weighed and over-priced. All of 'em had stickers reading "Ground Sirloin" when they was nothing but plain, old hamburger meat. Hamburger meat, in case you don't know, ain't nothing but ground up scraps. It's the cheapest ground meat there is. It don't cost nearly as much as ground sirloin.

When Ralph come back from taking a leak—like a fool—I piped up and said, "Ralph, there's something screwed up here. I put each and every one of these here packages on the scales. I put 'em on one at a time. And you know what? They're all over-weighed. And on top of that, they ain't got ground sirloin in 'em. They've got hamburger meat. They're all labeled wrong."

I could tell right off Ralph didn't like what I had said to him. I wasn't tryin' to make waves or give him a hard time. I was just tellin' him what I'd found out. But I could sense Ralph was gettin' upset in a hurry. When he gets upset, like I've told you, his face turns fire-engine red. Which is what his face was doin'.

Sometimes when Ralph takes a leak he forgets to zip up his pants. I noticed his pants were unzipped. So I said, "Ralph, you better zip your pants up."

While he was zipping up his pants he said, "Beulah, I didn't tell you to weigh the packages. I told you to put 'em in the display case.

Why in the hell didn't you do what I told you to do?"

I said, "I was just passin' time while you took a leak. On the spur of the moment I weighed a package and it was wrong. So I weighed another one, and lo and behold it was weighed wrong too. I weighed another one and another one. And—there ain't no doubt about it—they're all overweighed. You put your thumb on the scales."

By this time Ralph was getting really steamed. Of course it don't take him a long time to get steamed. Ralph can get steamed up in the snap of a finger. Or in the blink of an eye. By the way he was acting so huffy I could tell I'd caught him trying to screw our customers. I'd caught him red-handed puttin' his thumb on the scales when he done his weighing. And I'd caught him passing off hamburger meat as ground sirloin. I'd caught Deacon Ralph Rainey being as dishonest as a one-legged Jew in a Saturday-night crap game. I hadn't intended to catch him. Me catching him was strictly an accident.

All of a sudden Ralph blew up on me. He exploded like he was a volcano. He yelled, "Damn it, Beulah, are you accusing me of being dishonest? If you are I'm gonna whip your little tail off!"

I stepped over to the garbage can and pulled out the plastic tube that had "Hamburger Meat" printed on it. I held it up and in a quiet voice I said, "This here is the tube you dipped the meat out of. It don't have 'Ground Sirloin' printed on it. What does it say? It says 'Hamburger Meat.' Ain't that right?"

Usually when Ralph flew off the handle I got scared—like I done the night he got mad about the preachers and the fried chicken. But day before yesterday I didn't get scared. The reason I didn't get scared of Ralph was because I'd made up my mind to leave him. So I didn't care no more what he thought or said. Which is why I was thinking to myself, "Play it cool, Beulah. Remember—you don't have to take his crap no more."

Ralph screamed at me. He said, "It ain't a wife's place to question what her husband does. She's supposed to be submissive. That's what the Bible says. And you ain't being submissive when you accuse me of puttin' my thumb on the scales."

I come right back at him. I said, "What about them sirloin stickers? You can eyeball that meat and tell it ain't no sirloin. It's got too much fat in it."

He said, "If I say it's sirloin, it's sirloin! It's that simple. And besides, our nigger customers don't know the difference between ground sirloin and a hole in the ground."

I said, "Niggers or not, it ain't right to pass off greasy hamburger meat as sirloin when it ain't. And it ain't right for Ralph Rainey—a big time deacon in the New Jerusalem Baptist Church—to put his thumb on the scales when he's weighing meat!"

I tell you right now—when I said that—I thought Ralph was gonna go through the ceiling. He picked up a meat mallet, drew his arm back, and threw the mallet across the store. It hit the Coca-Cola clock that was hanging on the wall and busted it into a hundred pieces. The pieces from the Coca-Cola clock went everywhere.

The next thing Ralph done—which I thought was crazy—was to turn over the wrapping table. By the wrapping table I mean the metal table we use to wrap packages of meat on. Ralph—mad as a wet rooster—flipped it completely over on its side. It hit the floor with a loud bang. So did the scales that were sitting on the wrapping table. The rolls of paper and PVC film that were sitting on the table went bouncing across the floor. After the table hit the floor, he said, "By god, I don't appreciate people accusing me of not being honest!"

While Ralph was doing all this I stayed as calm as a cucumber in a pickle jar. I kept saying over and over to myself, "Remember, you've decided to leave him. He can't hurt you no more."

I decided I didn't want Ralph to think I was being cowed. On the spur of the moment I decided to tell him then and there what I was gonna do. I wasn't gonna let Ralph Rainey bluff me no longer. So I said to him, "Ralph, I don't want to be your wife no more. I want a divorce." In other words, I upped and spilled the beans. I know me saying I wanted a divorce was farting in Ralph's face. But I didn't care.

This startled look come over Ralph's face. In a snide, sarcastic voice he said, "Oh, you want a divorce! How about that! Beulah Rainey wants a divorce. I'll be damn!"

I said, "That's what I want. It's all over between you and me. Our marriage is dead. It's been dead for years."

Ralph mimicked me. He said, "Oh dear. Oh dear. Now ain't that nice. It's all over between you and me. Our marriage is dead."

I said, "That's right."

He said, "And just where do you plan to go? And what do you plan to do? I suppose you're gonna move in and live with the Pettigrews." Everybody in Jones County knows who you're talking about when you mention the Pettigrews. They're the richest family in Laurel. Frank Pettigrew is president of the Main Street National Bank and owns half the town. He lives in this big house on Seventh Avenue. Mr. Pettigrew comes by the barbecue cafe once a month and always buys three barbecue chickens to go. And a quart of barbecue beans.

I was still keepin' my cool. The fact is, I was kinda enjoying watching Ralph get mad and act the way he was acting. I could enjoy it because I didn't care no more. I was like a bird let out of a cage— flying around and enjoying myself. Maybe if me and Ralph had a bunch of kids I wouldn't have felt the way I was feeling. But we didn't have no kids. When you don't have no kids you've got more maneuvering room than you do when you've got a bunch of mouths to feed. Cause I felt like a flying bird and didn't give a damn no more, I said something I knew was gonna piss Ralph off. I said, "Sunday I drove down to the Confederate Truck Stop and had a long talk with Velma. She told me if I divorce you I can have a job working for her anytime I want it. And she'll give me a place to live too."

I reached in my pocket and pulled out the Confederate Truck Stop key ring Velma had give me. I held it up for Ralph to see. I made sure he saw the metal tab that showed it'd come from the Confederate Truck Stop.

I said, "You see this? This here is proof I've been down to Hattiesburg to see Velma. If you don't believe I talked to her and that she promised me a job, go call her. She'll tell you I'm telling the truth."

Ralph tried to cut me down. He said, "So you think you can go to work for that asshole on high heels?"

That wasn't the first time I'd heard Ralph call Velma an asshole on high heels. I'd heard him call her that a lots of times since she divorced his cousin. But I didn't like Ralph callin' Velma an asshole on high heels. She'd gone out of her way to be nice to me when I'd talked to her. I took the key ring and started twirling it on my finger. I twirled it like it was an airplane propeller. I twirled it right in Ralph's face and I said, "I'd rather work for Velma who you call an asshole on high heels than to kiss your butt anymore."

I knew saying that was gonna be like sticking a pin in Ralph. But I didn't care. He screamed, "Ain't nobody gonna talk to me like that. If you want to talk about butts, we'll talk about butts. We'll talk about *your* butt. By god I gave your little butt a good whipping last week and I sure as hell can do it again. Just let me put this meat that I ain't used back in the freezer where it belongs, young lady, and you're gonna get it. I'm gonna chastise you again in the name of the Lord!"

I knew what that meant and I wasn't about to let that happen again. No way! My body juices got to racing. And percolating like crazy.

Ralph picked up the second tube of hamburger meat he'd taken out of the walkin freezer and hadn't used. He headed toward the freezer to put it back in before whipping my ass again. At the same time he was taking off his belt. He was taking it off just like he done when he gave me the fried chicken whipping.

When Ralph stepped inside the walkin freezer I went on the attack. Believe you me, I hit the warpath. Everything happened so quick I didn't have no time to think. Or to plan. I just did what I done next. I looked inside the walk-in freezer and I seen Ralph was down on his knees. He was kneeling and bending over while puttin' the tube of hamburger meat back on the bottom shelf. I saw his rear end was stickin' up high. It was stickin' up real high like a rooster's tail. I stepped inside the freezer and shoved his rear end with both hands as hard as I could. My shove caused Ralph to topple flat on his stomach. He hit the floor as flat as a pancake. He done that because the floor where he was kneeling was slippery with ice.

He yelled, "Beulah, what in the hell are you doing?"

I yelled back, "I'm shoving your big ass as hard as I can."

I stepped back outside the walk-in freezer as quick as I could and slammed the door shut on Ralph. Quick as lightning I locked the freezer door. You can open the freezer door from the inside if it ain't locked. But if it's locked, you can't. I knew right off I had Ralph locked inside the walkin freezer and I knew right off he couldn't get out unless I unlocked the door which I wasn't about to do. He was like a rat caught in a rat trap. The light switch that turns the light on and off inside the freezer is right beside the lock. Just for the hell of it, I turned the freezer ceiling light off. I had Ralph right where I wanted him. I had him locked inside the freezer where it's colder than the North Pole and where it's darker than midnight when the ceiling light's turned off.

Ralph started yelling. He yelled, "Beulah, you open this goddamn door!"

I yelled back, "I can't hear you!"

He yelled, "I said open this goddamn door!"

I yelled, "I still can't hear you. What did you say?"

Ralph answered, "You can hear me, Beulah. You open this goddamn door and you open it right now. If you don't you're gonna be in trouble!"

I yelled, "It seems to me like you're the one in trouble!"

Ralph may have been a deacon in the New Jerusalem Baptist Church, but he was goddamning all over the place. Which is why— just for the hell of it—I yelled, "Ralph, you're a deacon. You shouldn't say 'goddamn.' That's using the Lord's name in vain."

He come back at me, "Screw you, Beulah! Open this door!"

We yelled back and forth at each other for at least fifteen minutes. I wasn't about to unlock the door. As mad as Ralph was, he'd of killed me if I'd let him out. I knew he was cold as ice and was in the dark. But that was his problem. It wasn't my problem.

Ralph stopped yelling and started beating on the door with his fists. He banged against the door with his body. He did that again and again. But as thick as the freezer door is and as strong as the lock was, there wasn't no way Ralph could knock the door down and get out. He'd had a real strong bolt and lock put on the freezer door so if somebody tried to rob the store at night, they wouldn't be able to get in the freezer where all the meat was. I've heard Ralph say, "Somebody would have to have a sledge hammer and a blow torch to break in my freezer."

Me locking Ralph in the walk-in freezer happened past closing time. The butcher shop was closed. So was the cafe. The neon sign was turned off, and I'd already closed the window blinds. Nobody was around but me and Ralph. And Annabelle. Annabelle is a cat. She turned up at the store three years ago and the help started feeding her. When she turned up she wasn't nothing but skin and bones. She's now as fat as a prize pig at the county fair. Ralph lets Annabelle stay in the store cause she's murder when it comes to mice. We used to have trouble with mice gettin' in the store. Since Annabelle came nobody has seen a mouse. Annabelle takes care of 'em.

I walked out of the butcher shop and sat down at one of the tables in the cafe. Annabelle come over to where I was and climbed up in my lap. I gave Annabelle a big hug and a kiss. She started purring. Somehow hearing Annabelle purr helped me to calm down. Ralph and me arguing and yelling and me locking him up in the freezer had got me uptight. The main thing I seen before I slammed the freezer door on Ralph was his rear end. He was bent over putting the hamburger meat on the bottom shelf. I'll always remember the way Ralph's fanny was sticking up real high right before I gave him a hard shove.

What I needed to do was to figure out what to do next. It dawned on me Ralph hadn't taken the money out of the cash registers. After he closes the store he always figures up the day's receipts and puts 'em in a bank bag. I decided to take the money out of both cash registers and put it in a bank bag.

Which I done. I could tell I had over three thousand dollars. We had really done the business. I could still hear Ralph yelling and cursing inside the freezer. But I let what he was yelling go in one ear and out the other. I figured spending a night in the freezer would teach Ralph a good lesson.

I picked up Annabelle and gave her another big kiss. I whispered in her ear, "You're a sweet cat." I put Annabelle back down on the floor and picked up my purse and the bank bag with the day's money in it. The bank bag felt like it weighed a ton. I started to step outside and lock the door. But at the last moment I walked back over to the walk-in freezer where Ralph was. He was still bashing against the freezer door. I got real close to the door and yelled, "Hello, Deacon Rainey, how're you doin' in there?"

Ralph yelled back, "Beulah, if you don't open this door I'm gonna kill you."

I said, "You are?"

He said, "You're damn right I am."

A moment or two passed by and Ralph screamed, "Beulah, you open this goddamn door!"

I was gettin' a bang out of listening to Ralph yell and scream. I yelled, "Ralph, there you go usin' the Lord's name in vain again. I'm gonna tell Brother Ledbetter about you usin' the Lord's name in vain. He won't like that. I bet next Sunday he ain't gonna let you flip your light on the 'Let Your Light Shine for Jesus' board."

Ralph yelled, "Kiss my ass Beulah and open the door."

I answered, "You kiss my ass. Goodnight Ralph, I hope you get a good night's sleep."

The last thing I heard Ralph scream was, "Screw you, Beulah!"

I called back, "Screw you, Ralph."

Before I left I made sure all the lights were turned off. I made sure all the grills and stoves and fryers were turned off too. I made sure Annabelle's water bowl was filled with fresh water. I stepped outside and made sure the cafe door and the meat market door was locked. I unlocked the car trunk and hid the money bag under my clothes. Then I got in my car. I sat there for a few moments and thought: where am I goin' to go? I thought about goin' to Earline's. But it was Monday night and I knew that was one of the nights she worked late at the beauty shop. I thought about checkin' in at the Blue Gables Motel. But I finally decided to go back to Ralph's house in New Jerusalem. I figured I'd be safe there. There wasn't no way under the shinin' sun that Ralph was gonna get out of the freezer. Somebody would have to unlock the door and that wasn't gonna happen because I had the key with me.

As I was driving away from the store it dawned on me I was hungry. I'd worked hard all day and I was hungry as a horse. So I went by the Jitney Jungle Grocery and bought me some cheddar cheese, some Crown-Prince sardines, and some Nabisco crackers. I went home and ate cheese, sardines, and crackers for my supper. I then went to bed. You ain't gonna believe this but I slept like a log.

I got the best night's sleep I'd had in a long time. Maybe the reason I slept so good is because I took two sleeping pills before I lay down. I don't ordinarily take no sleeping pills. But I figured after what I'd been through I needed something to help me sleep. Them sleeping pills knocked me out and I slept like a baby floating on a cloud.

9

TUESDAY MORNING the phone started ringing like crazy and it woke me up. I looked at the clock and it was almost eight o'clock. I couldn't believe I'd slept that late. I picked up the receiver and said, "Hello." It was Ebenezer the nigger butcher. Ebenezer said, "Miss Beulah, this here is Ebenezer. Do you knows where Mr. Ralph is?"

I waffled and said, "Eb, I'm not sure. I'm guessing he's at the store."

Eb said, "Me and the rest of the help has been at the store ready to go to work since seven-thirty. But there ain't no sign of Mr. Ralph. His pickup truck is here but he ain't. The doors is locked. So there ain't no way we can get in to start things up. What do you suppose we ought to do?"

I asked, "Where're you calling from?"

Eb said, "I'm calling from Casey's Hardware. Mr. Casey is letting me use his phone."

I knew what Eb was talking about. Casey's Hardware is right next door to Ralph's store. Eb was asking me if I knew where Ralph was. I knew damn good and well where he was. He was locked in the freezer along with slabs of meat and frozen french fries.

I knew I had to face the music sooner or later. Which is why I said, "Eb, you and the help wait there at the store. I'll be there as quick as I can."

Eb said, "Thank you, Miss Beulah."

When I want to or need to I can dress in a hurry. I put my clothes on in a snap of my finger. I didn't know what was gonna happen when I let Ralph out of the freezer. I knew he'd be mad. I knew I'd better be able to protect myself. That's why I took Ralph's pistol and put it in my purse. Ralph's always kept a pistol around the house. He kept it hung on a nail inside the back bedroom closet. He said that sooner or later—given what the world was comin' to—somebody was gonna try to break in the house and when they did he intended to be ready to meet 'em head on. Ralph's pistol is a snubnosed revolver. He had taught me how to shoot it. One Saturday afternoon he took me down to the Okatoma River and made me shoot it over and over until he was sure I knew what I was doin'.

I got in the car and took out for Laurel as fast as I could. While heading up the highway I said to myself over and over, "My name is Beulah Rainey and I don't care no more what people think. My name is Beulah Rainey and I'm gonna soon be free." Saying stuff like this to myself time and again made me not be afraid of what Ralph might say and do when he come out of the freezer. Since he'd spent the night in the freezer I figured he wouldn't be too frisky. Particularly since I figured he'd wore himself out banging time and time again against the door. And yelling about how he wanted out. I bet getting locked in the freezer is the only time in Ralph's life he wasn't callin' the shots. That's the kind of fellow he is. He likes to ride in the saddle and call the shots.

In my mind I decided what I'd do when I got to the store. I'd let Ralph out of the freezer. And I'd say to him, "Goodbye, Ralph, it was nice to know you. But I hope I never see you again as long as I live." I'd then walk out and drive away. I'd drive away as free as a bird let out of a cage. Not giving a damn no more.

When I got to the store Ebenezer and the rest of the help—Jesse, Rosie, Melinda, and Pearl—was standing outside. As I got out of the car, Ebenezer said, "Mr. Ralph still ain't showed up. His truck is parked on the side like it always is. But there ain't no sign of him."

I said, "Is that right? Something must have happened."

I had keys to both the cafe and the butcher shop. I had them on my old key ring. I'd decided they'd never be put on my Confederate Truck Stop key ring. No way was I gonna let that happen. I opened the café's front door. We all went inside—me, Ebenezer, and the rest of the help. After we'd gotten inside the cafe and turned on the lights, me and Ebenezer headed for the butcher shop. I expected to hear Ralph yelling. But he wasn't making a peep.

Eb looked around and said, "Miss Beulah, something ain't right. Just look here. The wrapping table is turned over. Everything that was on it is scattered on the floor."

I pretended to be surprised. I said, "Oh my goodness."

Eb then said, "And look at the Coca-Cola clock. It's been busted. The first thing I do when I come to work in the morning is look at the clock and figure out how long it is to opening time. Just look on the floor. That clock is busted into a thousand pieces."

I acted like I was puzzled. I didn't say, "Ralph hit it yesterday with the meat mallet." Instead, I said, "What do you suppose has happened?"

Eb said, "I don't know."

Lying like a sailor, I said, "Me neither."

Eb asked, "Do you suppose the store has been robbed?"

I said, "Maybe it has been."

Eb went to the door leading into the cafe and yelled, "Jesse, you folks come over here quick and take a look at what me and Miss Beulah has just found."

The cafe help—Jesse, Rosie, Melinda, and Pearl—came running into the butcher shop. Eb showed them the overturned table and the broken Coca-Cola clock. They said, "Something sho is funny." "We smell a rat."

By this time I was beginning to wonder about Ralph. He still wasn't making a sound. I knew the sooner I let Ralph out of the freezer the sooner I could be on my way. I was expectin' Ralph to come out like an angry cat. Or like a mad dog. So I handed the freezer key to Eb and I said, "Go ahead and unlock the freezer. We can tell if we was robbed if some meat is missing."

As soon as I handed the key to Eb I took a few steps back. I got ready for all hell to break loose. Which is why I had my hand inside my purse. I was lookin' for Ralph to come out cold and mad. I was gettin' ready to catch holy hell from him. If Ralph come at me too mad I'd make him back off with my pistol. Say what you want to, Beulah McRainey knows how to handle a Smith & Wesson revolver when she has to.

Ebenezer unlocked the freezer door. He turned on the freezer ceiling light. As soon as he turned on the ceiling light, he yelled, "Oh my god! Help me Jesus! Oh help me Jesus!"

Rosie asked, "What's wrong?"

Ebenezer said, "Mr. Ralph is in here laying on the floor!"

I asked, "He's what?"

Ebenezer yelled, "Miss Beulah, something bad has happened to Mr. Ralph. He's on the floor face up! I believe he's out! Maybe he's dead!"

I looked in the freezer. Ebenezer was right. Ralph was stretched out on the freezer floor on his back. He wasn't moving. He was as still as a piece of lead. Or a piece of wood.

The help went haywire. They started crying. They yelled, "Help us, Jesus!" "God have mercy!" "Oh Lord, come down and save us!"

Rosie, one of the cooks, asked, "Miss Beulah, do you wants me to call an ambulance?"

I said, "You'd better. Dial 911."

Rosie dialed 911 on the phone by the cash stand. I heard her say, "My name's Rosie. I works at Ralph's Barbecue Cafe out here near the Masonite plant. We need an ambulance and we needs it in a hurry!"

There was a pause. Rosie said, "That's what I said. We needs an ambulance at Ralph's Barbecue Cafe and we needs it right now! Somebody's hurt! Don't mess around!"

I didn't know Rosie could talk that fast. But she did. She talked as fast as a yankee from Chicago. Or a yankee from Boston.

Everyone got as quiet as church mice. The only noise was made by Annabelle. She walked into the butcher shop and started meowing.

Ebenezer asked me in a soft voice, 'Miss Beulah, do you want me to close the freezer door?"

I said, "Leave it open."

Annabelle walked over to the freezer. She started looking inside. Ebenezer said, "Get away, Annabelle. Don't you try to go in there!"

Several minutes passed. Then from way down the street I heard a siren. It got louder and louder as it got closer to the store. I looked out the window and an orange and white ambulance was pulling up in front of the store. The ambulance had flashing red lights on all sides. Two men got out of the ambulance. They were wearing white coats.

Ebenezer rushed to the front door of the butcher shop and opened it. He yelled to the men who had gotten out of the ambulance, "He's in here!"

The two men rushed into the butcher shop.

Somebody—it may have been Ebenezer or it may have been Rosie—yelled, "He's in the freezer."

The two men with the ambulance walked into the freezer. One of them knelt beside Ralph and tried to find his pulse. I heard him say to his partner, "I can't feel any pulse. See if you can feel one."

The other man knelt and tried to find Ralph's pulse. I heard him say, "I can't either."

They bent over Ralph's face and looked at his eyes. They opened Ralph's shirt and one of the men put his ear on Ralph's chest. He kept his ear on Ralph's chest for at least a minute.

The two men stood and walked out of the freezer. They were rubbing their hands. One of the men—the tall one with a moustache—said, "We can't find any pulse. I'm afraid he's dead."

The help went haywire again, screaming, "Help us Jesus!" "God have mercy on Mr. Ralph!" "Oh Lord in heaven above, come down and help us we pray!"

For a moment or two I felt like I was gonna faint. Everything in the butcher shop started going around and around. I felt for a moment like I was riding on a merry-go-round at the Jones County Fair and I was about to fall off because it was goin' too fast. I had wanted Ralph taught a lesson. And that lesson was he couldn't bully me no more. I hadn't counted on seeing him dead. Which I was now doing.

But I'm gonna be honest with you: a feeling of peace—or maybe I ought to say a feeling of sweet revenge—began to creep over me. It began to sink in that Ralph Rainey—the man I'd lived with for six years—was dead. He was laid out on the freezer floor like a slab of beef. Or like a plastic tube of frozen hamburger meat from the Superior Meatpacking Company in Meridian. I knew things about him nobody else knew. I knew his body was a fucking machine. He wanted pussy three times a week. Always on his own terms. And with no love. Just get on top, stick it in, and pump away. Then roll over and start snoring. Snoring so loud you could hear him a mile away.

He was the man who married me and then made me his unpaid employee—expecting me to work my fanny off in his cafe and garden. Nobody but me knew he put his thumb on the scales when he was weighing hamburger meat. Nobody but me and Sumrall and

Velma knew Ralph had set old JR on fire with gasoline. He was the man who flew off the handle and gave me a whipping for not frying enough chicken for the pot-bellied preachers. And he was on the verge of giving me another whipping before I pulled a fast one on him and locked him in the freezer. I can still hear him yelling, "Beulah—damn it—let me out of here!"

Before we married Ralph was a pot of honey. After we married he was a bastard. So deep down on the inside I was glad he was dead. Him being dead meant a problem—or a pain in the ass—was solved. Of course I wasn't—so I knew—gonna broadcast the way I felt from the housetops. I'd keep the way I felt to myself. But I'll bet you a silver dollar and a cold bottle of buttermilk that a lot of wives feel the way I do. Their husbands being dead would be a blessing. A load would be lifted off their backs. Instead of seeing dark clouds every morning, they'd see the sun shine again. Some people would think I'm a sinner for feeling this way. And having these thoughts. But they ain't walked in my shoes. All I can say to 'em is they ain't been Ralph Rainey's wife. If they'd been, they'd know why I feel the way I do. Getting rid of a mean husband ain't no different from gettin' rid of a bad disease. Or shootin' a mad dog.

I found myself up a tree. I didn't know what to do next. It ain't everyday you find your husband stretched out dead in a walk-in freezer.

Me and the help was quiet as ghosts all the time the ambulance men were examining Ralph. After they was through and had said Ralph was dead—and while the help was going haywire shouting "Help us Jesus!"—the ambulance men looked at me and asked, "Do you know who he is?"

I said, "He's my husband."

The help joined in, "That's Mr. Ralph. He's our boss."

Rosie said, "He owns this here place. He's Mr. Ralph Rainey. Everybody in Laurel knows Mr. Ralph!"

Ebenezer spoke up and said, "I think Mr. Ralph was robbed."

The ambulance attendants looked surprised. One of them asked, "Why do you say that?"

Ebenezer answered, "Because of the way things is messed up. When we come in this morning the wrapping table was turned over. That ain't ever happened. And the Coca-Cola clock was busted. I bet Mr. Ralph was robbed before he left the store last night."

Good old Ebenezer. His skin is as black as coal dug out of a Kentucky coal mine. The reason I know Kentucky coal is blacker than black is because summer before last I went to Kentucky with a quintet from the New Jerusalem Church. We give a series of singing concerts to three primitive Baptist churches around Hazard. Hazard is a town in eastern Kentucky in the coal country. While I was up there in Kentucky I seen a coal mine. That coal was the blackest coal I ever seen.

I decided right on the spot to go along with Ebenezer's idea that Ralph had been robbed. Which is why I spoke up and said, "The money ain't in the cash registers. And I just noticed the bank bag is gone." Of course I knew exactly where the money and the bank bag was. I had taken the money bag and put it in my car trunk. I put it way down under my clothes so nobody could see it.

The ambulance attendant—the short one with the big ears— said, "I believe somebody ought to call the police."

When he said that my heart almost jumped up into my throat. Thinking about the police coming out and asking questions made me feel weak at the knees. But I kept saying to myself, "Remember, Beulah, you don't care no more. If you keep your cool you can wiggle through this mess. You didn't kill Ralph. All you done was lock him up in the freezer. The temperature was what got him. Or maybe he had a heart attack. And don't nobody know you locked him in the freezer. Nobody knows that but you. And you can keep that to yourself." That's the way I was reasoning to myself.

The ambulance man with the big ears spoke up again, "Do you want me to call the police?"

I didn't want to say yes but I knew it'd be wrong if I said no. So I said, "I wish you would."

He asked, "Where's a phone?"

I pointed to the cash stand and said, "Over there beside the cash register."

The ambulance man dialed the number for police headquarters. He dialed it from memory. My guess was he'd dialed the number a lot of times and had it memorized. I heard him ask, "Who's the desk sergeant on duty this morning?"

Next he said, "Let me speak to him."

He then said, "Robert, this is Erskine with the ambulance service. I'm out here at Ralph's Cafe and Butcher Shop on Fulton Street. You better send some men out here. I'm afraid you've got a murder and a robbery on your hands."

He paused for a moment and said, "That's right. I'll stay until you get here."

He hung the phone up and turned to me and said, "Mrs. Rainey, the police are on their way. They'll be here in a few minutes."

Time creeped while we waited for the police. A crowd of some fifteen or twenty people gathered outside the store. The ambulance had got their attention. Through the front door I could hear them asking questions. Questions like "What happened?" "Is somebody sick?" "What's the trouble?" One person in the crowd was Carl Casey. Carl owns Casey's Hardware Store which is right next to Ralph's place. Carl was a regular customer at the cafe. So he and I knew one another.

Carl opened the butcher shop door and took one step inside. You could tell he was bein' cautious. He saw me and asked, "Beulah, may I come in?"

I said, "Sure, Carl, come on in."

He said, "Beulah, what's wrong? Is somebody hurt?"

I said, "I'm afraid we've lost Ralph."

Carl said, "You mean Ralph's dead?"

I said, "That's right."

He said, "Beulah, I don't believe it."

I said, "It's true." I pointed toward the walk-in freezer and said, "He's in there on the freezer floor."

Carl said, "In the freezer?"

I said, "Yep. In the freezer. You can take a look if you want to."

Carl said, "I'd rather not. Dead bodies give me the heeby-jeebies."

Ebenezer spoke up and said, "Mr. Ralph was robbed last night when he was closing down the store."

Carl said, "Robbed?"

Eb said, "He sho was."

Carl asked, "How do you know?"

Eb said, "Because of the mess we found this morning. The wrapping table was turned over. Things was scattered about. The Coca-Cola clock was busted."

I added, "Yesterday's receipts are missing."

Carl scratched his head and said, "I'll be damn."

Eb said, "Somebody held Mr. Ralph up and locked him in the freezer. He's in there on the freezer floor froze like he was a block of ice."

Carl said, "I'll be damn. Knowing Ralph, I bet he put up a fight. I saw him yesterday and he was fit as a fiddle. We never know when we're gonna go."

Rosie said, "That's why we need Jesus."

Eb said, "Amen."

At that moment—right when Rosie said "we need Jesus"—two police cars pulled up out front. On top of both cars were flashing blue lights. Two policemen wearing uniforms got out of one car.

Two men dressed in street clothes got out of the other car. All four men walked inside the butcher shop. I recognized one of the men who was not in uniform. It was Howie Fisher. The reason I recognized him is because he's a regular customer at the cafe. I bet I'd waited on him a hundred times. He always orders two barbecue pig sandwiches, a side order of potato salad, and a glass of tea.

Howie came over to where I was standing. He asked, "Beulah, what's happened?"

I said, "Ralph's dead."

The ambulance man with the big ears said, "He's on the floor in the freezer."

The four police officers hustled over to the freezer. They looked inside. They shook their heads. I heard one of 'em say, "This is bad."

Howie turned to the two ambulance men. He asked, "Are you sure he's dead?"

The ambulance man with the moustache said, "There's not a sign of a pulse. He's gone."

Howie came back to where I was and said, "Beulah, I'm sorry."

I put on a good front and said, "I'm sorry too." Which wasn't really the way I felt but the way I pretended to feel.

Howie asked, "What's this about a robbery? When the ambulance attendant called the station he said we had a robbery on our hands."

I said, "Ralph was robbed last night."

Howie said, "I can't believe it."

Howie then added, "Beulah, I know all of this is bound to be heavy for you to handle. But do you feel like talking to us? We need to put our heads together and try to figure out what happened last night."

I said, "I feel like talking. You fellows have got to do your job."

Howie said, "I appreciate your saying that. When a job has to be done it has to be done."

Howie pointed to the other officer dressed in street clothes. He asked, "Beulah, do you know Mr. Cuningham? Or maybe I ought to say Billy. Billy Cuningham. He's a detective with the department."

I said, "I don't believe I've met him."

Howie said, "Billy, this is Beulah Rainey. She's the wife of the man we just looked at lying on the freezer floor."

I said, "I'm pleased to meet you." Which was a lie. I could tell right off I wasn't gonna like Billy Cuningham. I could tell by the look on his face that Billy Cuningham was a smartass. And I don't like nobody who's a smartass. But I wasn't about to let him know I thought he was a smartass. When you're around any kind of a policeman—particularly one you don't know—the best thing to do is to get humble. Get humble in a hurry. Everybody needs to understand that when a policeman or a deputy sheriff or a detective puts on a badge and a pistol it makes him feel important. Mighty important. And you always have to be careful when you're around somebody who thinks they're important.

Billy—I learned later he'd been an army officer—said, "I'm pleased to meet you too."

Right then it dawned on me I had one thing I had to take care of. There wasn't no way we could open for business. Which is why I turned to Ebenezer and said, "Eb, you and Jesse get all the help together and tell 'em we ain't gonna open for business today. Tell 'em to go on home. I'm not sure right now when we'll open back up. But you tell 'em I'll call 'em when we do." It hit me that with Ralph gone I was gonna have to make a lot of decisions. There wasn't nobody else to make 'em.

Eb said, "I sho will, Miss Beulah."

Eb hustled off and started telling the help what I'd said.

I looked at Howie and said, "Why don't we step next door and sit down at a table in the cafe. I think we can talk better in there."

Howie said, "That's a good idea."

He added, "Before we start talking I'm goin' to call the station and tell 'em to go ahead and send out the coroner."

Howie picked up the phone by the cash stand and called the police station. I heard him tell whoever he was talking to to send the coroner out to Ralph's Barbecue Cafe and Butcher Shop on Fulton Street.

After he'd made his call me and Howie and Billy Cuningham went into the cafe and sat down at a table. I looked out the window. By that time the crowd outside had gotten a lot bigger. But there wasn't nothing I could do about that. More policemen in uniforms had drove up. The policemen in uniforms wouldn't let nobody come in. They put yellow tape across the front of the store. The two men with the ambulance came over to the table and the one with the big ears said, "Miss Beulah, we're goin' to be on our way. We're mighty sorry about your husband."

I said, "How much do I owe you?"

They said together, "Let's don't worry about that right now."

I said, "That's mighty decent of you. Send me a bill and we'll settle up later."

The ambulance man with the moustache said, "That'll be just fine."

After the ambulance men had walked out, Howie looked at me and said, "Beulah, this is not goin' to be easy for you. But Billy and I need to try to figure out what's happened. And when it happened. So let me ask you some questions. We've got to start somewhere. So let's start with yesterday evening. When was the last time you saw Ralph alive?"

I done some quick thinking. I said, "Well, last evening we closed the store somewhere between seven and eight o'clock. By that time I was tired. I was dog tired. So I told Ralph I was gonna go on home. Ralph told me that was fine with him. He said he'd stay here and count the money and get the bank deposit ready and make sure everything was closed down right. I left the store and stopped by the Jitney and bought me a few groceries. I then drove on home. I guess I got home around eight-thirty. But I can't be sure because I wasn't thinkin' about the clock. I fixed me something to eat. And since I was dog tired I hit the bed and went to sleep."

Billy said, "But Ralph never came home?"

I said, "Nope. He didn't."

Billy piped in and asked, "When he didn't come home, did you get worried? And did you try to find out why he didn't come home?"

Right then and there I smelled a trap. Billy was tryin' to put me on the spot. It would sound fishy if I said I didn't get worried or try to find out why Ralph didn't come home. So again I done some quick thinking. When you're in a tight spot and your butt is caught in a crack your brain goes on overdrive. You can think up stuff you wouldn't otherwise be able to think up. So I said, "I didn't get worried. The reason I didn't is because Ralph told me he was gonna spend the night with his mama and daddy. The reason he was gonna do that is because him and his daddy planned to go fishin' early this morning on the Okatoma Lake. So I wasn't expectin' him home last night." My stomach got in knots when I said that because I knew what I said wasn't so. But it was true that from time to time Ralph spent the night with his folks so him and his daddy could get up real early and go fishing on the Okatoma Lake. Ralph and his daddy went fishing together at least once a month. When they did Ralph always spent the night with his mama and daddy.

Howie said, "So you weren't expecting Ralph to come home last night?"

I said, "I sure wasn't."

Howie said, "I see."

Howie scratched his head and said, "Okay, tell Billy and me about this morning. What happened that led up to findin' Ralph in the freezer?"

I said, "Well, Eb called me at the house about eight o'clock. He told me that he and the help was here ready to go to work but Ralph wasn't here. He told me the doors was locked. Which meant they couldn't get in to get things started. And he told me Ralph's pickup was parked outside but there wasn't no sign of Ralph. I told Eb I'd get to the store as quick as I could. Which I done. I got here and unlocked the front door to the cafe and let the help in. Then me and Eb walked over into the butcher shop to turn the lights on and to get things started over there. But the butcher shop—it turned out—was a mess. The wrapping table was turned over on its side. Things were scattered all over the floor. The Coca-Cola clock on the wall was busted into a thousand pieces. Right off the bat Eb said he thought we'd been robbed. That's when we decided to open the freezer. If somebody is gonna rob a butcher shop, the meat in the freezer is one of the things they're looking for. I gave the key to Eb and he unlocked the freezer door. The first thing he saw when he opened the door and turned on the light was Ralph stretched out on the floor. I knowed something was wrong because Eb yelled, 'Oh my God! Help me Jesus!' I looked in the freezer and there Ralph was on the floor. On his back face up. He wasn't moving. And somewhere along in there I realized yesterday's money was missing. There wasn't no money in the butcher shop cash register. And there wasn't none in the cafe cash register. And the bank bag was gone. Every night at closing time Ralph bags the money and takes it home with him. When I seen the bag and the money gone—that's when it really hit me we'd been robbed."

Howie said, "And your guess is that whoever robbed the store locked Ralph in the freezer before they left."

I said, "That's what I'm guessing."

Billy said, "That was a dirty thing for them to do."

I said, "I agree. It was a dirty thing for them to do."

Howie said, "And poor old Ralph froze to death."

I said, "I'm guessing he did."

About that time so much started happening I couldn't keep it all straight. I felt I was in the middle of a three-ring circus. I believe every policeman in Laurel all of a sudden turned up at the store. There was so many police cars parked in front of the store I couldn't count 'em all. All of 'em had blue lights and they was all flashing back and forth—like the eyes of big crocodiles. Even the chief of police come out to the store. His name was Rodney Bricker. Mr. Bricker was dressed in a fancy uniform. His uniform reminded me of the uniforms you see drum majors wear in a parade. His hat had some kind of a gold ornament on it. And gold braiding.

Howie introduced me to the chief. He said, "Chief Bricker, this is Beulah Rainey. She's the wife of the man whose body was found in the freezer."

The chief said, "Mrs. Rainey, I want you to know I'm sorry this has happened."

I said, "I'm sorry too."

He went on to say, "There's one thing you can count on. We're gonna find the thug or thugs who did this to your husband. We always get our man."

I said, "I appreciate that."

The chief asked Howie, "Have you called the coroner?"

Howie said, "I've already called him. He should be turning up any moment."

The next thing that happened was my relatives started turning up. Laurel is a small town and news travels fast. The first one to turn up was Earline. As you know, she's my baby sister. Earline makes her living being a beautician. The police was not lettin' people come in the store. But they let Earline come in when she told them she was my sister.

She come in and said, "Beulah, what in the world has happened?"

I told her from A to Z everything I'd told the police.

Earline said, "I can't believe this. I can't believe Ralph is dead."

I said, "He is though." I then asked, "How'd you know something was wrong?"

Earline said, "Sally McQuire—she's one of my customers—come in the beauty shop and said she'd just passed Ralph's Place and it was ringed with police cars. She said something bad must have happened. When she said that I took off like a streak of lightning."

Dewey and Harold was the next to turn up. They're Ralph's brothers. Dewey is an automobile mechanic and Harold works at the Masonite plant. The police let them come in since they were Ralph's brothers. They had confused expressions on their faces. Which was unusual. You seldom see a Rainey with a puzzled look on his face.

Dewey and Harold asked the same question that Earline had asked, "Beulah, what's happened?"

I told them what I'd told Earline and the police. They listened and then went in the butcher shop and took a look at Ralph's body. They come back and asked, "Has anybody told Mama and Daddy?"

I said, "Not that I know of."

Dewey looked at Harold and said, "Somebody has got to tell 'em and it might as well be us."

Harold said, "Let's go."

I said, "After you've told Ralph's mama and daddy, I wish you'd go to Ellisville and tell Oscar."

They said they'd tell Oscar. And away they went.

Talking about Ralph's mama and daddy caused Earline to ask about my mama and daddy. She asked, "Has anybody told 'em about Ralph?"

I said, "I don't think so."

Earline said, "I'm leaving right now to tell 'em. Then I'll come right back. I'm guessin' you'll still be here."

I said, "I'll be here for sure. I've got to ride this storm out."

Earline took off to tell Mama and Daddy that Ralph was dead.

After Earline left things speeded up again. The coroner came. I can't remember for sure what his name was. I think his last name was Spell. Then again his last name may have been Bell. I do remember his first name. His first name was Grover. Grover I'd say was about fifty years old. He was a little fat man with a bald head. He reminded me of a baseball or a basketball he was so round. When he came into the store he was carrying a black satchel and a clipboard. I tried to figure out one day how many people when they come into the store have a clipboard. The Sysco man always has a clipboard. So do the health department inspectors. So do the men with the state tax commission. So do the fire department inspectors and the insurance folks. So do people who come by asking you to give to outfits like the Salvation Army and the community chest. And so did the coroner. I could tell the detectives with the police department knew who he was. When he walked through the door Howie said, "Hello, Grover. How're you doing today?"

Grover said, "Well, well, well: if it's not old Howie. It's been a long time since we've seen each other?"

Howie said, "That's right."

Grover asked, "What was the last case we worked?"

Howie said, "I guess it was the McHenry case." What the McHenry case was I didn't know. But I could tell Howie and the coroner knew.

The coroner got right down to it. He asked, "Where's the body I'm to examine?"

Howie pointed in the direction of the freezer and said, "Grover, it's in that walk-in freezer."

Grover said, "You've got to be kidding."

Howie said, "Nope. It's in that freezer."

Grover said, "I've been in this business for twenty years. I've examined bodies on boats and in swimming pools and in barns and in creeks and in watermelon patches and in the woods but never in a walk-in freezer. But there's a first time for everything. So here goes."

With that the coroner disappeared into the freezer. He stayed for what seemed to me an eternity. While he was in the freezer Howie said, "Grover is the best coroner Jones County has ever had. He always does a thorough job. When he was young Grover studied to be a doctor but for some reason he never made it out of med school."

When Grover finally came out of the freezer he was rubbing his hands and he said, "Boy, I tell you right now it's cold in there."

He then looked at Howie and said, "Who was that fellow?"

Howie said, "He was Ralph Rainey. He owned this place."

Grover looked surprised. He said, "He did?"

Howie said, "Yep. Ralph ran this place for years. Most everybody in town knew who he was."

Up to this point Grover hadn't said nothing to me. I don't think he'd even noticed me. Howie ended that by saying, "Grover, I want you to meet Beulah Rainey. She was Ralph's wife."

The coroner said, "Pleased to meet you, Mrs. Rainey. Of course I'm not pleased to meet you under these circumstances. I'm mighty sorry about what happened to your husband." After that he turned to Howie and asked, "Howie, what do you folks believe happened?"

Howie said, "We don't know for sure. As best we can tell Ralph was robbed yesterday evening when he was closing his store down. That's the theory we're going on."

Grover asked, "Do you have any idea who did it?"

Howie said, "So far we don't have a clue. Not the first clue."

Grover said, "Well, I'll tell you one thing: I'm glad I wasn't one of the robbers. I say that because Mr. Rainey put up one hell of a fight. While I was examining him I could see his knucklebones. His flesh was completely worn off. He must have hit whoever was robbing him with fists that felt like sledgehammers. And his face is bloody and swollen. Like I just said: he put up one hell of a fight. By the way, the inside of the freezer door is as bloody as a battlefield. You'd better check that out."

Howie said, "We sure will."

Grover then said, "I'll be on my way. I've got to hustle to my office and write up my report." He looked at me and said, "One more time, Mrs. Rainey: I'm sorry about what's happened to your husband." I said, "Thank you." With that the coroner left. For a few moments I almost felt sorry for Ralph myself. I could imagine him inside the freezer beating on the door with his fists. Maybe he went crazy. I'll never know. But I wouldn't put it past him.

After the coroner had gone, Howie and Chief Bricker asked me, "Beulah, what funeral home do you want us to call?"

I'll be honest with you. I hadn't even thought about a funeral. Or a funeral home. The only one I could think of was the Gates of Heaven Funeral Home. That's the funeral home in Laurel my folks have always used. They buried Uncle Robert. And they buried both of my grandparents on Daddy's side. And so I said to Howie, "Would you call Gates of Heaven for me?"

He said, "Sure I will."

About that moment a man named Duane Purvis turned up at the store. The police let him in because he was a reporter for the *Laurel Leader Press*. That's the name of Laurel's newspaper. He was carrying a notebook and had a camera strapped over his shoulder. He introduced himself and said, "Mrs. Rainey, I'm sorry about your husband. The paper has sent me out here to get an account of what happened. I know you're upset and under pressure, but I'd sure appreciate it if you would tell me what's gone on here at the store." Mr. Purvis seemed like a nice young fellow. He wasn't doin' nothing but doin' his job. So I told him the same story I'd told Howie, Earline, Dewey, and Harold. All the time I was talking he was writing down everything I said on this pad he had with him. I ain't never seen nobody write as fast as he was writing.

When I was through Mr. Purvis said, "Mrs. Rainey, I really appreciate you talking to me. And if you don't mind, I'm goin' to take one or two pictures inside the store and one or two pictures outside."

I said, "That'll be okay with me."

By the time I got through talking with the reporter for the *Laurel Leader Press* I could tell I was drained. I felt like a flat tire. Which is why I think I went into a kind of daze. Or into a trance. When I was a little girl I used to walk down to the Okatoma River in the fall of the year. I'd stand on the bank and watch leaves floating down the river. Some of 'em would be red. Some would be yellow. Others would be orange. They'd float along—going whichever way the river took 'em.

The rest of Tuesday and all day Wednesday I found myself feeling like one of those leaves floating on the Okatoma River. Only I wasn't being carried along by a river of water but by a river-of-things-happening. Things were happening all around me and I didn't have no control over them. It seemed to me that police were everywhere in the cafe and butcher shop. And it seemed that the telephone didn't stop ringing. A big crowd of people were standing outside the store. Some of 'em were smoking. Some of 'em were laughing and horsing around. I didn't see nothing funny to laugh and horse around about.

I wished they'd go away. People said things to me, but their voices sounded far off—like a voice sounds when you hear somebody calling you in a dream. At times this river-of-things-happening acted like it wanted to drown me. But I was determined not to let it drown me. I kept saying over and over to myself, "Beulah, you're free. Ralph can't hurt you no more. You're like a bird let out of a cage." Time and again the picture come into my mind of me slamming the door on Ralph and locking him inside the freezer. I could hear him yelling, "Beulah, you open this goddamn door!" But when this picture come into my mind, I'd think, "Ralph was taking off his belt and getting ready to give me another whipping. I have a right to defend myself. If Ralph froze to death, that's his problem. Not mine. I don't care no more."

A long, black Cadillac hearse from the Gates of Heaven Funeral Home pulled up in front of the store. Two men dressed in dark suits got out of the hearse. They come into the store pushing what looked to me like a little bed mounted on wheels. It had a blanket over it. They acted real dignified. They come over to where I was and introduced themselves.

One of 'em said, "My name is Mr. Holly."

The other one said, "And my name is Mr. DeArmy."

I'd never heard of anybody named DeArmy before. That seemed to me like a funny name.

They said they was from the Gates of Heaven Funeral Home and that they'd come to pick up Ralph's body. Or as Mr. Holly put it, "the remains of the deceased." Mr. Holly said, "Mrs. Rainey, Elton Wright has asked me to deliver a message to you."

I didn't know no Elton Wright. And so I said, "Who's he?"

Mr. Holly said, "He's the man who owns the Gates of Heaven Funeral Home."

I said, "Oh, I see."

Mr. Holly went on to say, "Mr. Wright has asked me to tell you that you can come down either this afternoon or tonight or in the morning to pick out a casket for your husband. At that time he would like to meet with you to work out the details of the funeral service."

I said, "That'll be fine with me. I'll call and let you folks know when I'm coming."

Both Mr. Holly and Mr. DeArmy said, "Thank you so much."

With that they turned and headed for the walk-in freezer. Two policemen helped them pull Ralph's body out of the freezer. They lifted it up and put it on this bed or stretcher—whatever you want to call it. They rolled Ralph's body out of the store and put it in the hearse. With that they drove off.

The next thing I remember was Earline turning back up at the store from goin' and tellin' Mama and Daddy that Ralph was dead.

I asked Earline, "How did they take it?"

Earline said, "They acted stunned—like they'd been hit with a two-by-four." She added, "Daddy said Ralph was tough as leather. And it was hard for him to believe he let somebody lock him in the freezer. But I told him that was sure what happened."

The store was still full of police. They was all over the place. Howie said they was looking for clues and evidence. While Howie was explaining what the police were doing—checking for finger-prints and stuff like that—Earline spoke up and said, "Beulah, you need to get away from here. I want you to come on home with me and spend the night. You don't need to be by yourself."

I said, "I can't leave. I've got to stay here and lock up."

Howie heard me say that. Which is why he said, "Beulah, I think you ought to do what your sister said. I'll tell you what, if you'll trust the store keys to me, I promise you that me and Ebenezer will lock this place up tight before we leave. We'll lock it up tighter than a bank vault."

I didn't know Ebenezer was still around. But he was. The rest of the help had left like I'd told 'em to. But Ebenezer—may God bless his soul—was standing just inside the kitchen door. He was takin' in all that was goin' on.

Howie called to Eb and said, "Ebenezer, how about comin' out here for just a moment."

Ebenezer walked out of the kitchen and came over to where I was sitting.

Howie said, "Ebenezer, I think Beulah needs to leave and get some rest. I told her that if she'd trust me with her keys, you and I would make sure everything was locked up right. Is that a deal?"

Ebenezer said, "It sho is. We'll close this place down right."

I trusted Ebenezer. He'd worked for Ralph for years. And so I left the store and rode home with Earline. When I got to Earline's house I drank two cups of black coffee and ate a piece of her yellow pound cake. I decided to put off picking out Ralph's casket until the next morning. So I got Earline to call the funeral home and tell 'em when I'd be there. The person Earline talked to at the funeral home told her to tell me that I needed to pick out one of Ralph's suits for him to be buried in. And that I needed to bring the suit—along with a shirt and tie—with me when I came to the funeral home. I hadn't thought about that.

When you have a funeral you have to think about a lot of things you've never thought about before. So later on in the day me and Earline got in her car and drove down to Ralph's house in New Jerusalem. I picked up Ralph's blue suit, a white shirt, and a maroon tie.

While we was picking out a suit for Ralph, Earline asked me, "What dress are you gonna wear to the funeral?"

When she asked me that it dawned on me that all my best clothes was hid in the trunk of my car. It was still parked at the store. I said, "I'm gonna wear that cream-colored dress I bought at McRae's. And I'm gonna wear them new cream-colored shoes I bought at the Smart Shoe Store."

She said, "Where are they?"

I said, "They're in the trunk of my car."

Earline said, "My lord, what are they doin' there?"

I said, "I was gonna take a little trip." Which—when you stop and think about it—was the truth. I added, "Later on today we'll have to go by the store and get my car."

Earline said, "Okay."

Me and Earline drove back to her house in Laurel. Sammy,

Earline's husband, had heard about Ralph and had got off from work early and he was home when we got there. And when we got there the telephone was ringing and ringing. It was Ralph's people. I bet they called a hundred times Tuesday afternoon and night asking questions. The calls come mostly from Ralph's two brothers and from his sister who lives over in Baton Rouge.

"Where is the funeral service goin' to be? At the funeral home or at the church?"

"When's it gonna be?"

"When are you goin' to pick out the casket?"

"What time do you plan to go to the funeral home?"

"What about Oscar?"

"Did you know Ralph had a burial plot laid out in the New Jerusalem Cemetery?"

I was too wore out to answer all them questions. I let Earline and Sammy handle 'em.

About seven o'clock that night Bessie called by long distance. Bessie is Ralph's sister who lives in Baton Rouge. She and her husband both work at the Standard Oil Refinery. I've always hated Bessie's guts. She reminds me of a porcupine. She don't know other people have feelings. Earline took her call and Bessie said she wanted to talk to me. Earline told Bessie I was too tired to talk. Bessie insisted, "I must talk to Beulah." So I took the phone and Bessie said, "Beulah, I'm real sorry about Ralph."

I said, "I appreciate that."

She then said, "Beulah, about a year ago Ralph told me something you need to know."

I said, "What's that?"

She said, "Are you sure you won't get upset?"

I said, "I won't get upset." How could I get upset after all I'd been through?

Bessie said, "Ralph told me that when he died he wanted to be buried in the New Jerusalem Cemetery next to his first wife Ruth Ann."

When she said that, I said, "That'll be just fine with me!" I slammed the phone down in her face.

Earline asked, "What brought that on?"

I told her and Sammy what Bessie had said about Ralph wantin' to be buried next to Ruth Ann.

Earline said, "Bessie shouldn't have said that."

Sammy said, "Bessie is a bitch."

10

I SPENT ALL Tuesday evening and night with Earline and Sammy. We drove to the store and got my car. I took my dresses and shoes out of the trunk. I checked and the store money I'd hid in the trunk was still there. I left it right where it was. Earline helped me iron the cream-colored dress I'd bought at McRae's. It was the one I was gonna wear to the funeral. I finally went to bed but I had a hard time sleeping. I couldn't sleep for thinking about Bessie callin' and sayin' Ralph wanted to be buried beside his first wife. I felt that was hittin' below the belt. Ralph hurt me when he was alive. Now he was hurtin' me when he was dead. But maybe I didn't have no right to complain. After all, I was glad he'd soon be six feet under. I didn't know where Ralph was. Maybe he'd gone to heaven. Ralph said he believed in the blood, and Brother Ledbetter always preached you went to heaven when you die if you believed in the blood. Then again maybe Ralph went to hell. That's where anybody oughta go who sets an old mule like JR on fire. But I hoped—wherever he was—that Ralph knowed how I felt about him wantin' to be buried next to Ruth Ann. For the past six years I hadn't been nothing but Ruth Ann's shadow.

All day yesterday—yesterday was Wednesday—Earline and her husband Sammy was as nice to me as they could be. They knowed me and Ralph didn't get along too good together. I'd told Earline about that. But they didn't know how rough things had gotten between us. They didn't know about Ralph whipping me and givin' me a black eye. I was too ashamed of it to tell Earline. They didn't know about Ralph settin' the mule on fire. They sure didn't know about me lockin' Ralph in the freezer.

Early yesterday morning Earline brought me my breakfast on a tray. I was still in bed. That was the first time in my life anybody ever brought my breakfast to me while I was still in bed. She brought me two scrambled eggs, some bacon and toast, and a cup of coffee. Along with some strawberry jam. When Earline brought that tray to me I couldn't believe my eyes. I felt like I was the queen of England.

She also showed me a Tuesday copy of Laurel's newspaper. I'm talking about the *Laurel Leader Press*. I almost flipped when Earline showed me the front page. Ralph's murder was the headline. The headline read LOCAL MERCHANT MURDERED. Under the headline was two big pictures. One was an outside picture of the store. You could read the sign that stands in front of the cafe. It read RALPH'S PLACE. The other one was a picture of Ralph sprawled out on the floor of the freezer. He was flat on his back with his mouth open.

Under the pictures was an article written by Duane Purvis. He's the young fellow from the newspaper who talked to me at the store. I got Earline to read the article out loud to me. This here is what it said:

> Ralph Rainey, owner of Ralph's Place—a barbecue cafe and meat market—was found murdered Tuesday morning in his store on Fulton Street. Police theorize that one or more persons entered the store Monday evening after Mr. Rainey had closed for business. They also theorize that a fierce struggle ensued between Mr. Rainey and the person or persons who robbed him. Equipment in the meat

market was found in disarray. A wall clock was smashed. Mr. Rainey's hands were bruised and bloody. Howie Fisher, one of the detectives who investigated the murder, stated, 'Mr. Rainey's mutilated hands suggest he had a violent fight with the intruders.' Mr. Rainey's body was found lying on the floor of the meat market's walk-in freezer. The evidence suggests he was forcibly locked in the freezer Monday evening and that he remained there all night. His body was found by Ebenezer Fortenberry, a veteran employee of Ralph's Butcher Shop. Police report also that Monday's cash receipts were missing from both the cafe and the meat market. They reached this conclusion after talking with Beulah Rainey, widow of the slain merchant.

A contingent of detectives and police from the Laurel Police Department spent all day Tuesday investigating the Rainey murder and robbery. At the present time they have uncovered no incriminating clues. They have interviewed scores of people who either live or work in proximity to Mr. Rainey's store. No person interviewed reports seeing anything unusual Monday evening. Nor does any person interviewed report seeing strangers entering or leaving the establishment. The last person anyone remembers exiting the store was Mrs. Beulah Rainey, the owner's wife.

Mr. Rainey was a familiar figure in local food circles. He served two terms as president of the Laurel Restaurant Association. He was a veteran of World War II and during that conflict served his country in the United States Navy. While in the Navy he learned the food business. Fellow restaurateurs recall Mr. Rainey saying, 'Before I joined the navy I didn't know how to boil water. When I left the Navy, I knew how to prepare a Christmas dinner for a thousand sailors.' His cafe on Fulton Street, a regular for employees of the Masonite plant, has the reputation for serving 'the best barbecue in Jones County.'

An avid hunter and fisherman, Mr. Rainey was an active

member of the New Jerusalem Baptist Church. He is survived by his wife, Beulah Rainey, the former Beulah Buchanan of the New Jerusalem community. He is survived by Oscar Rainey, a son from his first marriage. He is also survived by his parents, two brothers, and a sister.

Funeral arrangements are incomplete. It is anticipated that the Rainey funeral will be conducted in the New Jerusalem Baptist Church with burial in the New Jerusalem Cemetery.

After Earline had finished reading the article, she said, "Lordy me, that's something, ain't it?"

I said, "It sure is."

I took the paper from Earline and looked again at the headline and the pictures. The RALPH'S PLACE sign stood out. Under those two words in smaller letters the sign read, "The Best Barbecue in Jones County and the Best Meat Market in Mississippi." Ralph had the sign made three years ago by the Headrick Sign Company. That's a big outdoor sign company in Laurel. The sign is electric and shines at night. When it was first put up Ralph would wait until it was night and then he'd drive around the block time and again so he could look at it. He'd say, "That sign is the prettiest thing I ever saw."

I looked again at the picture of Ralph stretched out on the freezer floor. I looked at it real close. The picture showed his mouth wide open. That made the picture look creepy.

Sammy come in the bedroom where me and Earline was. I was still eatin' the breakfast Earline brought me. Sammy said, "Beulah, you'd better go ahead and get up. You've got to go to the funeral home to talk with Mr. Wright and get the funeral details worked out."

So I got up and took a bath and dressed. Sammy and Earline took me in their car to the Gates of Heaven Funeral Home. I carried Ralph's suit, shirt, and maroon tie with me.

The Gates of Heaven Funeral Home is in the middle of downtown Laurel right next to the City Hall. It's made out of red bricks and on the outside it looks like a castle. Or at least that's what everybody says it looks like. I ain't never seen a real castle.

Mr. Wright was waitin' for us when we got to the funeral home. He wasn't the only one waitin'. Ralph's mama and daddy was there. So were his two brothers—Dewey and Harold. And so were Pauline and Luella. Pauline is Dewey's wife. Luella is Harold's wife. I was particularly glad to see Pauline and Luella. I never got along at all with their husbands. But I got along just fine with them. Especially with Pauline. Pauline and me has got together from time to time and talked about what it's like to be married to a Rainey. She says all the Raineys have a crotch mentality. They think about sex most of the time. I told her one time about how Ralph never was tender with me but always jacked off in a hurry—like he was a fireman on his way to a fire. She said Dewey done her the same way. She said every time Dewey jacked off in her pussy he'd always turn her over and slap her on her butt and yell, "Good girl!" Pauline said him slappin' her on her butt every time they had sex made her feel like a cow. The reason it made her feel that way is because when she was a little girl she used to watch her daddy milk cows on his farm. He owned a dairy and ever time he got through milking a cow he'd slap the cow on her rear and say, "Good girl!"

And guess who else was at the funeral home? Bessie and her husband was there. Her husband is named Leonard McDowell. Bessie is Ralph's sister who called me by long distance from Baton Rouge to tell me Ralph wanted to be buried next to Ruth Ann. Her call burned me up. Me and Bessie never saw eye to eye on anything. Ever since I've known her she has drove me nuts over astrology. Astrology is her religion. Bessie believes in the signs of the Zodiac more than preachers believe in the Bible. She's all time goin' up to people she don't really know and sayin' things like, "You're a Virgo!"

"I can tell by the way you talk you're a Cancer!" "You come across as bein' a Capricorn."

The first time I met her she said, "Beulah, you're a Scorpio. I can tell by the look in your eyes!" I didn't have the foggiest idea what she was talkin' about. I think all of her Zodiac stuff is a pile of turtle crap. But she really believes in it.

I could tell by the way Bessie behaved she knew she'd made me mad when she'd called me from Baton Rouge about Ralph wantin' to be buried next to Ruth Ann. She acted toward me like she was a bowl of sugar. She put her arm around me and said, "Beulah, honey, we're all thinkin' about you."

I started to say, "If you're thinking about me, why did you call me from Baton Rouge last night and tell me Ralph wanted to be buried next to Ruth Ann?" But I held my tongue. I didn't see no need of making a scene.

Mr. Wright invited all of us to come into what he called the "Conference Room." This room looked to me like the lobby of a real nice motel. There was a rug on the floor. And there was a lot of stuffed chairs and sofas for people to sit on. There was also a bunch of green plants. They was in big brass pots. I couldn't tell whether they was real or artificial. But I think they was artificial. In the middle of the room was a low table. On the table was a bouquet of roses in a silver vase. They most definitely wasn't artificial. They was really pretty. They reminded me of the bouquet of roses Mrs. Pittman gave me to put on the dining room table the night I fixed supper for Brother Ledbetter and Brother Claypool.

Mr. Wright said, "Let me suggest we all take a seat." Which we all done. There was me and Earline and Sammy. And Ralph's mama and daddy along with Ralph's two brothers and their wives Pauline and Luella. And of course zodiac Bessie and her husband both from Baton Rouge. Mr. Wright sat down too. He sat down behind a desk. On the desk was a pen and some paper. Along with a lamp that had a dark-green shade on it. Mr. Wright looked mighty important sitting behind that desk. He reminded me of a lawyer or a banker.

Mr. Wright looked around at all of us and said, "Folks, let me say—first of all—that the Gates of Heaven Funeral Home is at your service. I want you to know that we are going to do everything in our power to make Mr. Rainey's funeral the kind you want it to be. I want all of you—particularly Mrs. Rainey—to make any suggestions you want to make. I tell all of the people who use our funeral home, 'Your desires are our commands.'"

I could tell Mr. Wright was tryin' to be nice. The only person nicer than an undertaker plannin' a funeral is a politician twenty-four hours before election day.

Mr. Wright said, "Let me begin by posing a few questions. I think one or two questions will get our discussion started. First of all, where do you want the funeral service to be conducted?"

Dewey—Ralph's brother—spoke up and said, "I think all of us want it conducted at the New Jerusalem Baptist Church. That's where Ralph went to church all his life."

I started to speak up and say, "Wait a minute, Dewey. I'm the one who's supposed to make that decision. I'm the widow woman here."

But I decided to keep my mouth shut. Particularly when Mr. Wright said, "That's where I thought you would want it."

Ralph's daddy spoke up and said, "Ralph's been a deacon there for over twenty years."

Mr. Wright said, "That speaks mighty well for him."

I thought to myself, "A deacon, my fucking ass."

Mr. Wright looked at me and said, "Mrs. Rainey, when do you want us to have the service?"

As far as I was concerned, the quicker, the better. I wanted to get Ralph's funeral over with. I wanted it behind me. Which is why I said, "How about in the morning at ten o'clock?"

Dewey spoke up and said, "Don't you think that'll be rushin' it?"

Ralph's mama said, "I don't think so. We're all here. We ain't got no relatives comin' we need to wait for."

Ralph's mama sayin' what she said settled it. Everybody agreed the funeral would be at ten o'clock on Thursday morning.

Mr. Wright then asked, "Who will be the minister?"

Ralph's daddy popped off and said, "There ain't no doubt about who we want to conduct the funeral. We all want Brother Ledbetter to do it. Ralph worshiped the ground Brother Ledbetter walked on. Him and Ralph was best friends. We all want Brother Ledbetter to conduct Ralph's funeral."

When Ralph's daddy said that I could have croaked a grasshopper. In my mind I could see Brother Ledbetter taking his pants off and puttin' a rubber on his dick. I was glad to get rid of Ralph. So I wasn't uptight about his funeral. To be honest with you: I didn't give a damn about his funeral. But for reasons I think you understand I didn't want Brother Ledbetter to conduct his funeral. It didn't seem right. But I was outnumbered and knew it. So again I kept my mouth shut.

All of us kept on talkin' and planning. We agreed Aunt Laura would play the piano. And that the choir would sing "In the Sweet By and By" and "When They Ring Those Golden Bells for You and Me." We agreed that Winston, Dewey, and four of Ralph's first cousins would be the pall bearers. And that the funeral home would carry Ralph's body down to the New Jerusalem Church around nine o'clock on Thursday morning so it could lie in state for about an hour before the funeral began. We all agreed we'd meet at the church between nine and ten o'clock.

On the spur of the moment I happened to think about Sumrall and Ebenezer and the rest of the colored help at the cafe. The thought went through my mind: I bet they'd like to come to Ralph's funeral.

So when Mr. Wright asked if there was anything else we needed to talk about, I spoke up and said, "Ralph has had six darkies who've worked for him for a long time. I'm thinking about Sumrall, Ebenezer, Jesse, Rosie, Melinda, and Pearl. If any of them want to come to Ralph's funeral, would it be okay?"

Me asking that set Ralph's daddy off. He got huffy and said, "We got a strict policy at New Jerusalem about niggers. We don't let 'em inside our church. I'm Ralph's daddy, and I'm sittin' here to tell you I don't want no darkies at my boy's funeral."

That was that. What Ralph's daddy said jogged my memory. I remembered Ralph sayin' one day, "A nigger has about as much chance attendin' our church as a celluloid cat being chased through hell by an asbestos dog." So I let the matter drop. I hoped Ebenezer and the rest of the help wouldn't ask if they could come to Ralph's funeral. Fortunately for me, they didn't ask. Thank the good Lord in heaven above for that. I sure would have felt bad tellin' them they couldn't come to the funeral.

After we got the details of the funeral service worked out, Mr. Wright looked over at me and said, "Mrs. Rainey, I believe the only thing left for you to do is select a casket for your husband."

Him sayin' that made chills go up and down my spine. I'd never picked out a casket before. I didn't know how you did it.

Mr. Wright went on to say, "Let me suggest we go to the coffin gallery."

That's the word he used: a "gallery." I didn't know exactly what a "gallery" was. It turned out it was a big display room.

He added, "Our funeral home prides itself on having a wide selection of coffins for families to choose from. Each coffin in our gallery has a price card on it. The price of the coffin you choose will cover the cost of Mr. Rainey's funeral."

I wasn't sure what Mr. Wright meant by this. Neither did Sammy. Which is why he asked Mr. Wright, "Are you sayin' that what the casket cost is what the funeral home will charge for doin' Ralph's funeral?"

Mr. Wright said, "That's correct."

With that Mr. Wright stood up. So did everyone else. The thought goin' through my mind as I stood up was: I ain't got no money to pay for Ralph's casket. What was I gonna do? I didn't know what I was gonna do. Particularly when all of Ralph's people decided to get lost. Which meant I was left holding the bag.

Ralph's daddy said, "I'd better be on my way. I gotta get my suit pressed for the funeral. Me and Minnie will come back this afternoon." "Minnie" is the first name of Ralph's mother. Dewey and Harold said they needed to go too. There was things they "had to take care of" so they could be at Ralph's funeral tomorrow. So they took off like hounds chasin' a rabbit. Pauline—Dewey's wife—said, "I think we ought to stay and help Beulah pick out a casket." Dewey got horsy and said, "Pauline, you heard me say I've got some things I've *got* to take care of. Beulah can pick out Ralph's casket by herself. Let's go!"

Harold acted the same way. So out the door Harold and Luella went. I could tell Luella and Pauline didn't like the way Dewey and Harold was actin'. But there wasn't nothing they could do. They looked at me and rolled their eyes.

Bessie said, "Me and Leonard need to go too. We got to eat breakfast. We left Baton Rouge real early this morning and we ain't had nothing to eat. I think we'll go to the Waffle House." With that they was on their way. As they was walkin' out the door, Bessie said, "We've also got to find us a motel to stay in. After we've eaten breakfast and checked into a motel, we'll be comin' back."

Me and Earline and Sammy was left by ourselves. The Raineys ran. I was hopin' they'd help me pay for Ralph's casket. I could tell that was a hope I could forget.

Mr. Wright led me and Sammy and Earline to the coffin display gallery. When we walked into the gallery I saw a sight I'd never seen before—a room full of caskets. It looked to me like there was a hundred coffins in there. All of 'em was opened up so you could see on the insides. The insides was lined with what looked to me like expensive silk with a lot of tufting. Most of 'em was white on the inside. But some was pink. And some was blue or cream-colored. Some had pillows. And some of 'em had a lot of lace.

They all looked real soft on the inside. The thought goin' through my mind was: if a person is dead and can't feel nothing, why does he need a soft casket? On the outside most of the caskets was gray. But a few was bronze-colored. One or two was black. One coffin was made out of wood. It turned out—so Mr. Wright explained—that it was a Jew casket.

And like he had said, each casket had a price tag. Or as Mr. Wright put it, a price card. Each price card was layin' inside the casket.

I looked at the coffins' insides. I looked at their outsides. But mostly I looked at the price tags. I couldn't believe what my eyes was tellin' me.

Some of them caskets cost ten thousand dollars. One cost fifteen thousand. A lot of 'em was priced between three and six thousand. The cheapest one I could spot cost two thousand. It looked to me like a cardboard box covered with dollar-store cloth.

I bet I looked at every coffin the Gates of Heaven Funeral Home had. After I'd looked at 'em, I got Sammy and Earline off to one side and I whispered to 'em, "There ain't no way in God's good name I can come up with enough money to pay for Ralph's casket. I can see it's gonna take three to four thousand dollars. I ain't nearly about got that kind of money."

Sammy said, "I know you and Ralph didn't get along too good together. But I thought you and him had a lot of money. He traded for a new Buick every year."

I said, "Ralph had money. But not me. I don't have a pot to pee in. Ralph never let me have no money."

Earline said, "Then use his money."

I said, "I ain't sure I can get to it."

Earline asked, "Why?"

I said, "Every checking account we had was in Ralph's name. And his name only. I can't write no check on 'em."

Sammy asked, "How many accounts did Ralph have?"

I said, "He had three. One for the cafe. One for the butcher shop. And his own personal checking account. He always told me he was the only person who could write a check on 'em. Cause they was all in his name."

Sammy said, "Oh shit."

I said, "Shit or not, that's the way it is."

Earline said, "If worse comes to worse, me and Sammy will loan you the money for Ralph's casket."

I could tell Sammy wasn't too hot on that idea. But I appreciated Earline suggestin' it.

Sammy said, "Let's talk this whole situation over with Mr. Wright. Maybe he can give us some advice."

So all three of us walked over to the door where Mr. Wright was waitin' for us to make up our minds on what casket to choose. Sammy is a smooth talker. He could sell a pair of glasses to a blind Jew. Or ice to an Eskimo. So I let Sammy do the talking.

He said, "Mr. Wright, my sister-in-law has hit a snag. Let me tell you what it is. Ralph—as you know—was a hardworking farmer and businessman. He owned a big farm down at New Jerusalem. And he owned a barbecue cafe and a butcher shop here in town. And—so Beulah has just told me—he had three checking accounts. One for his cafe. Another one for his meat market. Plus a personal checking account. All three of 'em was in his name and his name alone. From what Beulah has just told me, Ralph strictly held the reins on his money. Since Beulah here can't write checks on them accounts, she isn't sure she has the money on hand to buy Ralph's casket. Or at least she doesn't have the money right now."

Mr. Wright couldn't have been nicer.

He looked at me and said, "Mrs. Rainey, don't you worry. We encounter problems like this all the time. The funeral home will be glad to wait for payment until your husband's will and estate pass through probate court."

I didn't have the faintest idea what Mr. Wright was talking about. Particularly I didn't know what he meant by "probate court." But I heard him say "husband's will." Which is why I spoke up and said, "Ralph ain't got no will."

Sammy asked, "How do you know he ain't got no will?"

I said, "Because I heard Ralph say over and over he didn't believe in wills. He said wills wasn't nothing but a way lawyers have of making money and screwin' people."

Mr. Wright said, "If that's the case, then your husband has died intestate."

That's the word he used: intestate. For a moment I thought he'd said "intestines." But he said "intestate." I didn't have no idea what that word meant either.

Mr. Wright went on to say, "That's the term lawyers use to designate a person who dies without a will. We run into this situation all the time. When a person dies intestate, the state of Mississippi moves in and takes charge of dividing up the estate. Mississippi law right now is that the estate of a husband who dies intestate is divided equally between his wife and his children."

I'd never heard of that before. Neither had Sammy. Which is why he said to Mr. Wright, "Could you say what you just said one more time? My skull is a little thick."

Mr. Wright said, "If a person dies without a will, the state of Mississippi in effect writes a will for him. As the law stands now, the property of a husband who dies without a will is divided equally between his wife and his children."

Sammy said, "I didn't know that."

I said, "Me neither."

Mr. Wright asked me, "How many children do you and Mr. Rainey have?"

I said, "We ain't got none. Ralph has one boy from his first marriage. I'm talking about Oscar. But Oscar don't have all of his marbles. He lives in Ellisville at the feeble-minded home."

Mr. Wright said, "I see." He went on to say, "Mrs. Rainey—if you don't mind me saying so—as soon as the funeral is over, you need to sit down and have a conversation with a good lawyer. I know a lot of people don't like lawyers, but at times you have to use them whether you like them or not. If your stepson is in Ellisville, my uninformed guess is the court will turn all of your husband's property over to you. But I'm no lawyer. That's just my gut judgement."

He then said, "You go ahead and pick out a casket for your husband. We'll wait until his estate is settled for our fee. We'll charge interest but it won't be much."

Mr. Wright sayin' what he did was the first time I'd thought about what was gonna happen to Ralph's farm and cafe now that he was dead. Me ending up owning them was something I hadn't thought about. That idea hadn't never crossed my mind one time. But wouldn't that be something? Me—Beulah Rainey who ain't but twenty-two years old and who's never owned a pot to pee in—owning a big farm on the Okatoma River and owning "Ralph's Place" in Laurel. That thought made goose pimples break out on my skin. If I owned 'em I wouldn't have to kiss butts no more. Or take static off my mama and daddy. Maybe I could buy me a Cadillac like Velma's. That'd make old Ralph turn over in his casket. Or maybe buyin' a Cadillac would make Ralph fart in his grave. If I ever bought me a Cadillac I'd want it to be pink like the Mary Kay sales ladies drive.

But I had to stop thinkin' about things like that and pick out a casket for Ralph to be buried in. Which is what I done. I picked out a casket that cost five thousand dollars. I knew Ralph had three times that much in his own checking account. I knew that because I've kept his books. I thought: if maybe I'm gonna get his five-hundred acre farm and his barbecue cafe and his meat market, I might as well bury the bastard in style. The casket I picked out was bronze colored. It really looked nice. The silk on the inside was cream-colored. The least I could do, like I've just said, was send Ralph out in style. That was the least I could do—particularly since I was the one who locked him in the walk-in freezer.

Sammy and Earline—after I'd picked out the casket—took me back home with 'em. When we got to her house about one o'clock Earline said, "Beulah, I'm gonna fix you something to eat. How about a good ham and cheese sandwich? Or maybe some tuna-fish salad? I can whip it up in no time. I've got a can of cold tuna and two cold hardboiled eggs."

I said, "Earline, I ain't hungry. I don't think I could eat a bite."

Earline said, "I say you ought to eat something. If you don't, you're gonna get weak as water."

I said, "Just let me play it by ear. What I want to do right now is get a little rest. I feel drained."

So I took off my clothes. I lay down on the bed in Earline's guest room and closed my eyes and tried to get some rest. Mr. Wright had told me that the afternoon newspaper would have a notice about Ralph's funeral. And that the notice would say that friends and family could visit the funeral home and pay their respects on Wednesday night. So I knew I'd have to go back down to the funeral home in a few hours and act like I was sad Ralph was dead. Which I knew was gonna be hard to do. But you do what you have to do.

Particularly when you ain't got no choice. As I lay there on the bed it seemed to me like my mind was goin' around and around—like it was ridin' on the merry-go-round at the Jones County Fair they have once a year in Laurel. I thought about the crap I'd walked through for the last five or six years.

For some reason I can't figure out, I thought mostly about Ralph settin' old, decrepit JR on fire. That's the meanest thing I think Ralph ever done. In my mind I could see JR burning like a torch and runnin' around the garden like he was crazy. And I could hear the awful sound he made while he was runnin' back and forth across the garden. And I could hear the crack—the explosion—of Ralph's shotgun when he took old JR out of his misery. I thought about the argument me and Ralph had in the butcher shop. I could see me shoving Ralph's ass and locking him in the freezer. And I could see the way he looked the next morning stretched out on the freezer floor—as dead as Methuselah who the Bible says lived to be nine hundred and sixty-nine years old. I've always wondered how anybody could live to be that old.

And the thought hit me that I was now free. Free like a bird let out of a cage and I would never again have to take shit off of Ralph Rainey of New Jerusalem, Mississippi.

I lay on the bed I guess for two hours. But I didn't get no nap. A time or two I almost dozed off. But the telephone ringing again and again kept me from goin' to sleep.

Sammy and Earline finally come in the bedroom where I was. They had a copy of the afternoon newspaper with 'em. Sure enough—like Mr. Wright said—there was an article in there about Ralph's funeral. It said it was gonna be at ten o'clock Thursday morning at the New Jerusalem Baptist Church. And it said that visiting hours Wednesday night at the funeral home would be between six and nine o'clock.

I looked at my watch. It was already past four. I said to Earline,

"I'd better get up and take a bath and get dressed. I gotta be at the funeral home by six."

Earline asked, "You didn't eat nothing at noon. Don't you want something to eat now?"

I said, "I couldn't eat nothing if my life depended on it."

Earline said, "Beulah, you're bound to be gettin' hungry. You need food to give you strength."

I said, "I swear to God I ain't. When I get hungry I'll eat. But not before."

With that I got up and took a bath and washed my hair. Since I was a primitive Baptist I'd always wore my hair real long. That's what all the ladies in the New Jerusalem Church do. Washing and drying long hair is a lot of trouble. After I'd washed and dried my hair, I got dressed.

And then about a quarter til six we left Earline's and Sammy's house and went to the funeral home. We drove in their car. When we got to the Gates of Heaven Funeral Home a bunch of folks was already there. All of Ralph's people were there. So was Mama and Daddy. Between six and nine o'clock more people than I could count come by to pay their respects. Ralph knew a lot of people around Laurel and in Jones County. Some of the folks who came to the funeral home to pay respects was cafe customers. They said things like, "Ralph's Place won't seem the same without Ralph there." A lot of folks who came by last night was from the New Jerusalem community and from the New Jerusalem Baptist Church. They said things like, "What happened to Ralph was mighty bad. Beulah, we'll be thinkin' about you."

All of the members of the Okatoma Swamp Club come by. They was Ralph's huntin' buddies. Ralph and six other men had what they called the Okatoma Swamp Club which was a huntin' club. During deer season they went deer huntin' together. During squirrel season they went squirrel huntin' together. And during turkey season they went turkey huntin' together. They always met at Ralph's house before they went into the woods to hunt. They done this over and over because Ralph's farm is close to the Okatoma swamp. They always turned up at the house between four and five o'clock in the morning—way before the sun come up. I dreaded them coming because Ralph expected me to get up and fix breakfast for his huntin' buddies. Ralph expected me to have homemade biscuits for 'em. He'd say, "I don't want my huntin' buddies to have to eat them little refrigerated biscuits that comes out of a Pillsbury can."

Gettin' up at four o'clock in the morning and fixin' breakfast for seven men ain't no fun. Particularly when none of 'em ever said "Thank you." But all of 'em come by the funeral home last night and told me they was gonna miss Ralph. I said, "I'm gonna miss him too."

And—as you'd expect—Brother Ledbetter was there too. When I seen Brother Ledbetter I wanted to puke. But I kept that feeling to myself. Brother Ledbetter come up to me and said, "Beulah, in a moment like this I ain't got but one thing to say."

I said, "What's that?"

He said, "Hold to Jesus."

With that he turned and started talking to other people. He didn't waste no time talkin' to me. I could tell the vibrations between me and him wasn't no good. I think he knew I didn't like the way him and Brother Claypool acted when they ate with me during the revival.

The person I was gladdest to see last night was Velma. She really looked good. As usual she had her hair cut short and had make-up on. She always looks snazzy. When I seen her I put my arm around her and gave her a big hug. I said to her, "Velma, it's so sweet of you to come." I knew she'd drove up all the way from Hattiesburg.

I pulled her aside and said, "Velma, you'll never know how much I appreciate the way you talked to me. I left the Confederate Truck

Stop last Sunday feeling like I was a new person."

She said, "I was glad to talk to you. I could tell you were down in the dumps. My offer of a job still stands."

I said, "I may not need it." I told her about what Mr. Wright said about a wife gettin' what her husband owned if he died and didn't have no will.

She said, "I wish you luck."

Velma lowered her voice and said, "I read the article in the newspaper about Ralph. The article said the police don't have a clue on who did Ralph in. Do you have any idea who did it?"

I said, "Yeah."

Velma asked, "Who?"

I whispered, "You really want to know?"

She said, "I sure do."

I whispered, "You're sure you won't tell?"

She whispered back, "You have my word."

I said, "You're talkin' to the person who done him in."

Velma put her hand on her forehead. She smiled and said, "Beulah, good for you! When I read in the article that you were the last person seen leaving the business, I thought to myself: I bet Beulah had something to do with this."

I said, "I sure did."

She whispered, "How'd you do it?"

I answered, "It was simple. Ralph was about to give me another whipping. So I locked him in the freezer and wouldn't let him out. My guess is he had a heart attack or froze to death."

Velma said, "Serves the bastard right."

She gave me a hug and said, "Let's get together when all of this is over and talk some more."

I said, "Let's do."

The last thing Velma said was, "Getting back to what Mr. Wright told you, as soon as the funeral is over you do what he said.

Get you a lawyer. I know the Raineys. I bet Ralph's daddy and brothers are already tryin' to figure out a way to get their hands on what Ralph owned. If they had a chance, they'd steal the Lord's money out of a collection plate on Sunday."

Velma gave me another hug and left.

By nine o'clock most everybody had left the funeral home except me and my relatives and Ralph's relatives. I took another look at Ralph in his casket. A thought dawned on me: he looks like he's made out of wax. Every year the fair comes to Laurel. The fair always has a wax museum as a side show. Last year the wax museum had wax statues of Harry Truman, Adolf Hitler, the Pope, Babe Ruth, and Al Capone. I couldn't help but think that Ralph looked just like one of them statues in the wax museum at the Jones County Fair.

After nine o'clock me and Sammy and Earline left the funeral home. Before we left we told Mr. Wright we'd get to the New Jerusalem Church sometime between nine and ten in the morning. He told us again he'd take Ralph's body down to the church and let it lie in state at the church beginning at nine o'clock.

On the way back to Earline's house I said, "Sammy, I'm hungry. Let's go get something to eat."

Earline said, "I knew you'd get hungry sooner or later. You hadn't eaten nothing since breakfast."

I said, "Where can we go?"

Sammy said, "The only decent place open this time of the night is the Waffle House."

I said, "Okay. Let's go there."

So we drove to the Waffle House just off of Sixteenth Avenue. All three of us ordered coffee, pecan waffles, and ham. Sammy told the waitress, "Be sure and tell the cook to put lots of pecans in our waffles. Sometimes you order a pecan waffle and you have to have a magnifying glass to find the pecans."

The waitress said, "I'll tell him."

When the waitress brought the waffles they was loaded with pecans. I poured maple syrup on mine and ate like it was the first meal I'd had in a month. While we was eating our waffles and ham, Earline said, "It was thoughtful of Velma to drive up from Hattiesburg. She really looks good."

I said, "She sure does. You'd never know she was born and raised as a country girl in New Jerusalem."

Sammy said, "Most people in New Jerusalem hate her guts."

Earline said, "That's because they're jealous of her."

Sammy said, "You're right there. Velma can tell 'em all to kiss her ass."

I said, "That's what I'm gonna do. I'm gonna start tellin' people to kiss my ass."

Sammy asked, "When do you plan to start?"

Just for the heck of it I said, "I'm gonna start tonight. Beginning tonight I'm gonna do what I want to do. Which I ain't never done before."

At that moment a thought hit me. All my life I'd worn my hair either long or tied up in a bun. I wore it that way because the Bible says it's a disgrace for a woman to have her hair cut.

At least that's what Brother Ledbetter says the Bible says. Earline used to wear her hair long. But five years ago she started working in a beauty shop. A part of her job was cuttin' people's hair which you ain't supposed to do if you're primitive Baptist. So Earline quit being a primitive Baptist and became a Southern Baptist. Southern Baptists let you cut your hair. Brother Ledbetter really got outdone with Earline when she left the New Jerusalem Church and became a Southern Baptist.

I put my fork down on my plate and said, "Earline, what would you say if I said I was gonna get my hair cut short?"

She said, "I'd say 'praise the Lord.' Your hair has always looked to me like a dirty horse's tail."

I asked, "How long would it take for somebody to cut my hair?"

She said, "Less than a half hour."

I said, "Sis, I got something I want you to do for me."

Earline said, "What's that?"

I said, "I want us—after we finish these here waffles—to go to the beauty shop where you work." Earline works at a beauty shop named "Results." It's owned by a fellow named Mark. That's his first name. I don't know what his last name is.

Earline asked, "What for?"

I said, "I want you to cut my hair."

She said, "You've got to be kiddin'."

I said, "No, I ain't. I want you to make my hair look just like Velma's does. Real classy—just like I was from New York or Chicago."

Earline said, "Sis, I'll be glad to cut your hair. That's no problem. But Brother Ledbetter ain't gonna like it if you turn up at the funeral tomorrow with your hair cut short. It's gonna make him as mad as a wet rooster. You better leave your hair just like it is."

I said, "I don't care what Brother Ledbetter thinks. I'm turning over a new leaf. I'm goin' to the funeral tomorrow with my hair cut short. And I'm gonna wear rouge and lipstick. And maybe eye shadow."

Sammy said, " Brother Ledbetter ain't goin' to like that either."

Earline chimed in, "Nor are the members of the New Jerusalem Church."

I said, "That don't bother me none. From now on—beginnin' tonight—I'm doin' what I want to do."

Sammy said, "I can't believe what my ears are hearing."

Me and Sammy and Earline left the Waffle House and drove straight to the beauty shop. Earline turned on the lights and had me sit in a chair. She took a comb and scissors and in less than twenty minutes had my hair cut short.

When I looked in the mirror—after Earline was through—I didn't recognize myself. My face and neck had a shape I didn't know it had.

Sammy said, "I swear to God, Beulah, you look like a new person."

I said, "To be honest about it, that's what I am."

II

LAST NIGHT AFTER Earline had got through cuttin' my hair, we all went back to Sammy and Earline's house. Earline insisted I take a sleeping pill. Which I done. The sleeping pill Earline give me was one her dentist had prescribed for her after she'd had her wisdom teeth taken out. It was a strong one. It knocked me out and I slept like a cat full of milk.

This morning I woke up a quarter past seven. The moment I woke up the thought popped in my mind: in less than three hours I've got to be at the New Jerusalem Church for Ralph's funeral. I could hear Earline in the kitchen. So I got out of bed and put on a housecoat. I went into the kitchen where Earline was. She'd fixed everybody a fruit plate for breakfast—cantaloupe, bananas, and orange slices. Along with wheat toast and tomato juice. And a good, hot pot of coffee.

Earline said, "Since we ate heavy last night at the Waffle House, I thought I'd fix us something light for breakfast."

Sammy and Earline and me sat down at the kitchen table and ate breakfast. We didn't do much talkin' during breakfast. Sammy had the kitchen television set on. What we done while we ate breakfast was listen to the "Today" program on NBC. They was interviewing this big shot senator up in Washington. The senator was talking about taxes.

Sammy said, "All those bastards up in Washington do is tax the crap out of the working man and take his money and give it to people who sit on their butts all day instead of working like the rest of us."

He added, "I say to hell with 'em."

Earline asked me, "What time do you want to get to the church?"

I said, "It don't matter. The funeral starts at ten. I'd say let's get there around nine-thirty."

After breakfast I took a shower. I washed my hair and dried it with Earline's hair dryer. Earline combed my hair the way she thought it ought to be combed. When she was through combing it, she said, "Beulah—so help me—you look just like Velma."

I put on my very best dress—the cream-colored one I'd bought on sale at McRae's in Hattiesburg. I then put on my shoes. Instead of wearing low-heeled shoes like I'd first thought I would, I put on my high-heel shoes. They was white. I'd bought 'em over a year ago at the JCPenney store in Gulfport. A matching white purse come with 'em. Ralph never liked for me to wear high-heel shoes. Every time he saw a woman wearing high-heel shoes he'd say, "They make her look like a New Orleans hooker."

After I'd put on my dress and shoes, I decided to fix my face. Which I'd never done before. Like I've told you, primitive Baptists don't believe in using cosmetics. Brother Ledbetter was always saying, "Cosmetics is the work of the devil."

I borrowed Earline's powder, lipstick, rouge and eye shadow and fixed my face up. Or at least I thought that's what I done.

Earline took one look when I was through and let out this moan. She said, "Beulah, you've used too much. You look like a clown at the circus. Take it off and let's start over."

So I done what Earline told me to do. I took all my makeup off. I let Earline fix my face the way she thought it ought to be. She put on powder, lipstick, rouge, and eye shadow. She sprayed my head all over with sweet-smelling perfume.

When she'd finished she stepped back and looked at me. She said, "Beulah, you look great. I never knowed you could look so pretty."

Her sayin' that made me feel real good. I hadn't felt good about myself for a long time. That's what can happen to you when you're married to a Rainey. The last thing I done was transfer stuff from my old purse to the white purse I was gonna take to the funeral—stuff like car keys and my Confederate Truck Stop key ring. When I picked up my old purse it hit me that it was heavy. The reason it was heavy was because I'd put Ralph's pistol in it. I don't know why I done it, but I took Ralph's pistol out of my old purse and put it in my white purse. Maybe I shouldn't have done that. But I done it. If I hadn't put Ralph's pistol in my white purse, things would have gone different at the funeral service.

All the time I was gettin' ready Sammy and Earline was gettin' ready too. At nine o'clock sharp I heard Sammy yell, "Come on, everybody! It's time to go. If we don't go now, we're gonna be late!"

A whisker after nine me and Earline and Sammy left Laurel for the New Jerusalem Baptist Church—the church I'd belonged to all my life. I'd seen a lot happen at the church. I'd seen dinners-on-the-ground. I'd seen Velma voted out of the church because she divorced her first husband. I'd heard Brother Ledbetter preach at least a thousand sermons on the book of Revelations—explaining what all of them beasts and trumpets meant. I'd seen people flip the switch beside their names on the "Let Your Light Shine for Jesus" board. I'd practiced "Onward Christian Soldiers" on the church piano. I'd seen Mrs. Ledbetter wear her funny hats week after week. Once a month I'd seen all the members go down to the front of the church and wash each other's feet in tubs of warm water. And then dry 'em off with towels. Foot washing is what makes a primitive Baptist church different. Others churches don't practice foot washing. Or at least I don't think they do. And the New Jerusalem Church was where I married Ralph. And now I was goin' to the church for his funeral. Nobody could accuse me of bein' tightfisted about his casket. I'd bet Ralph's casket was the first five-thousand-dollar casket that has ever been inside the New Jerusalem Baptist Church.

As we was leaving Laurel, Sammy said, "We'll be at the church by half past nine. We'll get there at just the right time."

While we was drivin' down the highway all kinds of questions was floatin' back and forth in my mind.

What was I gonna do about Oscar? Him not playin' with a full deck of cards wasn't his fault. Even though I wasn't his mama, I felt I ought to look after him. If I didn't, who would? Nobody I could think of.

Which attorney in Laurel should I talk to about Ralph's farm and business after the funeral was over? I didn't know no attorneys. Maybe the best thing for me to do would be to talk it over with Velma. She could give me some good advice.

Should I open back up "Ralph's Place" for business?

Or should I leave it closed down and let somebody buy it?

Would I have any trouble with Ralph's folks after the funeral? I knew his sister hated my guts. Maybe she'd go out of her way to rock my boat.

Should I stay Beulah Rainey? Or should I change my name back to Beulah Buchanan? Either way, I knew I wasn't gonna be no man's doormat no more.

Questions like these was goin' around and around in my mind when all of a sudden Sammy's car started actin' funny. It started jerking.

Earline said, "Sammy, what's happening to the car?"

Sammy said, "I be damned if I know!"

The car really got to jerkin' and sputtering.

Sammy said, "Oh crap! Look at the gas gauge! I've run out of gas! This is the first time I've ever run out of gas. I can't believe it!"

Earline said, "Me neither."

Sammy said, "I knew two days ago my gas gauge was low. But with Ralph gettin' murdered and his funeral coming up I hadn't been thinking about the gas tank. The gas tank is the last thing that's been on my mind."

Sammy pulled over to the side of the road. All three of us knew that Mr. Bilbo's grocery store and gas station was about a mile down the road. We could see it from where we was sittin'.

Sammy said, "You two gals sit here. I'll run to Bilbo's store and get some gas."

Sammy got out of the car and started runnin' like he was a jack rabbit. He run all the way to Bilbo's store. In what seemed like no time here come Sammy and Mr. Bilbo in Mr. Bilbo's pickup truck. Mr. Bilbo parked right in front of Sammy's car. Him and Sammy got out of the truck. Mr. Bilbo reached back on the truck bed and picked up a can of gasoline.

I've known Mr. Bilbo all my life. So has Earline. When he saw me, he said, "Beulah, I'm sorry about Ralph. I read all about it in the newspaper."

I said, "I appreciate that, Mr. Bilbo."

Mr. Bilbo and Sammy was really hustling. Mr. Bilbo started pouring gasoline into the gas tank. He said to Sammy, "This can holds five gallons. Don't try to start the motor until I've poured all of it in."

He poured away. Sammy was sittin' behind the wheel with the car door open. He had his hands on the keys. He was ready to take off. When the gas can was empty, Mr. Bilbo yelled, "See if it'll start!"

Sammy turned the ignition switch and the motor come right on. He yelled to Mr. Bilbo, "That's got it!"

Mr. Bilbo answered, "Great!"

Sammy said, "I'll pay you later! I'll come by after the funeral!"

Mr. Bilbo said, "Don't worry about it!"

Ralph took off goin' what felt to me like a hundred miles an hour. I ain't never been in a car goin' so fast.

You ain't gonna believe what happened next.

I heard Sammy say, "Oh, shit!"

Earline said, "What's wrong now?"

Sammy said, "Look in the rearview mirror? There's a highway patrolman signaling me to pull over!"

And sure enough there was. Right behind us was a highway patrol car with blue lights flashing like it was the end of the world. Only it wasn't just one patrol car. It turned out there was three patrol cars all together.

Sammy pulled over on the shoulder of the road and got out of his car. As he did so he muttered, "Oh boy, I'm in trouble."

The three patrolmen got out of their cars. I heard one of them say, "Buddy, are you on your way to a fire? I just clocked you goin' almost ninety miles an hour."

I knew right off who the patrolman was who was talkin' to Sammy. It was Bobby Lott. The reason I knew is because Bobby is a member of the Okatoma Swamp Club. That's Ralph's hunting club that I've fixed breakfast for at least fifty times. I've gotten up time and again at four o'clock and fixed 'em homemade biscuits and scrambled eggs and ham and coffee for them to eat before they went into the woods to hunt. Bobby came by the funeral home last night and told me he was sorry about Ralph.

Sammy said to Bobby, "Officer, please let me explain. I'm on my way to a funeral at the New Jerusalem Baptist Church."

Bobby said, "Whose funeral?"

Sammy said, "Ralph Rainey's."

Bobby said, "I knew Ralph. He was a hunting' buddy."

Sammy said, "It's his funeral I'm goin' to. His wife is my sister-in-law. She's here in the car and we're late for the funeral because I gave out of gas about a mile from Bilbo's store."

Bobby asked, "Are you talkin' about Beulah?"

Sammy answered, "Yeah. She's sittin' on the back seat."

Bobby bent over and looked in the window. When he saw me he said, "Beulah, bless your heart. We've had trouble with teenagers speeding on this road and so this morning we set up a trap to catch 'em. I had no idea I was stopping you."

I said, "We're late because—like Sammy said—we gave out of gas. The funeral service is supposed to have already started."

Bobby said, "You sure do look different from the way you looked last night at the funeral home."

I said, "Earline here gave me a makeover."

Bobby turned to the other two patrolmen and said, "Fellows, let's go and I mean let's go. We've got to get these folks to Ralph's funeral. Do you guys know where the New Jerusalem Baptist Church is?"

Both patrolmen said they knew.

Bobby said to Sammy, "Get in your car and follow me!"

All three patrol cars took off like jack rabbits. All three of 'em had their sirens on and their lights flashing. Sammy was drivin' right behind 'em.

He said, "Damn, I'm not sure I can keep up with these bastards."

Down the road we went like we was a bullet fired out of a gun. I thought to myself: now ain't this something! Here I am being escorted to Ralph's funeral by the Mississippi Highway Patrol.

I looked at my watch. It was already fifteen minutes past ten o'clock when the funeral service was supposed to start. We roared down the highway until we came to the church. All three patrol cars and Sammy pulled up right in front of the New Jerusalem Baptist Church. The church yard was full of cars. I could tell a lot of people had come to Ralph's funeral. People was even standing outside the

church because there wasn't no room for them inside. I got out of
Sammy's car as quick as I could. So did Sammy and Earline. Mr.
Wright the undertaker was standin' out in front. I could tell he was
in a dither. I trotted up to him and I said, "Mr. Wright, I'm sorry
we're late. We give out of gas a few miles up the road."

He said, "I knew something must have happened. The church is
packed. The only empty seats are on the front row. I've saved seats
for you and your sister and your brother-in-law. I'll escort the three
of you to your seats and we can get the service started."

Mr. Wright added, "By the way, you sure do look different today
from the way you looked yesterday."

I said, "I've had my hair cut."

He said, "Oh, that's it. I knew it was something."

Me and Earline and Sammy stepped inside the church. Like Mr.
Wright said, it was packed with people. Mr. Wright led me and
Earline and Sammy down to the front row and sat us down right in
front of the pulpit and right in front of Ralph's casket. As I walked
down to the front I looked around at the people who was there. I seen
my relatives and Ralph's relatives. I seen members of the New
Jerusalem Church and people from the New Jerusalem community.
I recognized a lot of our regular customers.

Me and Earline and Sammy sat down on the front row. No
sooner had I sat down than I could tell the members of the choir was
staring at me. They was staring at me like I was the two-headed calf
or the crocodile lady at the Mississippi State Fair in Jackson.
Particularly was Miss Sadie, the preacher's wife, staring at me with
saucer eyes. If her eyes had been X-ray machines they'd of gone right
through me. Miss Sadie had on a hat I'd never seen before. Her hat
was a green derby. Where in the world she found that green derby I
don't know. So help me she'd decorated it with one-dollar bills.
How she came up with the idea of decoratin' a green derby hat with
one-dollar bills is beyond me. But that's neither here nor there. All

I know is she was staring at me like a hungry man staring at a broiled steak. So were other members of the choir. My guess was they was looking at my new hair-do. And maybe they was looking at the way Earline had done my face up with lipstick and eye shadow. I could tell Brother Ledbetter was staring at me too. The way they was all lookin' made me feel edgy.

Which is why I turned my eyes in the direction of Ralph's five-thousand-dollar casket. Which I'd bought on credit and signed a contract for with the funeral home. The casket was right in front of the pulpit and right in front of where I was sittin'. Ralph's people had gone together and paid for a big spray of pink carnations to put on top of Ralph's casket. I've got to admit that the spray of pink carnations and the bronze casket went together good. They was pretty.

As soon as me and Earline and Sammy sat down on the front pew, the funeral service began. Like we'd planned, Aunt Laura played the piano. She played a piano prelude, but so help me I can't remember what it was. I've always liked Aunt Laura. When I was a little girl she used to cook me oatmeal cookies. After the piano prelude, the choir sang three verses of "In the Sweet By and By." There wasn't time for "When They Ring Those Golden Bells."

When the choir got through singing "In the Sweet By and By," Brother Ledbetter stood up behind the pulpit to give the funeral sermon. I could feel my stomach twisting into knots. I didn't want to listen to him, but I had to. I didn't have no choice. You've heard about people gettin' diarrhea after eatin' something that don't agree with 'em. I'm here to tell you there's another kind of diarrhea. It's mouth diarrhea. Sometimes Brother Ledbetter gets this kind of diarrhea when he gets to preaching. Words gush out of his mouth like water does out of an open faucet. I've seen Brother Ledbetter get mouth diarrhea when preaching from the book of Revelations— talkin' about all them beasts and bowls of wrath. I've seen him get mouth diarrhea when preachin' against whiskey and lipstick and divorce and cuttin' your hair short. When he gets this kind of mouth diarrhea his voice gets real singsongy—kind of like he was an auctioneer at a cattle sale.

Brother Ledbetter hadn't spoken two sentences of Ralph's funeral sermon before I could tell he had a bad case of mouth diarrhea. He got to chantin' with his diamond stickpin flashing like a headlight on a locomotive puffing away between Laurel and Hattiesburg. Words don't smell. But if they could smell I'd say Brother Ledbetter's words smelled like a chicken coop or a pigpen. I'm tellin' you he cut loose. I remember what he said. He said "Ladies and gentlemen, friends, visitors, and neighbors: may I welcome you to the New Jerusalem Primitive Baptist Church. I think you will agree with me when I say this is for all of us both a sad occasion and a happy occasion. It's sad because we have come to this place today to conduct the funeral of a man we all knew: Ralph Rainey. But it is also a happy occasion because we all know that Ralph has now gone to heaven to be with Jesus. Ladies and gentlemen: we have all got to hold to *Jesus* like Ralph Rainey done. Ralph Rainey was an unusual man. He was born and raised right here in the New Jerusalem community. This is where he went to school. His mama and daddy and his two brothers and his sister are also from this community and I'm proud to say they are all with us today. As a young man Ralph served his country by going off and joining the navy where he served with distinction. We all know that in the navy he learned the food business. I'm sure most of you read the article about Ralph that was in the *Laurel Leader Press*. The article quoted Ralph as saying that before he joined the navy he didn't know how to boil water but when he left the navy he knew how to fix a Christmas dinner for a thousand sailors. We all know that when Ralph left the navy he came back here to Jones County and became a farmer and the owner of 'Ralph's Place' in Laurel. The Bible says we are to earn our bread by the sweat of our brow. And that's what Ralph did: he earned his living by the sweat of his brow. Oh thank you Jesus for a hardworking man like Ralph."

Brother Ledbetter kept on goin'. He said, "But Ralph wasn't just a hardworking farmer and cafe owner. Oh no! He was much more than that. He was also a highly respected member of the New Jerusalem Baptist Church. I'm here to testify to you that Ralph rarely if ever missed comin' to church on Sunday. I could always count on him being here to lead the singing and to help take up the collection. The first thing Ralph always did when he got to church was to flip the switch beside his name on the 'Let Your Light Shine for Jesus' board. I want all of you to look at this board right now."

I looked over at the "Let Your Light Shine for Jesus" board. The bulb beside Ralph's name was turned on. No other bulb was burning. I hadn't noticed the Jesus board until Brother Ledbetter told us to look at it. Which of course is what I done.

The preacher said, "You see Ralph's name? The bulb beside his name is burning. And it ought to be burning. Why? Because every day of his life Ralph Rainey let his light shine for Jesus. And where is he now? He is up in heaven with Jesus. And why do I know that? I know that because Ralph was washed in the blood and people who're washed in the blood go to heaven to be with Jesus when they leave this world of suffering and woe."

Brother Ledbetter kept on goin' with his stickpin flashing. He said that Ralph loved everybody in the New Jerusalem community. And that he loved his mama and daddy and his two brothers and his sister. And that Ralph was a humble and gentle soul who never hurt nobody. That statement about Ralph being humble and a gentle soul who never hurt nobody almost cracked me up. I wonder what old JR the mule would say about Ralph being a gentle soul who never hurt nobody. Velma told me one time that one of the reasons she doesn't have much respect for the church no more is because they give Christian funerals to every bastard who comes along. People can be so crooked that when they die they have to screw 'em in the ground. And what do preachers do? They preach 'em into heaven when everybody knows they were as crooked as a barrel of snakes. Velma says that's one of the reasons she thinks a lot of preachers are buttkissers. They don't shoot straight and tell it like it is.

Toward the end of his funeral sermon Brother Ledbetter got off on a subject that really pissed me off. Of all things, he got to talking about Ruth Ann. Why he wanted to talk about Ruth Ann is beyond me. My guess is Bessie got to him and told him about Ralph sayin' he wanted to be buried beside Ruth Ann. Brother Ledbetter told the congregation about how devoted Ralph was to Ruth Ann. And about what a good wife she was. He said, "If there was ever a saint on this earth, it was Ruth Ann Rainey." And then he made a remark that wasn't nothing else but a slap at me. I know it was a slap because he looked right at me when he said it. He said, "Ruth Ann was a genuine primitive Baptist. She never cut her hair or used makeup."

When he said that Earline punched me real hard in the ribs. She punched me real hard three times. I could feel my skin stingin'. And I could feel my face turning red. Why was he slapping and slicing me? Talkin' like he was talking he wasn't being Henry. No way was he being Henry. As Henry he'd come by my house time and again for his early morning visits. I'd been good to him. I'd been understanding. I'd listened as he told me about how stale it was to be married to Miss Sadie who didn't have no boobs and wore funny hats. I'd listened as he told me how bad her breath could smell at times. One morning he said Miss Sadie's breath sometimes smelled like four-day-old funeral flowers that'd been left out in the sun. He told me he loved me and I'd told him I loved him. I'd been sweet to him and I'd let him fuck my pussy. Me being fucked and loved by somebody who didn't smell like barbecue sauce and always wore a suit and understood everything there is to know about the book of Revelations made me feel important. It made me feel special and there hasn't been many times in my life when I felt special. But when he let loose about Ruth Ann and about cuttin' hair and about using makeup he wasn't being Henry no more. He was turning against me and I couldn't understand why. He was being Brother Ledbetter who can rant and rave and criticize. By saying what he was sayin' I could tell he was sucking up to the Raineys and to Ruth Ann's folks. Before Ruth Ann married she was a Landrum. They was members of the New Jerusalem church like the Raineys was. Brother Ledbetter was sucking up to the Raineys and the Landrums at my expense. By doing this sucking up he showed me he didn't care nothing about my feelings. If you love somebody you treat their feelings tenderly. You don't stomp on them. And all of a sudden it hit me: maybe Brother Ledbetter had never really loved me. Maybe I'd let him and his diamond stickpin play me for a fool. Maybe I'd been suckered. Nobody likes to realize you've been a sucker.

I don't think I heard another word Brother Ledbetter said. I was too mad to listen. Finally he got to the end of what he had to say. Brother Ledbetter always ends his sermons with what he calls "testimony time." And that's what he done at the end of Ralph's funeral talk. He wiped his forehead with a handkerchief and took a sip of water. Brother Ledbetter always keeps a glass of water on the pulpit. He says water helps his throat not go dry.

After he'd taken two or three more sips of water, he said, "Now brothers and sisters, we have got a beautiful end-of-the-sermon custom here at the New Jerusalem Baptist Church. Members of our congregation know what I'm talking about. But some of you are not members. So I'll explain what that end-of-the-sermon custom is. We call it 'testimony time.' This is a time when you—the members of the congregation—can stand up when the sermon is over and say whatever is on your heart. So what I want to know is: is there somebody here who wants to give a testimony about Brother Ralph?

Is there anybody here this morning who has something on your heart you'd like to say about this dear departed soul? If so, I'll recognize you at this time."

The moment he said that I stood up. I stood up so fast I surprised myself. I sprung up off the front pew like I was a jack-in-the-box. The reason I stood up so fast was because during Brother Ledbetter's funeral sermon I'd built up a head of steam. I was mad at Brother Ledbetter for embarrassing me about my short hair. And for embarrassing me about using makeup. I was still mad about the way he acted like a wooden Indian when Ralph blew up on me for not fryin' enough chicken when him and Brother Claypool ate supper at Ralph's. Most of all, I was mad about the ton of crap he'd packed into his sermon about Ralph—puffing and blowing about what a fine church member he was and how he was always lettin' his light shine for Jesus. And on top of all that singing the praises of Ruth Ann. As you can tell, I was like a boiler about to explode. I felt like a female cat tired of being pissed on.

Brother Ledbetter looked real surprised when I stood up. He looked at the congregation and said, "Just in case anybody don't know, this little lady standing here at the front is Ralph Rainey's wife. Her name is Beulah Rainey—now a widow woman. I believe she has something she'd like to say."

I turned around toward the packed congregation and said, "I sure do have something I want to say. The main thing I want to say is that most of the stuff Brother Ledbetter has said about Ralph this morning is a big pile of bullshit. He's popped off at the mouth about what a great Christian and kind person Ralph Rainey was. I lived with him for six years and I'm standing here to tell you he was one mean bastard!"

Maybe I shouldn't have used the words "bullshit" and "bastard" in church. But I was mad. Which is worser—for me to say "bullshit" in church or for Brother Ledbetter to describe Ralph in a way that ain't so? Which is worser? For me to say "bastard" inside the church or for Brother Ledbetter to be dishonest in the church? I agree with Velma: a lot of funeral sermons in Mississippi are dishonest bullshit. Or baptized lying.

I could tell a lot of people in the congregation didn't like what I was saying. They began making this murmuring or grumbling sound. A lot of it was coming from Ralph's kinfolk. Particularly from zodiac Bessie who wants to know if you're a Cancer or a Capricorn. But I didn't care. Like I've said, I was mad.

I could tell everybody was listening to what I was saying. They was hanging on to every word. They was paying closer attention to what I was saying than they did to Brother Ledbetter's funeral talk in which he preached Ralph into heaven. I looked right at Brother Ledbetter and said, "If you think Ralph was all so good and kind, let me tell you what he done a few days ago to his mule."

I was about to tell 'em about Ralph pouring gasoline on JR and settin' him on fire. But I didn't get to tell 'em because Brother Ledbetter interrupted me. He yelled, "Miss Beulah, you are out of order! I am the pastor of this here church and I am not gonna stand here and let you use in the church the kind of language you're usin'—using words like 'bullshit' and 'bastard.' It ain't right. Now you sit down and be quiet! Do you hear me?"

I come right back at him.

I said, "I ain't gonna sit down and I ain't gonna shut up. Instead of me shuttin' up, you ought to be the one to shut up. And the reason you ought to shut up is because for the past six months you've been tom-cattin' on Miss Sadie. You've been a sneakin' skirt chaser with a married woman who lives right here in the New Jerusalem community and who's here this morning in this congregation. I know her name and you know her name. And if you deny you've been tom-cattin' on Miss Sadie, I'll tell the people her name and she'll look everybody in the eye and tell 'em it's the truth that you're a pussy-chasing preacher! If you want her to, she'll do it right now! She'll even tell 'em about how your underwear has red and blue dots!"

You could have heard a pin drop. Everybody in the congregation froze. They didn't know what to say or do. It was just me and Brother Ledbetter glaring at each other like two rattlesnakes in a snake fight. When I said what I said about him tom-cattin' I could see fire comin' out of Brother Ledbetter's eyes. I could tell I'd landed a punch. In fact, I'd kicked him in his nuts. Which is exactly what I wanted to do. Since he'd done a job on me, I decided to do a job on him. Turn about is fair play.

Brother Ledbetter didn't say nothing. He stepped down from the pulpit and started walkin' toward me with this stern look on his face. I could tell he was gonna try to cow me. And stare me down to size. The way he was actin' reminded me of the way Ralph acted when he said he was gonna chastise me in the name of the Lord. But I wasn't about to let Brother Ledbetter cow me. Or hurt me. Which is why I opened my purse and reached in and took out Ralph's revolver.

You should have seen the expression on Brother Ledbetter's face when I took out that pistol. He looked so surprised and afraid he could have farted chicken gravy.

He stopped dead in his tracks. Then he started backin' up. In this real trembling voice he said, "Now Miss Beulah, don't you do nothing you may someday regret." He said that over and over. "Now Miss Beulah, don't you do nothing you may someday regret." And he'd say, "Remember, Miss Beulah, this here is the house of the Lord."

Every time Brother Ledbetter took a step backward, I took a step toward him. I can't explain it. I don't know why it was. But when I saw Brother Ledbetter backtrackin' and shakin' like a leaf in the wind and whining "Now Miss Beulah, don't you do nothing you may someday regret," it made me feel good. I didn't give a damn what nobody there in the New Jerusalem Baptist Church thought. I felt I was in charge—not them. I was like an unchained eagle—flyin' high up into the clouds and feelin' cool wind blowing on me and blowin' away all the doubts I'd always had about myself and who I was and what I could be.

Brother Ledbetter backtracked until he got beside the "Let Your Light Shine for Jesus" board. The lightbulb beside Ralph's name was turned on. It was the only lightbulb on the board that was burning. I decided to take a crack at it with my pistol. I aimed and pulled the trigger. The bullet hit Ralph's lightbulb and busted it all over the place.

The pistol shot sounded like a bomb had gone off. It jarred the church. The shot was so loud it surprised me.

Brother Ledbetter let out a whoop and started running for the door. People jumped up and followed him. You ain't never seen such runnin' in all your life. I aimed and fired a second bullet into the "Let Your Light Shine for Jesus" board. My second shot sounded like thunder too. After my second shot the ladies in the choir cleared out. Most of 'em—including Miss Sadie—went out the window. They was all whoopin' and hollering.

I fired away a third time. And a fourth and a fifth and a sixth time. After the sixth bullet hit the "Let Your Light Shine for Jesus" board it fell down on the floor. It sounded like a train crash when it hit.

Outside people was gettin' in their cars and leavin'. The first person to leave was Brother Ledbetter. He left in such a hurry he forgot Miss Sadie.

When I got through shootin' I looked around and there wasn't but five people left in the church. They was Mama and Daddy, Sammy and Earline, and Mr. Wright the undertaker.

Mama and Daddy was too shook up to say nothing. Mr. Wright looked shook up too. But he managed to say they'd get Ralph's casket buried in the cemetery across the road.

Sammy said, "Beulah, I think it'd be best if me and Earline took you home with us."

So we all got in Sammy's car and started back to Laurel. On the way back we got to Mr. Bilbo's store.

Sammy said, "I'd better stop and pay for that can of gas I got awhile ago." When we pulled into the store Mr. Bilbo was standing out front. Sammy got out of his car and said, "I've come back by to pay you for the can of gas you put in my car."

Mr. Bilbo took off his cap, scratched his head, and said, "Forget about it. I was glad to help you out." Mr. Bilbo then added, "Sammy, something strange is goin' on and I don't know what it is."

Sammy said, "Why do you say that?"

Mr. Bilbo said, "Traffic on this road in front of my store is usually as slow as molasses in winter. Yet in the last fifteen minutes I've seen at least twenty cars go by and each one of 'em was doin' a hundred miles an hour. What in the hell is goin' on?"

Sammy said, "I'll come back tomorrow and tell you."

With that Sammy got back in the car and him and Earline and me headed back up the road to Laurel. When I say "Laurel" I'm sure you know by now what I'm talking about. I'm talking about Laurel, Mississippi, where the Masonite plant is.

POSTSCRIPT

T HE WEEK FOLLOWING Ralph's funeral Brother Ledbetter resigned as pastor of the New Jerusalem Baptist Church. He moved from New Jerusalem to Biloxi on the Mississippi Gulf Coast where he now holds a job as a used-car salesman at Honest Harry's Auto Corral. Having gotten a divorce, Miss Sadie moved to Tupelo, Mississippi, where she works on an assembly line in a furniture factory which produces sofas and reclining chairs. She is presently living with her older sister.

Beulah hired the law firm of Travis and Travis to represent her in the matter of her husband's estate. The fate of the Ralph Rainey estate was determined in Chancery Court by Chancery Judge Ingram Weldy. Ralph's two brothers attempted to get themselves appointed guardians of the Ralph Rainey estate. But Judge Weldy decided, contra the Rainey brothers, to have half the estate deeded to Beulah and half to Oscar with the provision that Beulah would serve as the guardian and conservatrix of Oscar's share of his father's estate.

Sammy, Beulah's brother-in-law, resigned his job with the Charley Moorman Janitorial Service to become co-manager of "Ralph's Place." "Ralph's Place" re-opened for business one week after Ralph's funeral. The business has prospered under Sammy's and Beulah's joint management.

The Laurel Police Department continues to look for the person or persons who robbed Ralph and locked him in the walk-in freezer. Laurel's chief of police recently stated, "The Rainey robbery has got us stumped. We don't have the remotest idea who did it."

Recently Beulah bought a pink Cadillac Deville. Last week she and Velma took a trip together in this Cadillac to New Orleans. They enjoyed beignets and coffee at the Cafe du Monde across from Jackson Square. Later they had lunch together at Galatoire's on Bourbon Street. Beulah and Velma have two things in common: both love and own Cadillacs and both have been voted out of the membership of the New Jerusalem Baptist Church.